CURSED

A HAVEN REALM NOVEL

MILA YOUNG

For more information, contact Mila Young.

milayoungauthor@gmail.com

Cover designer: Covers by Christian

ISBN: 978-1980428589

DEDICATION

To my husband for showing me fairy tales and happily ever afters do exist.

CONTENTS

A NOTE FROM MILA YOUNG

This Beauty and the Beast reimagining has been so much fun to write, so enjoy jumping into this fantasy world and prepare to meet Bee and her four grizzly bear shifters.

Each story in the Haven Realm series is a standalone novel and can be read in any order, though the more tales you read, the more likely you'll meet familiar characters.

These are adult fairy tale retellings for anyone who loves happily ever afters with steamy romance, sexy alphas, and seductive fun.

Enjoy!

Mila

HAVEN REALM SERIES

Hunted (Little Red Riding Hood Retelling)
Charmed (Aladdin Retelling)
Cursed (Beauty and the Beast Retelling)
Claimed (Little Mermaid Retelling)
Entangled (Rapunzel)
Wicked (Snow White Retelling)

More on the way…

CURSED
A Haven Realm Book

**Beauty and the Four Beasts. A Deadly Curse.
A Fallen Kingdom.**

With magic banned in the human realm, Bee, a powerful
witch, has had to offer her services in secret. When a request
to break a curse comes from the dangerous mountains and
royal bear shifters, Bee is hesitant, but winter is coming and
funds are tight.

At the castle, Bee finds things are not quite what she was
led to believe. The curse Bee is meant to break has reached
its zenith, siphoning off the Prince's life while preventing
him from controlling his shifting abilities. He is volatile,
angry, and far stronger than she had imagined. His brothers,
who commissioned her, present her with a challenge - fix it,
or lose everything.

Soon the curse is spreading throughout the castle, taking
brother and servant alike. It's a race against the clock,
buffeted by dark magic, intrigue, and a strange attraction
that has her looking at the four princes in a new light.

HAVEN REALM

The realms of Haven warred for ages upon ages, laying devastation upon its lands and its residents alike. To put an end to the death and destruction, the realm was divided into seven kingdoms, one for each race, ruled by nobility, entrusted to maintain the truce. Over centuries, kingdoms rose and fell as the power of the ruling noble houses waxed and waned. And the peace between the lands persevered. But a corruption is growing, bringing darkness to the realms, and threatening the return of war and suffering to Haven.

CHAPTER 1

"*J*s this a raunchy story?" Ariella whispered, leaning toward me as her gaze swung left and right, eyeing shoppers wandering through the open markets. She tugged down her woolen hat, keeping her fae ears covered, and her white hair fluttered over her shoulders from the breeze. Non-humans were forbidden from entering Terra, but that didn't stop Ariella from living dangerously and traveling there to sell books. And I loved that about her. Well, she lived dangerously for a good reason — she made a decent wage from her sales. But I still loved her sense of daring.

She smirked, her pale blue eyes with flecks of lavender narrowing as if mocking me.

I rolled my eyes. Why did all my friends assume I wrote smut? First Scarlet, then Hans at the coffee store, and now Ariella. I admit, sometimes I composed *those* scenes because, when two people fell in love, it led to a kinky night of pleasure.

"It's a romance," I corrected her. Sex wasn't new to me, but true love wasn't something I'd experienced firsthand. I'd seen the way my parents used to be together. Supporting each other through hard times, laughing at each other's silly jokes, and kissing when they thought I wasn't looking. That was the kind of relationship I yearned to find with someone... someday. "It's about my heroine's adventure in a new world, and she happens to find the right person to share her life with. Geez, girl. Get your head out of the gutter."

Ariella laughed, her face changing into that pure vision of joy, and she nudged my shoulder with a shove. "You ought to join me at the dragon markets in the Wildfire realm. A few vendors sell kinky toys there. That's your audience, and you can even sign your books in person. They'll love you."

"Are you kidding? What if someone recognizes me and tells Dad?" Just the thought had me perspiring. "And I've heard how insane those markets get, there are assassins and voodoo witches there. No thanks. Though I might take you up on a visit to the area."

Ariella journeyed throughout Haven Realm while searching for jobs to make money, but I wouldn't swap my world with hers. As an exiled princess, she'd been wrongly accused of slaying her whole family. Never mind that she'd been under a spell that had put her into a deep sleep while the real assailant had murdered her kin.

The hairs on my nape lifted as if I was being watched, and I twisted my head to see an old couple at the nearby baker's stand glaring our way. Had they eavesdropped on our conversation? Getting tossed into prison for spreading stories they'd classify as 'wicked indecency' wasn't on the cards today.

Ariella pulled me closer, her vanilla scent flooding my nostrils. "I remember reading that scene you gave me a while back." She lowered her voice, twisting her fingers around one another. "It still burns me up. You have a wild imagination, but I'm sure men don't do half the things you write about."

I turned my back on the peeping Toms. "Come on. Don't

act all innocent. Most men are randy bastards. And women will love my story." I slipped the five leather-bound books into her hands. Dad had invented a small print machine to replicate all his written inventions, so I'd secretly used it to make copies of my book. "You said there were potential customers in Wildfire. If they like these, I can get more copies made. We'll split the sales in half." I held my breath, studying the way she glanced down at the book I'd spent months writing, and now with Dad not selling any of his inventions for weeks, I was desperate to help pay our debt before we lost the family home.

Her nose wrinkled as she studied the cover. "Who's Mila Young?"

I giggled. "It's my pen name. I can't let my dad find out I write these. I'll die from embarrassment."

The sweet aroma of barbecued corn found me, and my stomach growled, but I had food in the backpack to enjoy once I left the markets, and I pushed the strap higher on my shoulder. A flurry of voices hummed on the wind, the surrounding stores in the courtyard brimming with people. My attention returned to Ariella. I'd met her a few months ago here, and naturally, I'd been drawn to her stall. While I'd read most of the books she offered, they never held my interest. So instead, I scribed tales I'd love to read.

"Most people want to learn about visiting other realms, dealings with the drama in royal families, how to care for domestic animals."

"Gah. Snorefest." I took her hand. "Please, just try. That's all I'm asking."

A breeze fluttered through my hair, sending auburn strands across my face and a chill ran down my back as it always did when the goddess sent a warning. I scanned the rows of vendors selling foods, clothing, plants, and even handmade toys. At the corner of the markets was my father, his fists resting on his belly, facing two guards. My stomach dropped. Why were they speaking with him? Had someone found out about my books?

Guards reported to the priestess and talked to people for two reasons: either they wanted whatever you were selling for free, or were arresting someone.

"Look, I've got to go." I pushed the books back into Ariella's grasp. "For me, just try. Please. And if you need a place to stay tonight, my room is free. I'm traveling out of town for the next few days." And I had to get a move on. I was already several days late to meet a friend, Elliana, at the Golden Lock tavern in the White Peak realm. The likelihood that she'd given up on me bugged me. I prayed she hadn't.

I glanced over my shoulder as a guard fumbled with one of Dad's inventions: his armored bedside table with a removable top that transformed into a shield, complete with an arm strap and buckle on the underside. The single leg doubled as a club. The perfect protection if anyone broke into your house in the middle of the night, he'd insisted. Which was why I had one in my bedroom.

"Just for you." Ariella's voice drew my attention. "I'll read it first, then show it to a few customers who might be interested. All right?" She tucked them under her stall.

"Thanks." I hugged Ariella. "You're the best."

"Anytime, and I might take you up on that offer tonight."

"Good idea. Dad loves your company and listening to stories about Darkwoods." My parents had always brought me up to welcome anyone in need into our home, regardless of race. Fugitive or not. And Ariella always snuck into Terra in the early hours of the morning when guards didn't patrol the woods.

She broke free of our embrace and turned to a woman with a young child who was approaching the stand. Ariella tugged down her hat.

I fixed the bag strap sliding down my arm and rushed through the crowds. Three men insisted on blocking the narrow path, so I careened around them. Someone trod on my foot and I winced. This was why I hated the markets. People treated the place as if it were the end of the world, shoving and pushing for goods. What I wouldn't give to lounge in the sun, enjoy the silence, and write.

Bursting free from the cluster of bodies near the candy stand, I stumbled forward, catching Dad's eye. Behind him stood Santos, his newest recruit. Santos had worked with my friend Scarlet, who owned an herbal store at the edge of town, but she'd experienced guard issues lately and wasn't in town for the foreseeable future. Until Scarlet got her shop back in order, Santos assisted Dad with his inventions for a small commission on anything sold.

The guard, who didn't have an inch of hair, dropped Dad's creation to the ground, and the leg snapped in half. "Doesn't pass our quality test."

"What's going on?" I gritted my teeth and shoved past the guard, my insides fuming over the fact that they'd dare harass us. This wasn't the first time, either.

I crouched to pick up the broken pieces, tired of pretending it was okay for these morons to push people around, tired of backing down, tired of abiding by society rules that didn't favor the majority.

"It's nothing," Dad said, his words shaky as he collected the top section of the table from me.

No one stood up to the guards due to fear of imprisonment, but I'd had enough of their crap. They'd pulled this stunt last week when they'd destroyed our storage box. So I faced the meathead and raised the wooden leg in my hand, pointy end up. "I know why you're doing this."

His upper lip curled, and something shifted beneath the surface of his hardened expression. Compassion? Doubtful.

5

"Bee. This isn't your business. Your father's inventions are a danger to society." He spoke as if we hadn't had this exact conversation last week, and the previous one. Each time, he'd strolled past Dad's stand, kicking and destroying our belongings.

"Bullshit! You're just being an ass because of Tristan." I was the dumbass who'd dated a guard in the first place, and despite dumping him months ago, that apparently gave his friends the authority to harass my family.

"Bee." Dad grasped my arm, drawing me back. "Don't."

But I'd confronted my fair share of bullies in Terra, and standing up for myself was the only way to deal with them.

"Listen to your daddy." The second guard belched and kicked an automatic shoe-polishing machine. "I could arrest you now for threatening me with that weapon."

"We mean you no harm." Dad's apologetic words annoyed me. He shouldn't have had to grovel before boys half his age. Dad wrestled the broken table leg out of my grasp. "And we appreciate your input on the safety of my products."

I glared at the two guards, not appreciating a single thing they stood for. They didn't protect people. I patted the pouch of herbs in my pocket. With a few words and a pinch of my mixture, I could freeze them long enough for everyone to mock them. Maybe throw eggs their way.

Customers watched us, as if waiting for a fight to break out, and my heart hammered with the urge to make the guards hurt. Make them feel the agony of defeat, of being kicked back down. But I held myself still until the tension flowed away without a hint of retaliation. Considering magic was forbidden in Terra, I had no plans on outing myself as a witch.

I'd inherited power from my mother. Like her, I was a bloodborne witch, meaning I had two sides to my power and was born under the blood moon. A dark and light source.

Choose one, Mom would say, and *stay loyal.* I selected the latter, just as she had. *Dark magic came with horrific consequences,* she'd insisted, but she'd always reminded me that despite my choice, a darkness still lived within me, like it did in every bloodborne witch. And growing up, she'd taught me to control that urge, keep it at bay. Interestingly enough, whenever I crafted my romances, in particular the sex scenes, I found it easier to meditate and focus on keeping my two halves separate. So in a way, my stories served a purpose beyond entertaining readers. They gave me balance and aided me in skating the razor's edge between the dark and light halves.

Aside from Dad and a few close friends, no one else knew about my magic, and I pretended to be a normal girl in this backwater town. While I loved my dad, I never felt as if I fit in in Terra, but since Mom's death, I couldn't fathom leaving his side.

"We'll let you off with a warning this time." Baldy's brow creased, and he and his buffoon friend stalked away, chortling.

"You shouldn't anger them, Bee." Dad fiddled with the broken leg of the table, and I guessed he'd glue it back together tonight.

"They deserve a lesson in manners," Santos said.

"Yes! Santos gets it," I blurted out.

Dad handed me a honey pastry I'd baked last night. "Have you had lunch?"

Shaking my head, I accepted the offering and stuffed half into my mouth. "Listen, Dad." I swallowed the food. "I'm heading off to that tutoring job near the mountains I told you about last week." I hated lying to him, but it wasn't as if I could say, *hey, I'm off to the heart of bear territory because someone hired me to remove a curse.* He'd lock me in the house, thinking I'd gone mad. Considering I did side jobs, teaching kids to read and write, he'd bought my story when I'd first told him. He might have known I worked magic like Mom, but I'd never told him how at times it felt as if I might self-combust from the energy bubbling in my veins, how on some full moons, the darkness inside was on the verge of taking me over, and how hard I had to fight it to stuff it back inside. I wouldn't want to worry him, so I finished my pastry and smiled.

"White Peak Mountains?" Santos's expression fell as he gripped the shoe-polishing machine, his knuckles turning white. "Alone? You're going to let her go near the bear shifter territory?"

"Hush, boy," Dad said, glancing around at the crowds. "Not so loud."

When he faced me, he lost his lively expression, and worry crept behind his eyes. With each passing day, I swore he grew more wrinkled, and his hair had turned an ashen gray. He was clean shaven today. I used to remember as a child he'd tuck me into bed and tell me stories from when he'd been younger and would roam through the different realms as a nomad before meeting Mom at a fair in Terra. He'd stay by my side until I fell asleep, and when he kissed me goodnight, I would always feel his stubble tickling me.

"Maybe Santos has a point," he said. "Let me come with you."

I shook my head. "With your sore knee, you won't make the trip. Plus, the family I'm working for only lives near the mountains." Second lie. "There's a small community of humans living there, and they hired me for a week to teach their kids. They're paying well." Goddess, I was going to end up in the underworld because I lied so easily. Though the part about people residing in White Peak was true, so did that balance the untruths? "I'm nineteen and there are girls in town who have three kids already at my age. I can look after myself, and I have the switch blade you created for protection."

Over a week ago, Elliana had arrived on my doorstep, saying she had an assignment for me. People hired her for unusual jobs, and she searched for the right person to fulfill each request. Turned out Elliana could detect magic. So when I'd performed a tiny spell on a douchebag pinching my ass at the tavern, she'd gaped at me. After a dozen ciders, she'd gotten me to confess my abilities.

Now she threw opportunities my way. Like this latest one, for which she insisted a bear shifter needed a quick curse reversal.

"I'll get paid enough to pay off our debt," I said. The job offered half the amount paid upfront, whether or not I could help with the spell. "So we won't lose our home."

Dad sighed. "I hate putting us in this situation. After your mother…"

I took his hands in mine, loathing the rawness curling in my gut at the reminder of the illness that had taken her two years ago. Dad had been forced to borrow money for the funeral, as it was custom to invite everyone from town and put on a feast. The memory sat heavy on my chest. I had sat by her bed for weeks on end, watching her slowly dying. Losing weight. Seeing her sunken cheeks. Listening to her breath, ragged. And every day since, I'd fought the tears away and put on a smile for Dad.

"Don't be silly. We'll make this work. We're a team." I looped my arms around him, feeling his hand rubbing my back. Hugs were never long enough. In his embrace, I felt warm and safe, as if my worries had vanished. "I'll return in no time. I made three loaves of bread and chicken soup for you. Oh, and Ariella is staying over tonight."

"At the first sign of danger, come straight back. All right?"

"Of course." I swallowed the boulder in my throat, I had

no clue what to expect once I arrived at the shifter bear's home. "Don't worry about me. And who knows, if I'm lucky, the family will hire me for two weeks. But I'll send word if I stay longer." Not that I intended to, but traveling into White Peak was an unknown and I didn't want Dad worrying if there were any delays.

A strange tingling sensation crawled up my spine and over my nape; the same feeling I'd experienced earlier about something going wrong. Maybe because I was late meeting Elliana. I blamed Scarlet, as she'd only just delivered her powerful wolfsbane roots this morning. She'd turned up at my place with three wolf shifters who stared at her with so much admiration. I was super excited she'd found herself three potential men... I'd love just one.

Anyway, wolfsbane was poisonous and worked wonders at fighting curses, and I had an assignment to complete.

With a deep breath of confidence, I didn't care that I was late. The bear shifters were going to let me into their home to cure whoever was cursed if I had to blow down their door with my magic.

CHAPTER 2

J couldn't stop shaking, and it had zero to do with the chill in the air. Ever since leaving the markets and beginning to make my way through the Terra woods, I'd turned into a trembling leaf. The morning sun found me through the gaps in the canopy overhead, but did nothing to warm me. Heading to White Peak ought to have excited me, yet goosebumps had broken out across my arms.

I kicked a pebble on the dirt track, sending the rock into a shrub. Birds sang overhead, and I pulled the backpack up my shoulders, stepping over a dead log, when the faint smell of brewing coffee teased my nostrils.

The Hideout sat on the edge of town, a tiny shop selling the fresh brew to anyone willing to trek into the woods. I confess… I was addicted, and most mornings I made the pilgrimage to their shop. My mouth salivated… and considering I had a day's walk ahead of me, I'd be a fool not to grab a cup first. I swung left and followed the hypnotizing aroma.

Amid the trees, a wooden hut came into view. It had no roof and had a rustic look going for it. The place was big enough for only two people to stand inside, with tables and chairs peppered out front. A young woman I greeted most mornings waved my way, and I returned the gesture as I approached the covered stall. I lounged against the counter, staring into the small hut, which was comprised of a small room, shelves across the back wall, and bowls of coffee beans and stacked glasses everywhere.

"Bee, you're late today," the owner, Hans, said, wiping his hands on a kitchen towel. A drop of milk lay on the edge of his curled mustache. Normally, I'd have no qualms reaching up to wipe it off, but his boyfriend, who was serving another customer at the moment, would probably object if he thought I was flirting. "Your usual?"

"You know me. Heavy on the milk with a dollop of honey. Put it on my tab."

"Got it."

Someone stepped alongside me, their shadow blocking the sunshine.

"Still with the honey, Bee? Thought you were watching your waistline. Hans, make mine the same."

I gritted my teeth at the sound of Tristan's voice. "Hey, Hans," I said. "Add two dollops of honey to my brew."

Tristan sighed, and I responded as I walked away. "Still a dickhead, hey? Oh, no need to answer. You've somehow morphed into an asshole."

Footsteps closed in behind me, and he clutched my arm, forcing me to face him. I played it cool, not showing how much his grip hurt.

"I should arrest you for talking to me that way."

Lifting my head, I took in his short, cropped hair, his creased nose, and the flatness of his mocha eyes. The gray guard uniform jacket with golden buttons was pulled taut across his wide chest. Tristan wasn't ugly, and he carried great ammunition in the downstairs department, but that wasn't enough when paired with his vulgar mouth and attitude - something I'd been blind to when he'd first caught my eye, always falling too easily for a handsome face.

"Would that turn you on?" I arched a brow.

"Damn, Bee." He dragged me behind the hunt, and I stumbled alongside him. "Don't say shit in front of others. What you and I do is private. And why are you carrying such a huge bag? Looks too heavy for you. Where are you going?" he sneered, his face tense.

I smirked and yanked my hand free. "We are never doing anything in private or public again. And who are you to comment on what I carry? Are you the bag patrol? What do you want?"

"What happened to you?" He stuffed his hands into his pockets. "This isn't the Bee I remember."

With a deep huff, I rubbed my eyes. "We haven't been dating for months because you're a possessive psycho, and I don't dance that way. Told you before. Go get yourself a girl who wants nothing more than to marry and please her husband. That's not me." I craved a man who put me first, always asked me what I wanted and then delivered — and someone who loved traveling. Yep, the latter was a must.

He tilted his head, studying me, and I sifted through my thoughts on which rebuttal he'd come back with. We'd had this conversation half a dozen times already, and his argument toggled between giving me everything a good wife could want in her home, to arresting my dad unless I agreed to marry him. Yeah, the perfect way to start a strong relationship.

The fault was mine for ever dating him. Not a mistake I'd make again.

"Back in the markets, I watched the way you aggressively addressed those guards. What stops me from taking you into the dungeons right now?"

I gave a slight shrug, like I didn't give a rat's ass about

13

his threat, but my imagination was running amok when it came to how I'd end up being interrogated. How I might never see sunlight, or my dad, or drink a cup of coffee again.

Worrying a rock with the toe of my boot, I summoned my courage. "Because deep down inside, there's a decent person who knows it'd be a prick thing to do. And if you ever cared for me, you wouldn't." I played the guilt trip card because in all honesty, I didn't have the energy for our usual long-winded arguments that ended with him insisting he'd show me how much he'd changed. And I had to head off. Stopping for a drink had been a huge mistake.

"Bee, your coffee is ready," Hans called out.

Tristan's expression tightened. "All I ask is for a second chance. I told you before, I want to marry you. I can change." And there it was.

I held back the laughter. "Look, awesome chatting with you like always, but my coffee is ready."

He blocked my path. "I'll collect yours and mine, then let's chat. Please?" The pleading in his voice almost touched me… *almost*, but then I remembered whom I was dealing with. The boyfriend who'd once insisted I stay home from a party while he'd attended it. Who'd reminded me I had to keep my figure in check because once I fell pregnant I'd turn into a balloon. Who once followed me and punched a male friend because I talked to him. Yeah, husband material right there. And damn him, I embraced my curves.

"No thanks." I shoved him aside, but he stepped in my way again.

"Stay here." His voice hardened. "I'll be back."

I grimaced. This was idiotic, and my head screamed to leave now while my heart said I ought to hear him out and that people could change. Nope.

The moment he whirled around, I darted in the opposite

direction, and what pissed me off the most was that I had no coffee. *Bastard.*

Rushing deeper into the woods, I didn't need him following me or knowing I'd left Terra. That would give him a real reason to arrest me.

So I'd be fast. I quickly looked over my shoulder. No sign of him. Goddess, please make Hans burn his milk.

A neighing sound came from my left. I jerked and hid behind a tree, convinced it was Tristan's muscle-head friends on horses waiting for him. When I peeked out, I only found one animal, tied to a tree. *Must be Tristan's.*

Hans had asked Tristan not to keep his horse close to the shop after it had panicked once over a wild boar. The horse had gotten loose and bolted, trampling down a person. If the animal got spooked that quick, then keeping it far from customers made sense.

But staring at the gorgeous golden horse with a white diamond on the middle of its forehead, I had other ideas. Ones that could get me thrown into a dungeon, but maybe this offered a solution to reaching the Golden Lock tavern quicker, and avoiding Tristan tracking me down. Considering I was already late to the job and was praying Elliana had waited, well... I approached the horse.

"Hello there," I whispered, reaching my hand toward his nose and patting him. "You're so beautiful. How does a long ride sound?" My heart beat so fast, and I kept looking back for any sign of Tristan. In haste, I untied the horse's strap from a low-hanging branch and pulled the animal along a trail before stepping into the stirrup and swinging my leg over the saddle. And this was why wearing pants made sense on travel day. I'd keep my bag on my back until I got out of the woods, then I'd attach it to the horse.

With the reins in my hand and a slight nudge to the horse's sides with my heels, I guided him away from the hut and down the curving path through the forest. This path passed near the border between Terra and White Peak, so we loped past clustered pines.

Another glance behind me, and I'd lost sight of the Hideout. We broke into a gallop, and I jostled about, my bag slapping into my back, but my priority was reaching the tavern. Tristan could walk to the guard house and report his horse stolen. He had no proof I'd taken his transport if he hadn't seen me.

Following the curve of the trail, I looked back once more. No one followed. With a long exhale, we rushed forward. Fuck Tristan and his chauvinist attitude.

Anyway, I might have lost my coffee, but I'd gained something better. Transport.

THREE REST STOPS LATER, the sun had slid down the heavens, and my food had been gobbled by Elf. Yeah, I'd given the horse a name because he had the longest ears, reminding me of the fae with their grace and beauty.

We'd emerged from the forest surrounding White Peak and now I stared at giant peaks in the distance. It was a mountain range that stood like the spine of the world, snow-capped peaks, and covered in pines. At the foothills lay the small transition town made up of one street riddled with shops and bars. No laws regulated the area, which explained why so many races crossed through here. I'd heard tales of various races trekking around the White Peak Mountains to reach a glorious snowy wonderland farther north. Apparently, an ancient royal family lived there, but who they were, no one seemed to know.

Then again, a ton of stories floated around about Haven and the different realms - from a society living underground in tunnels to pirates visiting other lands with blood-sucking monsters. My guess was the tales were created to scare people away from certain realms.

I drew Elf to a halt, hopped off, and scratched his head. "How does a new owner sound?"

Elf nodded as if he understood. "Ted owns the tavern and said he knew someone looking to buy a horse. I'm sure they'll treat you better than Tristan did." I held on to the reins and we strolled across the grassy field as I led Elf to the rear of the Golden Lock tavern. I tied him to a railing near a water trough.

Collecting my bag, I rubbed his side. "Well, enjoy your new life, my friend. And thank you."

Without a response, not that I expected one, I marched down a tight passage between two cobblestone buildings and emerged in front of the Golden Lock.

Shards of brown wood flaked along the wooden railing encasing the porch. Dust coated the windows, and the sign needed a new lick of paint as the letters had worn with weather. At a fast glance, one might read the name as Golden *Cock* tavern. *Might add that into one of my stories.* With a giggle in my throat, I climbed the groaning steps and opened the door, its hinges protesting.

Laughter overpowered the tavern as I entered the stone building, and the stench of beer and sweat permeated the air. A roaring fire blazed to my right in an old stone fireplace. Round tables and chairs dotted the place. On one side stood two oversized wooden barrels about five feet high filled with the tavern's famous alcoholic cider on tap. Candles lit the room from circular hoops suspended overhead.

I surveyed the customers. A young couple who appeared to be human sat at the bar, a man with a hood over his head slouched at a corner table nursing a drink, and three women laughed at a table close by the fire, downing drinks. Maybe a girls' night out, but a strange location for such a celebration. It wasn't my place to wonder about it, though, as I needed no one prying into *my* business. Especially since I didn't see Elliana.

What if she had been here this morning, and I'd just missed her? *Damn.* All because I'd waited for Scarlet to bring me the amplified wolfsbane this morning.

Against the rear wall stretched out the bar. Ted, the owner, served someone a glass of beer.

I hoofed it closer and dropped my bag at my feet before climbing up on a stool.

Ted smirked and made his way over, rubbing his hands down his stained apron. "Remember our last chat, Bee? You weren't welcome back until you paid your tab." He spoke with a light accent, rolling his Rs.

"Sure do." I leaned on the bar with bent arms. Yesterday, I'd cleaned up an old bird pendant I'd picked up at the markets and with a small sparkle of illusion magic, it looked three times its worth. Except I had a different payment to use now.

"Got something for you out the back of your tavern. Go check it out. I'll be waiting."

He studied me, his arms planted on his narrow hips. The man might have been in his seventies and thin as a pole, but he was tough as nails; I'd once seen him punch a man half his age and knock him flat to the ground.

Without a word, Ted marched out the rear door. The girls near the fireplace howled with laughter. Once I completed this job and got paid, hell, I was holding a huge party with Scarlet and her three lovers to celebrate. Just remembering she had three partners made me so proud of her, since most of the time she blushed like a raspberry at the mention of the opposite sex. Now, she was probably getting laid by those wolf shifters like a bunny. Damn lucky girl.

"The horse?" Ted asked, and despite his stoic voice, a thread of excitement thrummed beneath his question.

"Well, if you don't like the payment, I'd gladly keep him. He's worth ten times what I owe you, so how about we can call this paying my tab and an advance?"

Ted chuckled and stuck out his hand. "You ought to consider taking up undercover work because you always surprise me. Many people pay well in that field."

I shook his hand and offered him a smug smile. "Who said I wasn't? But you may want to discard the saddle pretty quick, as it comes with a priestess emblem from Terra. And guards might come snooping."

Ted drew me toward him by my arm, wrenching me halfway over the counter. "Seems the innocence in your eyes is deceiving. I'll take the horse and we have a deal. Now, what will you have to drink?" He released me, and I fell into my seat.

"Pear cider, a plate of your famous chicken fingers, and information."

He narrowed his eyes and leaned on an elbow on the bar. "Keep talking."

The couple at the end of the counter was deep in conversation, and not paying us any mind. "I was meant to meet Elliana here a few days ago. You know, the girl with the long, blonde hair. We got drunk here a few months ago, then you kicked us out. Have you seen her? Maybe she left a message for me?"

Ted's lips twitched in a frown. "She owes me a bigger debt than you, and I don't take messages." He wiped his stubbled chin, the sound grating on my nerves. "Haven't seen her since last week."

I forced a brittle smile, weariness eating away at my confidence and the earlier excitement of getting this job.

"Has anyone hung out at the tavern most of this week?"

"Girl, everyone does that here. I don't keep record of who comes and goes." Ted looked over at the couple at the bar, who waved him over. "Sorry I can't be of more help."

Ted poured me a long glass of cider, placed it in front of me, and joined his other clientele.

I slouched, coldness washing through my body, and drank half the cider. Its sweetness churned in my gut. If Elliana was avoiding the tavern, she'd probably turn up disguised. Well, *she* had selected this spot as our meeting place. What if she'd given up on me and offered the job to someone else? And to make matters worse, it was too late in the day to head back home, *and* it would be on foot since I'd sold Elf.

So I'd stay for as long as my credit with Ted allowed me to rent one of his rooms, in case Elliana made a show. Nervousness chewed on my insides. Getting paid meant paying off Dad's huge debt, and no longer having to live hand to mouth.

I swiveled on my stool, tempted to check out the other bars and shops in town for Elliana. But what if I missed her popping into the tavern?

The man from the corner stared my way. Shadows danced across his hooded face, and a shiver raced down my arms.

Had he heard what I'd asked Ted? Did he know Elliana, or was he working with her?

He stood, and when he came in my direction, my heart slammed into my chest. Judging by his concealed face, was I dealing with a gang member? They were renowned for kidnapping loners and selling them on the black market.

When he put his hand into the inside pocket of his coat, I lost my breath.

CHAPTER 3

*M*y heart hit the back of my throat. The six-foot-two stranger glided toward me like someone who knew the finer qualities of not making a sound. His long, unbuttoned coat, dark as a winter night, reached his knees. Underneath he wore black. Though his hood covered the top half of his face, I caught the shape of his prominent jaw and the muscles in his neck. His lips parted as if he might snarl.

With a deep inhale, I turned my back on him to show him I had no intention of confronting him, whatever his issue. Ted wiped down a wet glass and didn't seem to bat an eye at the man behind me, but then again, he served all kinds of clientele here. On my last visit, I'd seen a man I swore could have been a lion shifter with his wild golden hair, and the fact that a growl had hung at the end of each of his words only cemented that theory in my mind. So what was hooded stranger's deal?

He slammed a hand on the counter inches from my elbow and pulled back, leaving behind several gold coins.

I shouldn't have trembled, but heck, something about his

presence had my nerves on edge. I blamed it on not being able to see his face. *Show who the hell you are, otherwise no one will trust you.*

As much as I wanted to twist around, I refused. Ted wasn't acting strange. So the fraying anxiety was in my head, along with the screaming urge to leave the tavern, but for once, the prickles down my flesh weren't there. No warning from the goddess. Talk about whiplash emotions.

"Why's a little girl like you alone in the bar today?" His question drifted over my shoulder, a deep, cultured voice reverberating through me.

I swallowed back a groan.

"Didn't your mother tell you it's rude to act all creepy?" I had no time for someone trying to belittle me, regardless of whether or not his voice tickled my libido.

"Besides, who said I was alone?" I continued. "And calling me 'little' implies I'm helpless. That's where you're dead wrong." I took a gulp of my cider and licked the last drops off my lips.

He swallowed loudly, and the hairs on my arms shifted. His breath washed across the back of my neck when he whispered, "Don't be so sure about that."

What!? Yeah right. I tensed, my hand flinching to my waist, brushing the knife's hilt, and I spun on my swiveling chair to confront him. Instead, I spotted the last wisps of his long coat as he stormed out of the bar, the door slapping shut behind him.

"Asshole. He's lucky he left."

I shook my head and finished my drink as Ted placed a plate of chicken fingers with roasted potato wedges in front of me. Their salty and greasy aroma left me salivating.

"Damn, who cares about some loser when there's food involved," I said.

Ted laughed, reminding me of my dad. What was he

doing now? Enjoying dinner with Santos while mesmerized by Ariella's tales?

"You sound like my daughter," Ted joked. "Food comes first, even before me." He set the dish down in front of me. Goddess, if Ted moved to Terra, he'd make a killing. Except he'd once told me he was a quarter bear shifter and three-quarters human, which was why he'd set up shop at the foot of the White Peak Mountains. He didn't quite fit into either world, so he'd carved out his own haven. Smart man, and being out of Terra meant no trouble from the priestess or her guards finding out he wasn't a pure human. Bear shifters didn't have such rules in White Peak. Or least so I'd heard... but who the hell knew the truth since they kept to themselves?

Figuring I might as well get comfortable while I waited and prayed Elliana would arrive soon, I grabbed my dish and hoisted my bag in my other hand, then headed to the back table, where the hooded man had nursed his drink.

Ted followed me with a fresh glass of cider. "Enjoy."

"Thanks." I glanced out the window to an empty dirt road. Returning to my meal, I sat and dug in.

* * *

TREPIDATION WORMED its way up my legs and coiled in my gut like a goddamn punch. The tavern buzzed with activity, people standing there as if it were a festival. Had to be close to fifty patrons crowding the room. The chatter was like cicadas in my ears, and I shifted in my seat, feeling as if I was wearing a dress two sizes too small. I hated crowds. And despite all these people, there was no Elliana. Would she arrive later? Goddess, I hoped so.

Night claimed the world outside, and considering I

wasn't going anywhere tonight, I threw back my fifth cider and picked at the second plate of chicken fingers.

A loud chuckle drew my eye to the bar, where two friends hugged, slapping each other's backs. They wore thigh-length tunics and matching sand-colored pants. Were they from Utaara, the desert realm where a sultan lived in his enormous palace?

Someone else pulled the chair out across from me and plonked himself down, grinning. "Hey, beautiful."

I rolled my eyes. "Not interested. Leave."

Surprise crossed his face, which told me everything: girls rarely turned him down. Not that I could blame them. I mean, with his golden hair, strong cheekbones, and sun-kissed skin, he was cute. Didn't make him any less of an ass.

I scanned the room when Blondie snatched my hand, squeezing. I wrenched myself away from him, but he didn't budge or release me.

"Listen, little girl," he began, causing rage to sear through my veins, sick and tired of being referred to as anything but a lady or woman. Come on, I was nineteen, sure only five-foot-two, but that made no difference. That was why heels had been invented. Not only did they give me height, but they came in handy as weapons when trapped.

"No, you listen, sugarplum." I smirked. "Unless you plan on giving me a spiritual palm reading, let me go before I break your nose."

His mouth widened in satisfaction like a wolf who'd cornered his prey. "I just want to talk." He peered over his shoulder at two men who looked his way and lifted his chin in acknowledgment.

Oh yeah, now I understood. A jerk completing a dare from his friends to pick up the lonely girl at the tavern. "What would you want to chat about?" I began. "The weather? What I like for breakfast? Or how you still live with your parents and this little venture with your buddies to White Peak makes you feel so tough?"

I tried to tug my hand free, but he held on. "Bitch."

"Been called worse things." I kicked him under the table.

He flinched, his grip loosening, and I leaped to my feet, grabbing the knife from my belt. I lunged past the table and pressed the tip to his neck before he could react. A satisfied smile tugged on my lips. I loved payback. "Now play nice and run back to your friends."

His cheeks blanched while the bridge between his nose pinched. He got up in slow motion, the seat scraping across the wooden floorboards beneath him. Hate flooded his wry expression. Yeah, rejection stung.

I swept my gaze over his group of buddies. None of them made a move toward us, and I gave them my one-finger salute. I lowered my blade from Blondie and withdrew. "Get the fuck out of my face."

Except he didn't back off, he jumped at me, his hands going for my throat.

But someone from within the crowd grabbed him by the back of the shirt and tossed him into the masses as if he weighed nothing. Blondie and a huddle of partygoers stumbled to the ground.

I raised my gaze to the stranger with the hood from earlier in the day. He stood there, his face still half-covered, his chest puffing in and out, wide enough to carry the entire world.

"You're back, I see." I lifted my weapon because I wasn't sure what his deal was; maybe it was a full moon out that had turned everyone into lunatics. "I appreciate the bravado, but I can look after myself."

The majority of patrons fanned outward, watching, waiting for a fight. Blondie and his buddies rushed up behind Hooded Man.

"Watch out," I yelled.

He spun so fast, I flinched backward, hitting the wall, the blade shaking in my hand. Yeah, this was a night of crazies, and I didn't stand a chance against the newcomer. First rule of attending any tavern... never engage in a brawl with someone twice your size. The stranger punched Blondie, sending him reeling into a group of people, bringing several bystanders down with him. Two other attackers surged forward, arms flying, grunts exploding, and the crowd cheered them on, bellowing in excitement.

Men were the same no matter where I traveled. And in all honesty, I didn't need to cheer on a fight now or ever, so I flung my bag over my shoulder and squeezed into the hordes.

Hoots exploded around me, and several jabs in my ribs later, I pushed free from the masses. Sure, I appreciated the big man standing up for me, but no one had asked him to, and he could take care of himself. Worse yet, what if he expected payment for saving my ass? At the front door, I caught one last glance of the fight. Hooded Man appeared to be winning as he drove a fist into Blondie's stomach.

Hell, that must hurt. I dashed outside, heading for one of Ted's rental room places down the street. If I rushed, no one would see which one I snuck into for the night. With the cold enveloping me, I pulled my long, black coat out of my bag and slipped it on.

Then I ran, dried dirt crunching underfoot, and twisted my head around. More people poured into the establishment, and the moment the doors opened, a thundering cheer escaped.

Nothing I hadn't seen before, but still the shakes hadn't left me, not to mention the chill running down my spine. *Yes, I know, Goddess. You're warning me, and that's why I'm leaving.*

Being alone in White Peak left me with few options. Ted

was an acquaintance, but what power did he have to stop anyone from tearing my throat out if they so chose?

Footfalls sounded from the tavern.

My heart raced, and I whirled, weapon still in hand.

No one had followed.

I turned and ran straight into someone, but it might as well have been a brick wall. I bounced backward, and my stomach roiled.

Gawking at the hooded man left me breathless for so many reasons, like how the hell had he got in front of me so fast? Did he now expect a reward for fighting those idiots in the tavern, but most importantly, why had he returned to the bar? Was he coming for me? Or was he helping me and just staying in town for the night? But I wasn't in a trusting mood tonight.

"You're welcome." His gravelly voice carried on the wind buffeting him from behind. The hood he wore ruffled, darkening his features.

"Who are you?" I grumbled. "What do you want?"

There was movement in my peripheral vision. Blondie and five other men stormed our way. Fear flashed through me. I swore two of them looked familiar. Hard to tell in the dark.

I growled and sidestepped him.

Hooded Man blocked my path, his hand stretched out, palm up. "Let me keep you safe," he said with caution, his gaze lifting to the gang approaching.

"Are you insane? Those hillbillies are coming for you."

The encroaching steps grew louder, their voices reaching us.

I zigged to my right between two buildings. Damn, could the night get any worse? Surely, Ted hadn't moved Elf yet, and I could ride him out of here. "Please be there," I whispered.

The moment I burst into the darkened meadow where I'd left Elf, a strong arm snapped around my waist from behind and lifted me off the ground. Hooded Man grasped my knife, ripping it out of my hold.

I cried out as he pressed me against his side as if I were a toddler, my bag squished between us.

He broke into a run.

I jostled about, screaming.

People got kidnapped this way, then they woke up in an underground market auctioned off as slaves, or had their organs removed and used for death magic. All kinds of things happened in the Darkwoods. Was that who this man was? A gang member making an extra coin?

I bucked and elbowed him in the chest. "Release me!"

"Enough!" he roared. "I'm trying to help you!"

"Fuck you." With no weapon, I dug into my pocket for my herbs, energy already bubbling in my chest.

Five men emerged, each grasping long knives. "Get her! I want her to pay," Blondie yelled. But when I recognized one of the men as the idiot guard from Terra who'd broken Dad's bedside table, I shuddered.

Once Blondie and his friends were done with me, the guard would drag me into a dungeon back in Terra to rot for life for leaving the realm. I lowered my head, praying he hadn't seen me in the tavern. Or had they followed the horse's tracks to the Golden Lock? I changed tactics and decided to take my chance with the big man, even if he was probably a bandit.

"Run faster," I said. "They're almost on us."

We veered past the last building and came out in front of a carriage drawn by two dark stallions. Each had red horns, as if they'd just climbed their way out of the underworld. Their snorted exhales misted into the night. There was no rider out front. The carriage itself was pitch black with golden trim and studs encasing the door and windows. Rose motifs and thorned stems curled along the top paneling.

"Fuck!" Was this a hearse? Shit had just got real. "You *are* kidnapping me, aren't you?" I wriggled, panic gripping my insides. Energy rolled through me as I frantically tried to open the pouch with one hand.

"Don't you dare put a spell on me." His hand clasped across my mouth and nose, cutting off my air, pushing the pouch out of my hands. It slipped through my fingers and fell.

No! I *was* going to end up an undead with my organs sold to the highest bidder.

He kicked the door, and it creaked open. Inside the seats were torn, as if someone had released a large feral cat to mangle the decor.

I drove my heels into his legs and flung my arm against his face, hitting him.

But he rushed us inside, and at his whistle, the carriage lurched forward.

We landed in a seat, with me constricted by a monster who was suffocating me, and stars were dancing in my vision. My lungs strained and darkness crowded at the corners of my eyes.

CHAPTER 4

*J*ostled about, banging my head on something hard, and snapped open my eyes. Iciness wrapped around me, and I rubbed the chill that had settled over my arms. The blanket over my lap did little to warm me. My breath floated in front of my face, and my pulse rang in my ears. Night filled the air. As my vision focused, I found myself still inside the creepy carriage.

A dimly-lit lantern swung from above the window, revealing a figure sitting across from me. Hooded Man. His arms were folded over his stomach, his posture curled forward, and his chin dipped into his chest. Was he asleep?

Memories crashed through me, and my brain ached. The Golden Lock tavern, Blondie trying to pick me up, and then this man kidnapping me with a freakin' carriage. The only people who owned carriages were royalty visiting Terra from Darkwoods. So did that mean I'd been kidnapped and was getting transported in the opposite direction to White Peak? The urge to scream and run pushed on my mind.

I scanned the floor and seats for my bag. Where was it? Had he pulled over when we were free from town and tied it outside to the carriage, so we had more leg room? It was a tight squeeze in here. But all my curse reversal ingredients were in the bag, and maybe I could conjure something together to keep the man asleep.

Outside, the landscape blurred, but on closer inspection, snow smothered the forest on either side of us, and we were moving so fast, I jumped from every hole and rock we passed over. Why were we speeding? Wait, it never snowed in Darkwoods. That meant we were headed north, into White Peak Mountains. How long had I been out?

All right, I ought to celebrate, as we might be racing toward the family in need and maybe Hooded Man wasn't a bandit. Elliana had said we'd meet someone to take me into the mountains. Was this the man?

He sure didn't act like a guide. What if someone else had gotten wind of me entering their realm and that was why he'd snatched me first?

Hooded Man hadn't moved.

Sweat rolled down my nape, and the tremor in my hands began. Holding my breath, I leaned forward and reached for the door handle.

"I wouldn't do that." His dry and crackly words filled the void between us, and a shiver crept over me, numbing my brain.

Still grasping the latch, my head battled between grilling his ass or jumping. I twisted to face him, and while the shadows concealed his expression, his eyes glistened, covering me in goosebumps.

"Give me one good reason," I wheezed. Dread pressed against me, ticking like a bomb under my breastbone.

"I'll give you three. You'll freeze to death before you reach town. If the cold doesn't get you, the bears will. But most likely, before any of those things happen, I'll catch you." A snarl hung off his last word.

Lowering my hand, my veins turned to ice, and nausea claimed me. "Okay." I gripped the blanket over my legs. "Well, you make some valid points, if this were a normal scenario. But are you a bear shifter? And why did you kidnap me? Are you Elliana's friend?"

He laughed, rough-sounding, as if he might clear his throat. "You can't tell I'm a bear shifter?" When he leaned forward, the lantern lit up his face. Disheveled, dark hair reached his shoulders, and the uneven light made his thick stubble shine. Full lips were pressed together in an impatient expression. And lashes so long they should be illegal encased the brightest green eyes. The man wasn't lacking in the attractive arena, but that didn't make him any less psycho.

He turned his head to show me the side of his face. Three healed scratches ran down his cheek and neck.

"Shit." I couldn't cover my surprise.

I'd once heard a tale that initiation for male bear shifters happened when they turned ten years old. Pitted against a wild bear, not only did they have to survive, but they had to receive a permanent scar on their faces, necks, or chests to show the world they were true warriors. Never on the back, as that declared weakness. Anyone without one was shunned and discarded by their families. Something about bear shifters only breeding the most powerful fighters. For too long, I'd suspected it was an exaggeration of the truth, but the healed claw mark now turned me into a believer. Yep, no way was I facing this man in a fight, and taking this assignment to reverse a curse had been a huge mistake.

"And," he continued, "I didn't kidnap you. I saved you."

"Is that what you call saving?" I pulled the blanket up to my neck because I couldn't stop trembling. "I'd hate to see how you treat your enemies."

His earlier words about chasing me down circled in my mind like vultures spotting a carcass for the taking. Considering he was talking and not killing me yet, I figured I ought to keep him occupied.

The land climbed upward, yet we hadn't slowed. "And what do you feed those horses?"

"They're dragon horses, originating from the Wildfire realm. Stronger than your average beast, they can withstand the cold. Plus, they occasionally snort fire."

"What? No way."

He smirked. "They're mostly from the horse family, but there's also dragon in their blood."

I shifted in my seat, scanning the surrounding night. A long animal shape darted through the woods. I did a double take. Had I just imagined that?

"Dragon horses are not the smartest animals," he continued, "But once you teach them to follow a path, that's all they'll know for their entire life. They're loyal."

Yeah, but they were still demon-like horses.

He stretched out his legs and crossed them at the ankles, studying me from head to toe, so I sat and pulled the blanket tighter around myself.

"So, are you friends with Elliana?"

He shook his head. "I just met her at the tavern when I went asking people for help with a curse. But a few days ago, she sent me a message saying she was tied up and couldn't meet with you. She described you, but honestly, I was ready to leave tonight if you were a no-show again." He reclined and glanced into the wilderness. "My name is Raze Ursa." A smile broke over his face, his sharp cheekbones perfectly accentuating his rugged features.

"I'm—"

"I know who you are. Bee Père from the Terra realm. You're nineteen, live with your father, love to sun-tan, and Elliana speaks highly of your abilities."

I clamped my mouth shut when I realized it was hanging

open. What else had Elliana told him? And what did sun-baking have to do with the assignment? Perhaps I'd misunderstood everything. Apparently in the bear world, 'collecting someone' must have translated into shoving them inside a carriage and scaring them half to death before introducing yourself.

"Why didn't you tell me this in the tavern, instead of acting all stalkerish?"

His thick eyebrows lowered. "I went to prepare our transport, as I'd let the dragon horses roam free in the meadow. Except the damned charges bolted, and I spent half the day chasing them. They got excited, as they rarely spend time in a green field." His voice dipped with that not-impressed tone.

I released a long exhale. After all the earlier commotion and alarm, exhaustion washed over me as if I'd dragged myself through an ocean of mud.

"Why were you so late?" he asked in a deep authoritative voice. I was glad the shadows hid his face because I imagined him scowling. And while I found the man handsome, he left me worried. I'd never met a bear shifter before. Were all of them grizzly and ready to bite your head off?

"To be fair," I started, "I was at the mercy of a friend who had to bring me a key ingredient, and she got caught up in a mess with wolves in the Den. Goddess, you don't want to hear what she got up to." And considering Scarlet had brought three of the wolf shifters illegally into Terra, I definitely hadn't heard the full story yet. But on our next catch up, she'd have to tell me every detail, especially where it involved the three shifters.

Raze tsked. "You sure you can break curses?" His patronizing voice carried the arrogance I expected from royalty.

I snorted and straightened my posture. "Magic comes from inside, not what I look like. Sorry I didn't battle a wild animal as a child to prove my worth."

Silence folded around us, and he studied me from his side of the carriage.

I broke the silence. "Once we get there, I'll check the patient, then cast my breaking spell, and I should be out of your hair by morning."

"Sure hope so. We're all counting on you. No room for failure." The intensity of his gaze seemed to pierce right through me. Okay, I heard the warning loud and clear: *Don't fail.*

Drawing a bent leg under me, I huddled under the blanket. "As long as you keep your end of the bargain and pay up, I'll do my best. But I made it clear to Elliana, there are no guarantees. Every curse is unique and temperamental."

I'd tackled a few curses in my life, and there was only one I hadn't been able to reverse. A farmer's cattle had stopped delivering milk for weeks on end. Nothing I'd tried worked, until I'd discovered he'd had two different spells put on him by two unrelated people; a jealous neighbor and his ex-wife. Turned out the spells had intermingled and locked on to the poor cattle so tight, I had no chance of removing that mess. Instead, I'd added my own incantation, which bent the existing hexes to only affect the animals during moonlight.

Raze didn't respond at first, and I waited for him to challenge me. After a pause, he nodded.

We traveled for several miles without a word exchanged. I had premade a paralyzing spell in case I needed to protect myself and run away, though I never knew when dealing with bears if it would work. Except the ingredients were in my bag, which was probably somewhere outside on the carriage.

"How much longer 'till we get there?" I rubbed warmth into my legs.

"Not long. Once we're over the crest, the castle is just to the right."

I choked on my next inhale. "Castle? Is the afflicted bear shifter a royal?"

Raze nodded. "Something like that."

Completing a spell for a normal bear shifter, I could handle. But arrogant royalty demanded the impossible. Plus, guards could toss me into prison for not healing the royal member. Back in Terra, they surrounded the priestess every moment of the day, treating her like a goddess, and the only time she spoke to ordinary folk was when she dished out punishment. How the hell would bear shifters behave? Irritation buzzed through me; I wasn't ready to meet some snooty king or queen. I hadn't even brought my best clothes or a dress, opting rather for thick, layered clothes to handle the freezing weather in White Peak.

Centuries ago when Haven had been divided into seven realms, a family had taken control of each territory and called themselves royalty. Some places had lost those bloodlines, but others still controlled their kingdoms with iron fists. Was that how it was in White Peak?

My breath fogged the window, which had tiny piles of snow along the sill. I cleared the pane with my sleeve, not confident in the slightest this was a simple job, judging by how turbulent it had been so far. And what if I couldn't cure the hex? Would they imprison me for life? I needed to return to Dad and look after him. My next inhale rattled all the way to my lungs.

"You seem worried?" Raze asked.

"I'm fine." A blur flitted between the trees, moving almost in pace with our carriage. I squinted for a better look. My thoughts flew to wolves, except they mostly resided in the west side of White Peak due to an agreement they had with the bear shifters.

"Your perspiration gives you aw—"

Another dark shape raced through the night, and my heartbeat sped up. "Hey, what are those things out there?"

Raze shuffled in his seat to sit across from me, our knees touching, and scanned the wilderness. His sudden intake of frosty air had my pulse speeding.

"Do exactly as I say." His words rushed, and I hated the way he'd said that. "Stay in the carriage, no matter what happens or what you see. The horses won't stop and will deliver you to our home."

"Am I in danger? Where are you going? And where's my bag? I need my stuff." I gasped for air, drawn out of my comfort zone. I gawked as another dark form leaped behind a few trees.

"Oh, my goddess. Is that a bear? Why are they running with us? I-Is it an escort?"

Raze toed his boots off, shrugged out of his coat, and unbuttoned his black shirt.

"What the fuck are you doing?" I hissed and curled in on myself on the seat, my gaze swinging from the brown bear that now raced alongside us, so huge I could die from a stroke, to Raze, half-naked and pushing himself toward the door.

My attention lowered to the most incredible flat stomach, the planes of which were pure muscle. Strong, powerful and—

A growl bellowed from the woods, and I flinched.

"I'll buy you time to arrive at the castle." His words rushed and his brow perspired. Was he worried I wouldn't make it? He undid the buttons on his pants, and Goddess, any other time I'd be gawking, but now I couldn't pull my gaze from the window. The bear twisted its head in my direction, snarling.

"Those bears aren't our escort, are they?"

"Nope!"

Numbness owned me as I pictured my death—being torn to shreds. "Why are they attacking us if you're from the royal palace? Will you be okay?"

"There are some royal issues right now." In a blur of movement, the door slapped open, and icy winds flooded the carriage. Raze jumped out, butt-naked, transforming in mid air so fast, I would have missed it if I'd blinked. His body expanded, his legs and arms thickened, and fur exploded across his skin. He changed so swiftly, it reminded me of an eagle battling against a gust with ease.

Raze hit the ground on all fours, wearing golden brown fur. He lunged at the other bear. Both rolled across the snow and slammed into a tree.

The carriage kept racing forward, the door flapping open and shut, and the night stealing the battle from my sight.

I reached over and yanked the door shut. "Oh, shit. Oh, shit! What now?"

Raze had said to stay inside, yet my knees kept bouncing. The horses would take me to the castle, he'd insisted. My teeth chattered as I conjured images of my death. If bears attacked their own kind, what in the world would they do to me? And what issues were the royal bear shifter family having? Had I walked into political drama? Or was this about the curse?

A sudden crash slammed into the side of the carriage, and my heart froze. I jerked around in time to see a massive bear darting out of my line of sight as the carriage trembled out of control, lifting upward on its side.

Arms flaying for balance, I slid along the seat, hitting the wall. The snowy ground rushed toward me, and I screamed.

CHAPTER 5

*S*hock jolted through my body and I screamed as the carriage tilted sideways on two wheels.

Out of nowhere, a shadow slammed into the falling cabin's side, sending it rocking back onto four wheels. The sudden move tossed me across the compartment. I hit the opposite seat hard, my hip screaming with a short, sharp pain, then I slid to the floor with a groan. The world swayed, and I scrambled to my feet, wobbling when I came to an abrupt stop. The carriage stayed in an upright position. *Thank you, Goddess.*

The wind whistled outside, shaking the carriage, and I now stood diagonally across the road. A fierce blizzard battered the night.

Stay put, Raze had said. Not as if I could outrun the bears. But sitting here meant waiting to get butchered, and what if Raze lay somewhere injured? Maybe the dragon horses just needed a little nudge to get them running again. They must be spooked from the carriage almost toppling over. But I couldn't hear them struggling.

Pressed up against the window, I searched the woods,

39

then did the same on the other side. All clear, except for the impenetrable dark woods, but if two bears had knocked over the carriage, why would they have taken off? Unless Raze was fighting them. Okay, I had to get the carriage moving. He might need a quick escape, or for me to go get help.

I pushed open the door and froze as a gale hit me. "Goddess, please help me. Don't let me get eaten," I muttered under my breath.

Once I jumped out, I rushed to the front, where both horses were upright, neighing, and snorting short flames from their nostrils. Okay, that was new.

A tremendous snarl erupted from farther up the road, and I flinched so hard, my head spun.

I plastered myself against a skittish horse. A scream bubbled on the forefront of my mind. Trembling, I peeked out and stared at the biggest mother of a bear on hind legs, snarling, drool seeping from long fangs.

My stomach churned. *Goddess, I don't want to die this way!* I scrambled alongside the horse toward the back of the carriage, searching for my bag. I needed my herbs.

Breaths came too fast. At the rear, I found my bag tied up with rope. Adrenaline soared through me, muscles taut. I tugged at the knots, my chest aching. *Hell!* The ropes weren't loosening. I might as well have been trying to rip the cord apart with my bare hands. *Shit!*

A thundering roar came from the bear, and the horses backpedaled, driving the carriage backward and into me. I shuffled aside, peeking around to the front. The grizzly hadn't budged, maybe put off by the flame-snorting horses. Rushing back to my bag, I kept pulling at the rope knotted tighter than a dead bug in a spider's web. *Fucking ropes. Come on!*

The wind howled in my ears, ripping at my hair and

clothes, icicles chilling me to the bone. When the crunch of snow came from behind me, I snapped around.

A huge bear the color of timber was on all fours, fifteen feet away, and it wasn't Raze. Was this a wild bear or a shifter? Tales painted them as brutal and unforgiving, carrying grudges for life. So that explained the death stares coming my way, and Raze had said royals had issues right now. What did that mean?

Facing the bear, I fumbled with the buttons on the bag behind me. My hands shook so hard I fought the restraints to pry the bag open so I could get my hand inside.

The animal inched closer, and when it unleashed an ungodly sound, a strangled cry fell from my throat.

It's going to attack!

My hand slid into the bag. I fumbled about, past clothes and pouches of ingredients, for spells. What I needed was a small, velvet sack. My fingers touched the fabric. I pulled it out and tore open the tiny purse.

The bear charged toward me.

I trembled and dropped the bag to my feet, herbs and powders spilling onto the snow.

"No!"

The insistent gale tossed them around my feet, and yet I stood there, fear sitting over my mouth and nose, suffocating me. The beast flew at me.

Another figure lunged out of the woods and slammed into the attacking bear. They both smacked into the ground, snow thrown in every direction and hitting me in the face.

My stomach lurched, and I snatched up my pouch of herbs.

Snarls filled the night. Teeth bared, ripping off fur, spittle, and a cacophony of growls. They rolled off the road, and I rounded to the front of the carriage to where the horses pulled away from the encroaching danger.

It felt as if my heart would break out of my ribcage, but I couldn't just sit back and wait to become bear food. I pulled out a pinch of herbs from my pouch and summoned the strength to hold myself still. The horses reared and nudged me aside. I stumbled into the middle of the track, right in the path of the other bear unleashing a deathly roar. It charged.

Clasping the enchanted powder, I trembled, and those few moments felt like a lifetime as I grounded myself. Magic flowed over my skin and I let it go. "Freeze." I blew the crushed herbs into the gale, but the wind seized the ingredients from in front of me and blew them into a tree, ice crackling around its trunk in an instant.

I recoiled, my fingers deep in the pouch. The horses pulled a hard right to avoid the attack. I screamed and tossed the contents into the bear's face as it reached me. "Freeze!"

The beast iced over mid-movement, its expression twisted into a snarl, and it fell at my feet with a dull thud.

Gulping for air, I gawked at the extended claws, teeth bared. *Hell!* That had been too close.

I darted to the rear of the carriage, where Raze had attacked the other bear, but the area was empty. Where was he? And it wasn't as if I could wait and put everyone into a frozen state. The magic only worked for a short moment, and as I checked the pouch, I realized I'd lost most of the powder.

But unless I intended to die, which was a *hell-no* in my books, I scrambled up into the driver's seat. The iced bear lay in the middle of the road.

I leaned forward and rubbed the horses' backs. "We need to get out of here. Need to return home."

They stopped pulling off the road, so that was something. I collected the reins tied to a wooden stake near my feet and scanned the woods for any sign of Raze. Nothing. And as much I hated leaving him, he was a goddamn bear in his territory. I was a shish kebab for the bears, ready for the killing. I whipped the straps into a wave across the horses' sides.

"Home!" I called out once more.

They lurched forward, throwing me into my seat, but I held on. Damn, they moved fast.

Wind buffeted against me, my eyes tearing up from the cold, my hands frozen.

A roar echoed at my back, and I glanced over the top of the carriage.

Two bears were chasing us. *Fuck no!*

Raze had said his horses knew where the castle lay, so I had to trust them. It wasn't as if I had any other ideas. Goddess, if I ever got out of this alive, I would grill Elliana about all future jobs before I blindly accepted. Who was hiring me, what the job entailed, and most importantly, would I be at risk of dying?

We rushed forward, and my gut knotted. The wind tore at me relentlessly. Darkness consumed the surrounding scenery, and I glanced back.

The animals still pursued, and urgency pressed on my chest. I nudged the horses with the reins. "Faster."

Where the road forked, the horses careened left, the land climbing upward. Trees thinned out on either side, replaced by jagged stone rocks towering over me. Up above, shadowy bear forms raced along the ledges.

More of the monsters! I yearned to return home, forget this assignment. But look how hard it had been getting this far, and who the hell knew how I'd get home. I prayed Raze had survived because I didn't need to turn up to the castle and announce that the guide who'd been sent to collect me had perished. I couldn't live with that on my conscience. But in any case, the quicker I got to safety, the sooner someone could go help Raze.

Grunts escalated behind me as I traveled farther along the narrow road, just wide enough for one carriage; if I stretched out my arms, I'd touch the rocky walls of the canyon. The bumpy passage had me jostling about.

If I had ingredients, I'd create a more elaborate spell to stop the attackers, but that took time and concentration, neither of which I had while fleeing for my life.

A sudden crash into the back of the carriage sent me reeling forward in my seat. The horses kept going, but I spun to find a bear scaling the top of the carriage.

Fear drenched my skin with perspiration, the internal screams rattling in my ears. Tendrils of energy zipped up my arms, and I retrieved the pouch from my pocket. I didn't have much of the powder left. Last time the wind had stolen the herbs, so I moved fast. I poured the rest of the contents into my palm and found maybe enough for one spell. I glanced at the beast crawling closer, teeth exposed, sharp, white daggers ready to slice my body.

His paws were rooted to the roof of the carriage. His fur fluttered left and right from the wind.

The animal swiped a claw outward, inches from my face. I swerved sideways, holding onto the stake that held the reins to stop myself from falling. I ducked down. Terror was a knife twisting in my gut, and it took every inch of strength to not scream and jump off the carriage and run.

I clenched the herbs in my fists, waiting for the animal to get closer. My hands sweated despite the icy winds. If I moved too soon, I might not get another chance. My heart stuck to my throat. What if I missed?

When a shadow fell over me, I tossed the ingredients into the animal's face. "Freeze."

He halted at first, staring, waiting. *Please, please let it work.* I slid back down into my seat.

Something shifted behind his black eyes: terror. Then, in

a sudden swerve of the carriage, I lurched sideways, about to get tossed to the rocky ground. I screamed and pawed the air for something to hold. My fingers grasped the back of the seat, and I hauled myself back up. *Shit!*

The bear flew backward and out of sight, collected by the night.

Pulling myself upright, I gulped for air and fought the impulse to turn the carriage around and go back for Raze. But I had no freezing herbs left. I picked up the reins again. I had to move—and fast—and get out of here.

Bears continued to follow me along the overhead cliffs that now sloped downward. They'd catch me in no time, and I'd die out here and no one would know what had happened. My throat thickened.

"Come on." I drove quicker, the horses' flaming exhales ripped from their nostrils by the wind.

Around the next bend, the cliff flanked outward in opposite directions but dipped fast. The bears wouldn't be far behind.

But when I focused on the path ahead, my gaze landed on an enormous castle atop a mountain, grand and majestic, just as I'd imagined in my wildest dreams. Torches lit a winding path from an open gate toward the building. More dotted the structure, lighting up the place as if it were a birthday cake. Weren't they bothered they'd attract these angry bears to their doorstep? I didn't even know if these attackers were shifters or wild animals.

We thundered onward. Behind me, bears closed in from both sides. I tensed and whipped the reins. "Faster. Faster."

They were so close I could make out their warped glares, their wild eyes.

We raced forward, the carriage jostling and jumping about. I held my breath as I burst through the iron gates. At that exact moment, a snap of energy rocked through me, lifting every hair on my body on end.

Magic!

The horses never stopped but galloped toward the castle, climbing a dark, windy road.

I twisted around but found the bears hovering near the gate, which slowly closed on its own.

I regretted everything about this assignment; I felt without a shadow of a doubt that the battle I'd just endured with the bears was child's play compared to the storm brewing in the air around the castle.

THE EARLIER ENERGY still lingered on my skin, its sharpness biting into my flesh. This was no ordinary power... not at all, but something dark, using death magic.

CHAPTER 6

*T*he horses galloped for the last leg of the curved road leading up to the castle. A rock face filled on the left-hand side, and a sharp descent into the abyss on the right. With the reins tied up, I curled up in the front seat, pulling my jacket tight around my chest as the cold wind slapped me in the face and stole my breath. These horses were resilient and incredible. They looked like normal creatures, except they snorted fire. Something glinted across their backs, and I squinted for a better look. Translucent scales ran the length of their spines.

Veering left, the horses pulled the carriage down a cobblestone road, their heads high, as if proud to return home—and they ought to have been after escaping a near-death encounter.

Ahead, the castle appeared to reach the clouds. Moonlight shone against the ancient castle drenched in snow. Walls stood silent, gray stone towers with cone-shaped turrets flanked the building, unapologetically reminding me of protectors of the realm. Flags fluttered from the roof.

Mullioned windows reflected darkness, as if no one was home.

The place had to be larger than the entire town of Terra, and how many hundreds of people did it take to maintain such a place and the grounds? Imagine coming home to this every day? It was like a fairy tale!

Snow claimed everything in sight. The only time I hadn't seen snow caps on the White Peak Mountains from back home had been during summer. I supposed one had to wear a thick fur coat permanently to live this high up in the realm.

The horses came to an abrupt halt in front of half a dozen steps. At the top waited double doors black as the night, in contrast to the pale walls.

Jumping down, I rubbed my hands together for warmth and hurried to the rear of the carriage to collect my bag, but the horses galloped onward, my bag in tow.

"Hey, wait up. I need my belongings." I waved to no avail and felt stupid standing there as they careened around the side of the castle. This was their home, so they had to know where they were going, right?

I spun on the spot, taking in the enormous terrain, snow sparkling beneath the moonlight. The edges of the land vanished into the dark, as if the castle floated in the sky. Aside from the whistling wind, everything else remained silent. Too quiet, perhaps. No sounds of bear shifters grunting and pounding the ground to reach me, and that alone had me breathing easier.

I imagined the place as manicured in the summer months, with animal-shaped shrubs, and riddled with fountains, while pompous bear shifters strutted around in frilly outfits. I laughed to myself. Sure, they might not have worn those clothes, but I preferred to picture them that way.

I hightailed it up the front steps and used the bronze door-knocker shaped like a bear's claw.

Thump. Thump. The sound rang loud, and when no response came, I tried again.

Behind me, the gale swirled, pulling me backward by my clothes. Night swallowed everything else.

With no one answering my knocks, I pushed open the door. My plan was simple: get the job done quickly and by morning they'd escort me back to the tavern. Then I'd never return to White Peak Mountains—ever! No matter how many gold coins Elliana promised.

"Hello?" I stuck my head inside and entered a dimly-lit hall, shutting the door against the cold outside. Uneasiness flooded me, making me feel like an intruder.

Okay, *hall* was an understatement, because this chamber was a mansion, and larger than my whole house. A golden marble floor flowed toward wide stairs that swept upward, splitting in two directions to an upper landing. Ornate handrails, the color of cherry wood, were carved with roses and thorns along the beams. At the base of the steps were two statues of young maidens in flowing gowns holding candelabras with lit candles. Opulent bronze chandeliers in the shape of flowers hung overhead, dotted with more candles, yet cobwebs also dangled from the arms.

"Anyone home?" Where was everyone? I approached the stairs, glancing up, and grasped the railing. Going upstairs didn't feel right, so I pulled my hand back, noting it was covered in dust. I wiped my hand clean on my pants.

"Hello!" I called out, my voice echoing. "I'm your hired help. Raze picked me up at the tavern." Well, technically, he'd kidnapped me. *Goddess, please let him be safe.*

I waited, expecting a thundering of footfalls to answer my call. Except there was nothing. Was this place empty?

I whirled, my boots tapping the marble floor. If anyone was upstairs, they wouldn't hear me, considering the size of this place.

Paintings littered the pale blue walls. In one, an older man embraced a beautiful woman. They stood in a rose garden and carried warmth in their gazes. The lady wore a golden gown, blonde hair falling over her shoulders, while the man had silver streaking the hair above his temples.

I rubbed the chill from my arms and studied the five young children in the next painting, four boys and a girl, dressed in white frilly shirts and black pants.

More family portraits of the kiddies with their parents, posing in gardens. What they all had in common were those contagious smiles. A joyous family. No paintings of the children grown up, though.

Added to that, all the boys had the greenest eyes, bright, like a freshly-cut lawn, identical to their mother's.

"This place sure could do with a dusting," said a male's light voice came from behind me, and I spun around.

A man in his early twenties leaned an arm against the railing, studying me as a smirk pulled his lips upward. Dressed in black pants covered in dust, no shoes, and a midnight-blue top with sleeves pushed up to his elbows, he must have been used to the cold. Yet my gaze fell to the rose ink stretching out from under his sleeves, crawling around his forearms.

Centered amidst his trimmed hair and short, dark beard, his stunning green eyes called to me. This man was scorching hot, and definitely a warrior judging by his size alone. He was flawless, from his high-bridged nose to his captivating sharp lips. And the three distinct healed gashes down the side of his neck had me cringing that these poor bear shifters faced off with a wild animal at the age of ten. Talk about barbaric practices.

Now, place him and me in a different situation with no creepy castle or blood-starved bears, and I'd be all over those muscles. Scarlet's words played in my head, calling me a horny hound dog. *Ha*. I loved it, I embraced it, but I had too many questions, and staying alive was a priority. I lowered my gaze, distracted by his strength. Was it a bear attribute to resemble a god? While I could gawk at this man for an eternity and never get bored, now wasn't the time or place to focus on him, so I tucked away my melting libido.

"I'm here for a job. If you can please advise the owners I'm here?"

He nodded. "You must be the *witch*, arriving days after the booked appointment." The way he pronounced "witch" carried a mocking tone.

I stared at his ghost of a smile. Was he being an ass on purpose? Swallowing, I lifted my chin. "Sorry I'm late, but I came as soon as I could. And actually, I prefer 'magic caster.' 'Witch' is like me calling you a beast 'cause you live in the White Peak, when I'm sure you'd prefer 'bear shifter' instead of 'bloodthirsty animal' — or maybe you'd prefer 'sugarplum.'" I dipped my voice with sarcasm and smirked to myself.

A small laughter rolled over his throat, and his eyes locked with mine. "'Beast' will be just fine." His voice deepened and that earlier grin widened.

Butterflies swarmed in my gut — and did my legs just wobble? I mean, that right there was grounds for me to back away, yet something inside me coiled tight.

"Well, anyway," I said, "Nice of you to share your fetishes, but we can get this started. As much as I love White Peak Mountains with all its snow and ferocious bears, I've had enough fun for today."

Shrugging, he didn't say a word, but his eyes didn't hesitate to slip down over my buttoned black coat, dark pants, and worn leather boots. I glanced at the family paintings, into the same green eyes I'd also seen on Raze.

My breath caught in my throat. With his attire and lack of

servants, I'd assumed he was a helper. "Is that you in the portrait? A prince?"

"Yes." His faced beamed with pleasure, as if my discomfort brought him joy.

My jaw dropped open as I intended to apologize, but no words came to mind. *Honestly*, could I be any dumber? And if I could, I'd roll my eyes at myself. I'd never been this close to royalty — what did one say to a prince? Well, so far, I'd insulted him.

Hopefully, the apologetic expression I plastered on my face looked real. Should I offer him a curtsy? With those chiseled cheeks and suave intensity, he probably had a dozen royal families throwing their daughters at him, women who I was sure behaved perfectly. I shouldn't have been surprised, and I refused to give his expectations any more thought.

Reversing the curse, receiving payment, and getting back home alive were all that mattered.

"Where's my brother Raze?" He glanced toward the front door.

Okay, so I'd gotten that part wrong too. Raze wasn't a guide, but a royal. "Why would you send a prince to collect me? Don't you have someone to run your errands?" I scanned the room to avoid his peering stare. Dust coated the frames on the wall, and cobwebs were suspended from the corners. "And not to judge or anything, but whoever you've hired to clean this place is doing a terrible job."

"Listen, sugarplum," he said, tossing back my insult wrapped in an endearment with just as much tart as I had. He closed the distance between us in three long strides. "Focus and tell me where Raze is."

I arched a brow and didn't even flinch. "Well, Beast, your brother is one interesting character. Not only did he toss me into his carriage near the Golden Lock tavern as if I were a criminal, but then he leaped out to fight freaking bears attacking us. Because this place is insane. Why would others attack him if they knew he was of royal blood? And why would he risk his life for me? Again, don't you have guards to do this job? He jumped into the woods, leaving me to face off monsters alone." I swallowed hard and held myself strong, but on the inside, I crumbled. What if Raze lay somewhere in the woods dying? He'd saved me, in his own way, twice. Once at the tavern and again on the way here. Panic now brushed aside my calm and throttled me.

"I think you should send help to go find him. Maybe he's in danger. And" — I leaned closer — "how the fuck am I supposed to get home safely with wild bears trying to kill me?"

"Criminal, you say?" He turned and walked across the hall.

I trailed behind him, my boots scraping the marble floor. "That's what you focus on out of everything I said? Your brother could be in the woods dying." Just like Raze, this prince didn't seem to bat an eye at the potential of his brother being injured. Why? Was Raze a rival for the throne and this one was just as happy to have one less contender? I clenched my fists. He better do something quick or I'd figure out how to make him.

To our right and left there were doors and more family portraits. Were these servant quarters? But why hadn't I seen anyone else in the castle? Something was amiss here, like the-end-of-the-world wrong and waking up to discover I was the last survivor.

In the kitchen, candles in the chandelier lit the enormous room with a wooden table running down the middle. There was a fireplace and a stove, and pots and pans hung from hooks on the wall. I drifted toward the blazing fire to warm the ice from my veins.

"Best you stay here," he ordered. "Make yourself some

food. Or better yet, be a sugarplum and create enough for all five of us."

"I'm not your personal chef." I faced him while I heated my butt. "I have a job to complete, and we still haven't discussed payment, as you owe me half upfront. Maybe take me to the person who's suffering from the curse, too, so I can get started. Also, can you get my bag from the carriage?"

His gaze was elsewhere, not paying me any attention as he walked out. "Whatever you do," he called out, "don't leave the kitchen. Stay here."

"Wait!" I yelled.

And he halted, glancing at me over his shoulder, concern pinching the bridge of his nose.

So many questions buzzed in my head. "What's your name? What do I call you? 'Prince'? Are you going to send help for Raze?"

"'Beast' is just fine." He stormed out and shut the door behind him, and the sound of a key jangling had me flinching.

No, he didn't! I raced after him and rattled the handle. Locked. I banged on the door. "Are you kidding me?"

Was this payback for me calling him a beast? Yep, a wonderful way to win over a royal prince… call him names.

I rushed to the window, unable to see much beyond the darkness outside. Tugging on it did nothing. There was no latch, and with the glass divided by metal bars, fat chance of me breaking through them.

Tonight was fast becoming a nightmare. My stomach clenched at the possibility of Raze being hurt or dead while his brother, very much a beast, had imprisoned me in the kitchen. I paced in front of the fireplace, hugging myself. I'd tried to help Raze but facing the bears myself wouldn't have been the smartest move if I intended to keep breathing.

Goddess, what had I gotten myself into? I chewed on my

lower lip until it hurt. On top of everything, why had this prince told me not to go into the rest of the house? Was he worried the rebel bears would burst into the castle and this was him keeping me safe?

Before I could work out what to do next, I crossed the kitchen and flung open the pantry, pawing for food. Better yet, I might find herbs to help me create a spell.

CHAPTER 7

I shoved a piece of smoked jerky into my mouth, chewing the salty deliciousness. I'd found a bucket load of the stuff in the pantry. They wouldn't miss a few, so I pocketed three more strips for later. With no herbs at my disposal, my bobby pin and a meat skewer I'd found in a drawer would have to do. I fell to my knees in front of the kitchen door and jammed the tools into the keyhole, then shook them. I'd done this a few times before to break into the locks of boxes Dad would buy on the market. Jiggling the two metal objects, I couldn't get my head around why such a huge castle was nearly empty. What had happened here?

The moment the lock clicked open, I punched the air. "Yes. Got you."

Dumping the tools on the table, I ripped open the door and entered the darkened corridor. A rush of cool air greeted me. Time to discover what in the world was going on here. Most kitchens were built at the back of a home, so I swung left. I followed the rug to an enormous ballroom drowning in darkness. Only the silvery moonlight sprinkling in from the windows lit the marble flooring, along with a dozen chandeliers dripping with crystals. Against one wall stood an oversized shield divided into quarters, two diagonal parts in white, while red colored the other two. In the center lay two crossed swords and a blossoming red rose on top, its thorny stem curling around the weapons. The family crest.

I made my way across the ballroom, my footsteps echoing behind me. Suspended between the chandeliers, more cobwebs filled the corners. And where in the world were the servants?

Regardless, I pictured grand balls, music filling the castle, food served on silver trays, women in glittery gowns, and men in suits asking ladies for a dance. I did a small spin, imagining myself doing just that. Except who was I kidding? The royals and their lavish lifestyle were in a world of their own, and unless one was born into the family, normal townsfolk were nothing more than potential servants.

I had a job to complete and money to collect. Attending a ball was my foolish fantasy; the reality was I had to ensure my dad and I didn't lose our home.

Next, I entered a waiting area with velvet-covered chairs lining the walls, perhaps where men courted women under the watchful eyes of their chaperones. Boring. Me, I'd drag a prince I eyed out into the garden and jump him behind the bushes. I smirked to myself and visited more rooms. All had the same thing in common: they were dark and empty of people. The place was desolate. Plus, somehow I'd missed a rear exit to take me out to the yard and find the stables so I could collect my bag. Instead, I'd ended up in the front hallway again, facing the stairs.

If someone in the castle was sick from a curse, wouldn't it make more sense to let me start treating them right away? And they would be up in a bedroom, not downstairs. Then I'd leave the house faster and put this whole experience to an end.

And I might as well get started before Beast came back, though I prayed he'd tracked down Raze alive and well.

Up on the second level, I found more stairs, one heading left, the other right. I'd need a week to explore this house before I could make my way around without getting lost first.

A creak sounded behind me, and I jerked around, my heart pounding. But no one there. Had to be the castle settling.

So I turned left because it appeared brighter. Dust coated the banisters. On the next level, I discovered nothing but empty areas, a few bedrooms that hadn't seen action in too long. But on the third floor, a light flickered, so I followed the circular stairs, the walls dotted with portraits of old people. Perhaps old kings and queens?

At the landing, my gaze swept to the door with light dancing out from underneath.

My gut tightened, and sure, I was exploring a castle without consent, but I wouldn't remain locked up. Dad had always brought me up to believe that only I had a right to make decisions that affected my life.

I collected the blade from my boot and tucked it into my belt for easy access as I approached. "Hello?" I knocked. "My name is Bee and I'm here to help with a curse problem." I didn't plan to bust in on someone in their home unannounced.

A guttural sound came from within. Was that a cough?

The wooden floorboards creaked from inside, as if a person paced back and forth. Okay, I wasn't alone after all. My stomach pinched, and my hands shook. I glanced down the hallway for any sign of life. Nothing.

I bit my lip. I'd come this far, so there was no turning back.

"Do you mind if I come in? I have a few questions." I

leaned an ear against the door, listening. More footfalls and a weird scraping sound. A shiver zipped up my spine like it always did when the goddess sent warnings.

But what was I supposed to do? Sit in the kitchen until the princes returned? What if they didn't come back until tomorrow? Besides, I'd already announced I was here, so wouldn't it be rude of me to leave? My brain churned, trying to work out the best solution. If it weren't for the nerves dancing beneath my skin, I'd already be in the room. Yet my imagination conjured up a bloodbath, the servants butchered, a bear watching over them. I grimaced.

Goddess, give me strength. My priorities were getting paid and getting home, and that meant discovering what curse I was dealing with. Then I'd track down the carriage, use the kitchen knife to cut my bag loose, and get started on my spell. By the time the smug Beast returned, I'd have the hex cured and then in the morning, I could leave with my big, fat payment.

Before I convinced myself to run away, I grasped the handle. "I'm coming in, okay?" I called out and pushed it open. At first, only the fluttering of candlelight washed across the walls, revealing shredded wallpaper and a wardrobe on its side, the doors off their hinges and laying in the corner. White feathers plastered everything in sight. Goddess, my first thought flew to a chicken butchery house. Please don't let me stumble across a bear tearing into a bird.

A copper and musty stink accosted me, smothering my senses.

I held my breath and stepped deeper inside to view the rest of the room. "I'm here—" My words vanished and a jolted spark ran through me as I faced a gigantic metal cage taking up half the room. Shredded fabric lay strewn on the floor. Inside, a man crouched in the corner with his back to me and made a strange huffing sound like an animal unable to get enough air into his lungs.

My heartbeat banged in my ears.

Why was this person imprisoned? Was this what they did to people they pretended to hire for supposed help, and Goddess, what if that was what had happened to all the servants? "Are you okay?" Fear tangled in my chest.

He gave no response, and while the whole situation creeped me the hell out, I couldn't walk away. Not if this man faced danger. He might have been cursed. Curiosity drove me closer, but I still kept my distance.

"Who's in there?" Nervousness burrowed through me. The situation reminded me of the time I'd found an injured bear cub in Terra, his leg caught in a trap. Worried he'd end up as someone's rug, I'd released him and taken him home to heal him with Dad's help. Then we'd freed him in the wilderness of White Peak.

Yet staring at the figure with torn pants and brown fur sticking out, as if only his legs had transformed into a bear's, pity flooded me. How was this different from anyone else needing help?

The hairs on my arms lifted as I inched forward for a better look.

But within a flash, the person whirled toward me, lightning fast, an arm striking out between two bars.

I flinched backward, but his fingers seized my forearms and hauled me toward him with a burst of intense strength. I tripped forward, face-planting into the cage. My vision twirled as my hip grazed the bars and the blade on my belt clanged to the ground.

I moaned from the ache across my skull.

But when I focused on the sharp fangs inches from my face, a hot, putrid stink of blood washing over me, a cry strangled my throat. His face was human, but his arms and legs were that of a bear.

My heart thundered.

Claws clutched my neck, drawing me closer, my cheek pressed against a metal bar.

"You…" His voice gargled, and he snarled so loud, my ears rang. "Smell delici—" He broke into a roar, and I shuddered.

I writhed against his hold, shaking like a leaf.

I'd been wrong. This wasn't just any man, but something hideous. He had long ears, and his shoulders were broad, brown and furry. But behind his gaze lay desperation and humanity. Those green eyes were familiar, and I didn't need to know anything more: this had to be the cursed brother.

Coldness washed through me, and when I tried to form words, none came.

He licked my cheek and sniffed me.

My pulse pumped furiously as I pictured my head ripped off my body. His claws pressed into my flesh, and a suffocating scream pushed past my throat.

With the knife near my feet, reaching it was impossible without ticking off the monster in half-bear, half-human form. I dug into my pocket and pulled out the jerky I'd stolen from the kitchen earlier.

A quick wave in his face, and the bear-man's nose twitched. His grip loosened. I tossed the food into the cage behind him, and he leaped after it.

I stumbled backward, gripping my neck where he'd broken skin, and gulped for air. He could have killed me, but for the smart move on my part with the beef jerky.

What sort of hex had they placed on him?

He crouched, eating, his lips smacking. Near him I spotted a pile of bones, and I choked on the urge to gag. Someone had cursed him to straddle between two worlds? Half-bear, half-human. I recalled the magic upon first entering the castle gates. A death enchantment. How was I equipped to handle this kind of curse? If Mom were alive, she'd demand I leave this very night and never return.

I practiced white magic, worked with the goddess. I'd never killed a single living thing for magic. But this here was something else. Even now, energy crackled down my spine. Someone had wanted this prince to suffer.

The bear-man snapped upright, slamming into the cage wall, arms reaching for me.

I jumped back and ran, unable to stop. I raced down the stairs, faster than I would have thought possible. Because now I knew I dealt with evil. And no way in hell I could fix this. Ice filled my veins. I refused to sacrifice another life. I didn't dance that way, now or ever. Worse yet, dabbling in death hexes came with side effects. Like opening myself up to a possession. Unbalancing my two witch halves, releasing the darkness within. *Nope.* I'd spent too many years controlling that side of me.

The solution became obvious. I'd tell the princes I'd made a mistake and couldn't help. Then back home, I'd get two jobs — cleaning toilets if I had to help Dad pay his debt.

When a growl boomed from upstairs, the sound reminding me of an attacking animal, I halted at the base of the stairwell, grasping the railing. Guilt twisted my insides.

Dad's words streamed through my mind. *Never abandon anyone in trouble, because what if that were you?*

$\mathcal{B}$ack in the kitchen, I resumed my pacing, gnawing on a hangnail. The scratches on my neck from the attack upstairs stung, but not as much as trying to decide what my next steps were. Should I head home tonight by any means necessary, which was risky, even if I could conjure up ingredients for a protection spell. Or should I wait for the other princes to return, with the chance that Raze might not have made it? Dread sat on my chest, squeezing my lungs. If I asked the men to take me down the mountain, what if they refused until I healed the cursed brother? I couldn't stop thinking about him, and the despair in his eyes.

Footfalls sounded in the house, and I recoiled toward the window, my thoughts flying to the prince upstairs. But if he'd escaped, he'd be running down here like a madman, not taking normal steps.

Beast walked in, his gaze on the door handle, then on me, his brow arching.

"No one locks me up." I crossed my arms. Before I could ask about Raze, he strolled in as well, wearing trousers and nothing else. He was laughing at something over his shoulder, not terrified that he could have died. Fresh gashes streaked his chest and arms, and he had a large bite mark on his bicep. Most were healed over, and the flesh blushed pink around the injuries. I'd heard shifters healed quick, but this was miraculous. And just seeing him alive had me beaming. *He hadn't died!*

When Raze swung to face me, he smirked, and his eyes sparkled in the candlelight. "I was afraid I'd lost you in the woods." The sincere concern in his gaze felt real, and he closed the distance between us.

"How did you escape those bears?" I watched the way his muscles moved across his solid chest and rippled stomach, and my gaze fell to the line of dark hair dipping into his pants. *Damn!* This was so unfair, dangling these men in front of me when they weren't on the menu. And why was it getting so hot in here?

"The forest is my backyard, and I can handle a few rebels. I was more worried about you." He reached over and lifted my chin gingerly with his thumb. "Did you get hurt?"

I shook my head, unable to find my words as Raze's brows pulled together while he studied my injuries. Back in the carriage, the shadows had concealed his features, but he had the same strong jaw and cheeks as his brother behind him. Raze's lips were thicker, and waves of darker chestnut hair sat off his face, falling to just below his jawline. He was slightly taller than Beast, and bulkier in the muscle area. Both men were incredible... yep, the handsome gene was generous in this family.

"Those scratches look new." Beast approached and tilted his head, staring my way.

But I didn't need them knowing I'd spied on the massive problem upstairs... at least not until I heard their side of the story and determined how deep in a hole I'd landed.

"I'm fine." I drew the collar of my coat to my neck, covering my injuries. "Shall we get down to business?"

Both men exchanged a knowing glance, and I noted the worry marring their expressions.

"Sugarplum," Beast started as he cracked his neck, not conducive at all to discussing a difficult topic, "It's late," he continued. "You've had a scary night. Let's start this in the morning?"

"But I'm wide awake. How about you make us all a cup of tea and let's talk? I have questions for you. So many questions."

He stared at me in disbelief.

"Oh, right! You probably don't know how to boil water," I said, maybe a bit too briskly, and I regretted my rudeness at once. These were princes, but my pulse still buzzed. When hyped up, I blurted out anything in my head.

Raze laughed and slapped Beast's shoulder. "She's got you worked out, Leven."

So that was Beast's name. Leven! Despite his thorny demeanor, his name rolled smoothly through my mind.

I slouched my hip against the kitchen counter and stuffed my hands into my coat's pockets. "Why were those bears attacking us if you're royalty? Why is there no one else is in the castle?"

The brothers stiffened at my questions.

But I didn't stop. "Why is there a protection ring surrounding the castle? I sensed magic in the air when I entered. Something dark. So speak to me if you want my help." I caught my racing breath, facing two huge bear shifters, and squared my shoulders.

"Or?" Raze asked before he shot a glance toward Leven. Both seemed to be sharing mental notes.

I licked my dry lips. "Or I'll head home." I wasn't some meek woman they could manipulate.

"Well, here's the thing." Raze pulled a kitchen knife out from the back of his pants and plonked it on the table.

The same weapon with a wooden hilt I'd dropped upstairs after being attacked.

Coldness washed through my body, and my head rang like a siren.

"As you can see, tonight we're not in a trusting mood." His gaze swept from me to the blade and back. "I just asked you to stay in the kitchen." Leven's voice hardened, the earlier flirting look replaced by a hooded glare. "You could have gotten hurt."

I felt the blood drain from my face. "Do you think I trust either of you?" I pointed at them. "Raze, you kidnapped me near the tavern, then made me pass out, and you, Leven, you locked me in the kitchen. If anyone has trust issues here, it's me."

"Raze, you abducted her?" Leven turned to this brother and sighed. "I've told you before, stop with all the heroic shit. Just talk to people. Girls don't like to be hijacked."

"Talk?" Raze raised his voice. "Talking to her is like trying to convince a bull to wear a tutu." His nostrils flared. "Nothing is happening tonight. If you want to leave, you know where the front door is. But I doubt you'd make it far. Alternatively, follow me and I'll show you to your room."

Okay, so everyone had a prickly personality. Fine, I could play that game too. "I'm not in the mood for sleep. What's with your brother in the cage? When did he first start changing?"

He shrugged, as if nothing in the world could touch him, his lips thinning to a straight line. "I don't have the headspace for this tonight. And I'll carry you to your bedroom if you prefer." Raze stood there, arms tight by his sides. Yep, someone was used to getting his way.

"Excuse me?"

Leven moved to stand between us. "It's for your own safety, Bee. And under no circumstances are you to return to the west wing on the top floor."

I stared from one shifter to the next, both were looking at me with judging expressions. While I agreed that maybe sleep might clear my thoughts, I hated to give in on principle alone. But if they refused to talk about the situation, we'd be going in circles.

"Then I need my bag from the carriage," I insisted.

"Leave it to me," Leven said before heading out of the kitchen, leaving me with Raze and his piercing stare.

I pushed past him and marched into the corridor. "Are you showing me to my room then?"

Raze stormed ahead of me, his arms swinging wide. I trailed after him to the next floor and along a long hallway until we reached double doors, which were wooden and arched, and golden trim decorated the edges. He opened them both and moved aside, waving me to enter.

I stepped into a room large enough to fit two carriages and horses, plus wriggle space. "Wow." A king-sized bed sat on one side, complete with four posts and a fishnet fabric hanging from them. I held back the squeal in my chest because I'd always wanted a bed like that, and I needed every inch of strength to hold myself back from rushing over there and jumping on it. A blazing fire crackled on the opposite wall, warming the room.

There was a wardrobe on the opposite end and even a sofa overlooking an oversized window covered by golden curtains. Damn, I'd move in here this second, and bring Dad with me to take one of the other bedchambers if there were no ravenous bears outside.

"We'll bring your bag up in a moment. Good night, Bee." His voice faded.

I listened intently as he retreated and shut the door. No

locking me in this time, but I noted the key was on my side, meaning I got to lock myself in, which I preferred.

At the window, I pushed aside the curtains and stared down at the torches lining the road leading up to the castle. I'd never been this goddamn high before. This must have been how birds felt, taking in the entire landscape in one sweep. Night swallowed the rest of the terrain. Who would have thought I'd spend the night in a castle in White Peak? Wait until I told Scarlet. She'd bounce on her toes with excitement and ask a million questions.

Still, I was here, and by daylight it would be safer to travel back home. I tracked my way to the cupboard and flung it open to find a plethora of outfits and gowns. I squealed out loud. Goddess, whose room was this? I reached over and touched the silver-threaded skirt, a silky blue chiffon dress, and a strapless black number.

If I owned these clothes, I'd wear a different one every single day. Giddiness swirled in my chest, the kind that made me deliriously happy. Who would own such clothes? A princess? I recalled the portraits with four brothers and one daughter. Where was she now? Married off to a lord in White Peak, most likely, but why leave her clothes behind?

To my right was a door and inside I discovered a bathroom. Perfect, as my clothes were damp from the snow.

Just then a knock came at the door.

"Come in."

Leven waltzed in, my bag held over his shoulder with one hand. He dumped it near the sofa and rubbed the back of his neck. "Is the bedroom to your satisfaction?"

"It's amazing. Is yours this big too?"

He smiled, his furrowed brow smoothing out, and nodded. "This is a visitor's room. My sister, Vivienne, filled the cupboard with clothes in case guests needed them, since we're so far from the closest town."

"Oh, where's Vivienne now?" I shuffled closer and sat on the other end of the couch.

He ran a hand across his mouth, his eyes darkening. "She died in an accident."

"Oh, shit. I didn't know." I lowered my head because what else was I supposed to do with such news? I detested people talking about my mom, as sometimes I felt as if they had no right to bring her up and resurrect emotions I barely controlled. Yet I'd done exactly that to someone else. "I didn't mean to pry."

"It's all right." He stared at something over my shoulder, his posture curling forward.

"When I lost my mother," I started, "I swore the world would swallow me whole because I wasn't sure how to face a new day without her. Even now, I miss her all the time."

He nodded. "My sister, Vivienne was taken too young." With a sigh, he patted my bag and cleared his throat. "Anyway, it's too late for such dark talk. Here are your belongings. Sleep well." His voice lowered.

When he left, I curled up on the corner of the sofa, hugging my knees, unable to get his words out of my head. So not only had the princes lost their sister, but now one of their brothers was cursed.

Having so much empty space left me feeling lonely. Maybe I missed Dad and our small living room, warming ourselves by the fire, chatting into the night.

Silence reminded me of things I'd rather not ponder. Like how I wished Mom was still with us. How I hated the world for taking her. How I loathed the universe for allowing her illness to steal her from us. And I detested myself for not having been able to do a single thing to help her. Magic hadn't saved her... I'd failed my mother. What if, even if I really wanted to, I couldn't fix the cursed brother?

CHAPTER 9

I lay on my stomach on a four-poster bed where a princess might have once slept. The first morning rays drenched the room with warmth and light while feathery snowflakes cascaded outdoors. With the door locked, I contemplated sleeping in for most of the day, pretending I wasn't surrounded by grizzly bears, or needing to face a dark curse, or deal with princes who had issues. And there was still one brother I hadn't met yet, but maybe he'd left home, or had something happened to him as well?

Looking down at my scribblings in my notebook, I chewed on my pencil. A new story idea had crossed my mind the moment I'd woken up and I couldn't write it down fast enough. It was about a lost princess being rescued by two men, but first she had to have sex with each to determine which one fulfilled her the most. In my tale, my heroes were based on Raze and Leven, with different names of course. Two brothers so similar, yet different. Raze jumped into action without thought, while Leven seemed more mature and thought through situations. Both brothers were wicked, and despite the princess's embarrassment, they insisted on taking her at the same time. In my head, I pictured Raze and Leven naked, and the princess quivered with desire.

I rolled onto my back, the chill in the air pebbling my nipples, and I let myself fall into the fantasy, picturing their strong hands on me. Raze taking me from behind, thrusting into me until I rocked from an orgasm, Leven's enormous cock filling my mouth, flooding into me with his seed, dominating me. A surge of heat slinked through my gut, diving south fast.

But guilt nudged forward and squashed my earlier desire. Upstairs lay a shifter in agony, and I had to help him.

So I shoved aside the desires and blankets tangled around my legs and climbed out of bed, pushing back the fishnet fabric encasing the four-poster. Before long, I'd washed up, combed my porcupine-like hair, and dug into my long backpack. I hadn't planned to stay too long, so I'd only packed one spare set of clothes, and several pairs of underwear, a habit Mom had ingrained in me. But the clothes were damp to the touch.

I should have taken them out last night to dry. I shook my clothes and laid them across the sofa facing the sunny window, along with my sachets of ingredients, to ensure they all dried. The underwear I'd packed was semi-dry, so I stepped into them, but what to wear?

I swung toward the wardrobe. It wasn't as if I had a choice. And Leven had said the outfits were here for guests to use, so I rushed closer and ripped open the doors, smiling.

The vast array of colors shouldn't have excited me so much, but I was bouncing on my toes. My collection at home didn't compare. I made a lot of my garments myself with materials I ordered from different realms, but these gowns were out of this world. I pulled out a red number, the bodice covered in sequins, but shoved it back.

"Too fancy for daytime wear." This morning, I'd find out

what kind of curse I had to break, so I needed simple, comfortable clothing.

The next dress was strapless with a layered skirt, and I pressed it to my chest, the fabric silky smooth. "So gorgeous. But not today." Flipping through the outfits, I found a more suitable option.

In no time, I got dressed and stood in front of the mirror. Black leather pants hugged me, and I spun to check out the fabric curving across my butt. "Oh, yeah." The bottom of the pant legs bunched up around my feet. Short girl problem. I rolled them up to my ankles and pulled on my socks and boots over them. The long-sleeved blouse I'd borrowed had buttons that kept pulling open. *Crap.* The burden of being busty—it was impossible to find a top that fit right.

This one was not going to work, so I ripped the shirt off and plucked out a mustard-colored one, also with long sleeves for warmth, a low V-neck, and a drawstring at the front. Yes, bar-girl style. This I could do, so I tied it closed.

A final check in the mirror to ensure the outfit embraced all my curves with some cleavage showing. The top stretched across my breasts, so I drew my long hair over my shoulders to cover my breasts and draw attention away from them. Up close, I noticed how dry my lips were, and how red my cheeks glowed. Must be the cold weather.

Okay, now that I was ready, I grabbed my coat, which was mostly dry, and a small satchel of sleeping herbs. While I had no more freezing powder left, I'd take the slumber ones. I made it a mission to always have a spell on me at all times, because you never knew what the universe would throw my way. I strolled out of the room.

When I reached the kitchen, expecting the princes to be there, I found the place empty. Though someone had been awake because a pot of water steamed over the flames.

From behind me, a waft of cold wind curled around my

legs, and I turned to find the door slightly ajar. Had someone gone to feed the horses? I did a quick check outside and found the yard had taken on a unique radiance, with the untouched snow glistening, and the picturesque image of mountains in the distance crested with white. Pines filled the landscape. Overhead, a hawk flew past, diving somewhere nearby, probably for a meal.

The cold nipped my flesh, and I tugged my hands into my pockets. Following a cobblestone path around the corner, I came face-to-face with an enormous glass dome. Green plants lined the inside walls. I'd never in a million years have guessed royalty had a greenhouse, but it made sense. If it snowed often, where else would they get their food from?

Up close, I peered inside to the abundant rows of vegetation and miniature fruit trees. Farther in the rear, a man wearing no top, with only pants hanging low on his hips, was shoveling a big pile of soil into large terracotta pots. *Leven?* I entered.

The chill faded, and I closed myself inside to keep out the cold. A narrow pebbly path ran down the middle of the enclosure, greenery bursting to life everywhere I looked. Tomato plants towered over me, bean vines and cucumbers curled up a trellis, a bed of carrots stretched as far as I could see, and much more. Some vegetation remained covered with a white fabric to probably combat frostbite. Damn, if I could get my garden at home to this level of production, we'd be able to sell them on the market and make a fortune.

"Morning, Leven." Passing a berry shrub, I picked a fresh raspberry and popped it into my mouth, emerging into a small area with a two metal benches facing each other. Beyond that, Leven straightened from his digging and turned to face me.

But I halted, frozen on the spot when a different man

stared back at me. Not Leven, but someone with the same hypnotic green eyes.

"You must be Bee." He drove the shovel into the soil and wiped his hands down his pants, striding my way.

Dirt sprinkled his wide shoulders, sun-kissed and utterly eye-googling worthy. He might have been bigger than his brothers, if that were even possible, and strong enough to haul a boulder on his back. Though I noticed his healed initiation scratch marks just above his heart.

"Yep, that's me! The witch you ordered. I mean magic caster." Goddess kill me now.

He smirked and stuck out his palm. I accepted, shaking it. His calloused hand swallowed mine in size, and I chewed on my cheek, staring at how big his fingers were. *Oh, my.* My thoughts flew to my story from this morning, needing to add him into the mix with the princess.

"My name's Ash. Nice to meet you. After Leven and I went out to search for Raze, I got into a massive brawl with rebels near our property, and I had a few injuries to tend to." He lifted an arm, revealing a healed gash from his armpit to his waist.

"Holy shit!"

"I'm okay. I heal quickly." He laughed and flicked the pieces of soil caught on the whisper of dark hair across his chest. His washboard abs had ridges that made up his eight-pack, and I couldn't stop gawking. I offered him a smile. *Keep your eyes up.*

"Thanks for coming to help my brother. Talin's in bad shape. The last three witches did nothing for him, then returned home." He retreated and took a seat on one bench, reclining his legs wide, and one arm stretched out across the back of the seat.

So Talin was the name of the prince in the cage. "Three witches?" I said. Okay, now that worried me, and I sat across from Ash. "Tell me everything you know about the dark magic used on Talin."

He leaned forward, elbows pressed into his thighs, and the light hitting the side of his face showed the slight bend in his nose. He'd probably broken it in a fight. But something about Ash epitomized regal, more so than in Leven and Raze. Even covered in soil and shoveling dirt, he exuded a striking majestic quality. Maybe it was the way he held my gaze, his facial expression neutral. When he spoke of Talin, he didn't lose himself to emotions and stayed composed. I could take some lessons from Ash.

"That's the tricky part," he said. "We don't know. Over three weeks ago, Talin started shifting in and out of his bear form, unable to stop, then he halted mid-transformation, frozen in that form. Neither bear nor man. Problem is that, in that state, the body is fighting itself, trying to tear him in two, literally." He swallowed, his Adam's apple sliding up and down, and his voice carried a panicked undertone. "He's dying."

I inched to the edge of my seat and reached over, placing my hand on his. "Fuck!" My throat dried, and I cringed on the inside. "Sorry, I didn't mean to swear in front of you. I'll do everything I can to help him."

"It's okay." Shadows crowded under his eyes. "But the last witch promised the same thing."

Sitting back, I laced my fingers in my lap. "There must be something else you know. How can you be sure it's a curse?"

He nodded, and his eyes narrowed. "At first, we thought he was sick. It started the night we arrived home from attending court at our cousin's mansion deeper in the woods. Talin had eaten a feast, like we all did, and he never left our side."

"So these cousins of yours," I said, "they've practiced charms and spells in the past and wanted Talin hurt?"

With a sigh, he reclined in his seat. "It's a long story. As the eldest, Talin cannot take the throne as king until he gets married, but he refuses until he finds the right person, insisting these things shouldn't be rushed. But we were summoned to the duke's court as a special invite to meet a prospective new wife for Talin. Ever since our parents passed ten years ago, our cousin, Rek, has demanded we merge houses and duchies. He's had his eye on the other two estates in White Peak as well to grow in strength, insistent that other realms in the south are looking to take over our land."

"Let me guess, he offered his daughter," I said.

He shook his head. "The duke presented his granddaughter, as he has no daughters of his own. But Talin refused the offer." Ash ran a hand over his mouth, his brow creasing. "The poor girl was a child of fourteen. Talin was furious, and we left halfway through the meal." He scowled. "Ever since, Talin has been ill."

I shifted in my seat. "And you think your cousin cursed him? Have you gone back to the manor and confronted him?" A horrible churning swirled in the pit of my gut.

Ash grimaced. "We tried, several times. Once, we got caught in the woods during the night and Talin's change kicked in and stuck again mid-transformation. A madness he can't control takes him over and he feels an urgency to return to the castle." Ash exhaled a long breath. "He almost killed me when I tried to stop him. The other times we reached the manor, Rek feigned surprise and even offered to help us find the witch responsible. He's undermining us and has no plans to admit the truth or help. We all know he wants Talin to die as payback for not accepting his granddaughter's hand." Ash lowered his eyes, breathing heavily. "Our only choice now is to find a way to break the curse ourselves, or we lose our brother." His voice darkened, and he sounded like a man whose spirit was on the verge of shattering.

He cleared his throat. "And Talin's condition has worsened; his episodes now extend for full nights, instead of short periods. Every witch we hired confirmed he'd been cursed by an enchantment so dark, they couldn't undo it. One said even if she could, she'd never touch it."

That was exactly as I feared, and that meddling with such a spell could unbalance my energies. I didn't need the darker side to take me over. It had happened once when I was younger, and I'd almost killed someone. The memory had never left me and it reminded me why I worked so hard to keep my magic leveled.

"What we know," Ash continued, "is that his episodes happen at night. And the last witch warned us to prepare for the worst, insisting that the hex used the moon cycle and, on the next full moon, he'd lose his battle."

"That's in two days!" My mind whirled with what I'd learned and the fact that Talin would die. When a spell involved the moon, the power came from the goddess. That lent itself to not requiring a sacrifice to reverse the spell, and my knees bounced from the exciting news. *I might be able to pull this off.* Mom always told me my power was stronger than any she'd ever encountered, including hers, and she'd traveled to all realms in Haven. *Anything is possible if you accept who you are and carry the right intent*, she'd say.

"So can you do this?" Ash asked, watching me with an expectation such that the only right answer would be *yes*. His expression held the complete opposite of the despair I'd seen in Leven and Raze's gaze when I'd tried to discuss Talin.

My body tightened, and it terrified me to poke at such a curse. "I'll try my hardest. If it's linked to the moon, there might be a way to utilize its power for Talin." Even as the words left my lips, I regretted showing confidence, especially with Ash now grinning at me. But the full moon wasn't for another two days, so I had time to perfect this. Whatever it took, I'd assist Talin. I hadn't been able to save Mom, but this was my chance to make a difference.

The three brothers might have put on a tough act, but on the inside, it must be killing them to watch Talin perishing before their eyes. That helplessness lingered in my chest. I remembered Mom in bed and coughing, growing frailer by the day. Every single damn spell I'd created had fizzled. Nothing had worked, as if the universe was blocking my efforts. And it had torn me to shreds to know I had the ability but couldn't use it.

So, despite my earlier trepidation, I couldn't walk away if I had the power to prevent Talin's death. I wanted to believe my ability could create extraordinary things.

What was the use of wielding magic if not to set wrongs right?

CHAPTER 10

I tucked a bent leg underneath me, leaning back against the metal bench, watching Ash shovel soil into half a dozen pots. "Still can't believe how much food you're growing. Everything is thriving, even while it's snowing outside. You may need to come to my place in Terra and help me with my garden."

Ash twisted toward me, the corner of his mouth twitching into a smile. If I could have frozen time, I'd have done it in that moment and memorized his glimmering eyes, the stubble on his jawline dark enough to give him an edge, and the way the longer strands of hair across the front of his head danced over his brow. Add to that the bonus of him being half-naked, sweaty, and dirty. Yep, I was sold.

Goddess, help me. What was it about these three princes? When they looked at me, my stomach coiled, and I lost my words.

"Let's make a deal," Ash said. "Save Talin, and I'll transform your garden into a paradise."

That sounded heavenly, particularly if he worked in my

yard and I lounged with a cold drink watching him. Yes, that was very doable.

"You've got yourself a deal."

He laughed, deep and powerful, and returned to his task.

"What's with the soil and pots?"

He glanced my way. "Trying to bring dead roses back to life."

I got up, stretching my back, admittedly I knew little about gardening, but why not buy new flowers? "Okay. You must love them."

"Something like that." He spoke while piling dirt into a pot with his shovel.

"Well, thanks for the information," I said. "I'm going to work on breaking Talin's curse."

"I'll be right in."

When I walked through the front doors to the castle, a waft of fried meat found me and I drifted toward the kitchen, following my nose. Raze was dressed and lounged on a chair, bare feet on the table corner, his hands behind his head. When he saw me, he lowered his legs to the floor.

"Is Ash coming to join us?" he asked.

Leven glanced over his shoulder my way and nodded his morning *hello*, then returned to collect the strips of cooked meat from the frying pan. Was it deer or rabbit?

"He'll be here shortly," I responded, though I wondered how they'd known I'd been in the greenhouse. Probably went searching for me when they'd found my bedroom empty. "He's planting a shitload of roses. He's into flowers, isn't he?"

Leven joined Raze at the table and set down a plate with a mountain of cooked meat. "Come and eat."

Raze took two pieces and stuffed them into his mouth, his cheeks full, reminding me of chipmunks. "Our family crest is a rose," he said, his lips smacking.

"Oh, yeah, I saw it last night in the grand ballroom."

Joining them, I sat next to Leven and grabbed a piece. The gamey morsel melted on my tongue. *Divine.* I kept helping myself.

Raze wiped his glistening mouth, and with his hair slicked off his face, still wet from a wash, his thick, dark brows brought out his eyes. He had one of those hard faces where frowning seemed to come naturally, but to see him laid back and not brooding brought out a softer, more approachable side.

Or maybe I was just fantasizing, instead of focusing on the issue at hand. These brothers were princes… royalty. And if I could help them, they'd be back to their fancy lifestyle without a second thought as to what a witch like me did. And I had enough of my own issues to worry about, like ensuring that Dad and I didn't lose our family home.

Leven swallowed the food in his mouth. "Ten years ago, every rose on our property died, and Ash kept the stems that never rotted or perished. He took that as a sign that one day they will grow again. The plant is called a snow rose, and apparently, our mother's grandma grafted the first flower to resist the icy chills of winter, and that's how it got its name. I still think Ash is wasting his time."

"The snow rose sounds impressive." I'd never heard of such a plant before, but Ash had said their parents had died ten years ago too.

"Ash thinks it'll bring peace back between the royal houses in White Peak and to all bear shifters," Raze added.

"Interesting. I'm assuming the roses all died after your parents' and sister's passing?" I wiped my mouth with the back of my hand. "Do you think there's magic in the plants?"

They both stared at me with widened gazes, and Raze responded, "Ash sure loves to talk. What else did he tell you? Where the family treasure is? Did he also mention he still keeps his old teddy bear in his closet from when he was five?"

The kitchen door swung open, and Ash stood there, filling the space. "Fuck you. I see you're in one of your moods today."

Raze shook his head, grimacing, and reclined in his seat. "Not me."

Leven pushed the plate across the table toward Ash, who joined us and sat next to me, snatching a handful of cooked meat strips.

No one said a word and only the sound of chewing filled the void. I didn't know if the brothers fought often or whether it was a stress thing. After all, they were minus servants or anyone to help them, and were dealing with a dying sibling. Tension was a guarantee.

"So, after breakfast, I think we can get started. Ash said the curse involves moon magic and that's given me some ideas to—"

The door slapped open, and I flinched against Ash's arm. In the entranceway stood a man—muscular, hair wild, and his body covered in fresh scratches. He wore only ripped pants reaching his knees.

My breaths jammed in my chest because I recognized Talin from the cage upstairs, but he was a full human now.

Around me, no one moved and kept eating. What the hell?

"You better be making another batch of those." Talin had a honeyed drawl that caught my attention. He marched inside, as if all was right, and while he might have been the smallest of the brothers, he carried himself with an air of importance.

Ash leaned closer to me, his warm meaty breath on my ear. "It's rude to stare."

"Are you kidding?" I looked up at Ash, and he winked so

sexily, I squeezed my thighs together to cover that tingling sensation. But no… no flirting to blindside me.

"Sugarplum," Leven said, "you've already met our brother, Talin."

The oldest brother sat across from me, sizing me up with the same ravenous expression he'd shown when I'd found him in the cage and he'd readied to tear my throat out.

"Does anyone see a problem with this picture?" I pulled back in my seat, scanning the counter for a knife.

"Relax." Raze leaned forward. "Talin's episodes come at night, and during the day, he's okay. Sometimes he's a prick, but we love him."

Talin chuckled, his facial expression softening, and the tense lines around his mouth fading. He threw a torn piece of meat at Raze, who caught it and stuffed it into his mouth.

Ash touched my shoulder, his fingers warm. "I checked on him before coming for breakfast and found him back to normal, so I let him out. You're safe."

I glanced from one man to the next, all four eating and unperturbed. "He could have killed me last night, and now it's all normal?"

"Yeah, sorry about that." Talin winked my way. "But you smelled so delicious. I have no control over myself at night these days. But Ash said you're here to help. Fantastic. Hope you're better than the last three Raze hired."

Raze cut his brother a serious look, both eyebrows climbing his forehead.

Surely, I was in some twisted world where they allowed someone who could morph back into a bloodthirsty beast wander freely through the house. What if the encroaching full moon triggered his humanity to slip faster away and he transformed during the day? Curses were tricky like that and never predictable.

"I'm not going to harm you," Talin insisted as he crammed

morsel of food into his mouth. His face was thin in the cheeks, and his short brown hair carried a golden hue. His lithe form might not have matched his brothers' bodies, but upstairs, his grip had been iron strong. He wore the healed marks of his initiation across his shoulder and collarbone.

"Sure you're not." I curled my hands in my lap. Okay, they were all loonies. "You know, his curse might accelerate as the full moon approaches, so maybe someone should chain him up when he's not in his cage."

Raze burst out laughing and slapped the table several times. What the hell was his problem?

"Oh, Talin," Raze began. "You are *so* getting added to Bee's erotica in a bondage scene. I see it now! You're tied to a wall, and she's in charge."

Fire hit my cheeks, and I burned up in an instant. Was he talking about my writing? "What did you just say?"

Leven butted in. "Am I going to be in it?"

My stomach plummeted, and my brain numbed at the realization that not only had Raze searched for me in the bedroom, but he'd searched through my belongings and read my tale. I balled my hands into fists. *How dare he!?*

"Leven, we're both already in the story, and damn, this girl has a filthy mind. You should *see* what she wants to do with us."

"Shut up!" I yelled, trembling as anger raged in my veins, while embarrassment had me blushing.

"I want to read this now!" Leven glanced my way, his head nodding, his mouth opened as if he were a starved dog.

Raze smirked. "I never knew you felt that way, but I'm ready whenever you are."

Mortified, I pushed away from the table. What I'd written that morning was a stupid fantasy, and *private. And* I hadn't done any editing on it yet.

Four sets of gazes watched me in awe as I stood with my

back to the fire, the heat wrapping around me. "I'm an author who writes romance. Not erotica. And you two"—I pointed at Raze and Leven—"are not in my story. They're fictional characters." I never should have made the characters bear shifters or described them like the two princes. I gripped my hips, refusing to admit I'd used them as my inspiration. "And who gave you the right to go through my stuff?"

"Your book lay open on the bed when I went to fix the sheets." Raze wiggled his eyes my way.

"Liar! No way in hell were *you* making my bed!" I gulped for air, no longer able to stand being in their company.

Ash's fingers found my hand, stroking me. "Hey, Bee, can I be in your story too?"

"Gah!" I spun and stormed out of the kitchen.

Behind me, their laughter boomed. Assholes, the lot of them. When I reached my bedroom, I slammed the door shut and locked myself in. "Bastard. Fuckwit. Dickhead."

I stared over at the bed, where the sheets were pristine and pulled tight over the mattress, as was the blanket. And right there on the puffed-up pillow was my book, left open. I marched closer and discovered on a new page with hand-writing that wasn't mine:

Bee, I will never just take you from behind. I'm not an animal. I'll strip you naked, lick every inch of you, and then tongue fuck you until you come in my mouth.

CHAPTER 11

I reread Raze's sexy sentence for the tenth time, my pulse thrumming in my ears, and I snapped the book shut. Except the words kept floating through my mind and already a tingling roused deep in the pit of my stomach. Damn, he wanted to do those things with me? For real? Or was he teasing and making fun of me? Because in all honesty, if we were anywhere but in our current situation, I'd be taking him into a private room this instant. That was how I rolled… I desired something, I went for it. But here, it felt wrong. Like they were being mischievous and, after all, when men got together, that pack mentality took over. Worse yet, now they all thought I wrote erotica and fantasized about them.

Okay, I did, but they hadn't needed to *know* that. Goddess, I blushed so hard. Raze had blurted out about my story out to everyone, and then they'd laughed. Now I felt as if a boy I had a secret crush on had seen me naked and poked fun at me.

I shook myself and stuffed the book into my bag. *Nope.* No more writing stories on this adventure. Once I got home,

I could scribble away to my heart's content and put my ideas for dirty tales with four bear shifters to paper. Now if only Ariella agreed to sell them and stop calling my writing "erotica."

With a huge huff, I collapsed on the couch. "Get your head straight." It was time to collect my ingredients and break the curse. First, I had to get my heartbeat under control and ground myself. I crossed my legs, balancing the backs of my hands across my knees.

Waterfalls. Tranquil mornings. In my mind, I followed a path in the woods. The sun slid down from gaps in the canopy overhead, warming my shoulders. Birds chirped, and a soft breeze washed through my hair, ruffling my clothes. Nothing could touch me. I was safe, calm, and protected.

Silence enveloped me, and I opened my third eye to the brightness around me. Outside, the falling snowflakes sparkled. The peace in my head.

"I call upon the goddess to protect me, to enhance my magic, and eradicate the curse placed on Talin Ursa." Tendrils of energy tingled at the tips of my fingertips, then swept across my palms and up my arms, the sign that she listened to my call.

Once my pulse slowed, I collected my prepared potion from my bag; herbs, salt, bones from a dead bird I'd found in my yard, and wolfsbane, all ground to a fine powder. Plus, the small sack of black salt.

I'd read enough in Mom's old spell books about reversing an enchantment, and I summoned the strength to make this work. It had to. At its core, all spells were vibrational patterns of an energy field around someone or an object being manipulated. And the best way to deal with that was to rebound the curse back to its owner.

Back downstairs, voices streamed from the kitchen, and I

crept closer, not because I was intent on spying, but hell if I didn't want to know if they were talking about me.

"It's getting worse out there," Raze said. "Rebels are surrounding the property, but it won't be long before they breach the protection circle. Then what? They beat us until we submit to Rek?"

Someone sighed. "And if I marry his granddaughter, he'll find ways to control White Peak, manipulate us, and how long before he kills us all? Then he'll take over the realm as he's always wanted." Talin's voice carried heavy tones.

Silence.

My throat dried. Wasn't Rek their cousin, but he wanted the throne for himself? The four royal princes had been left alone to face a life-and-death battle. I admired them for their courage and for sticking together. It said so much about who they were and how they treated people.

Ash spoke up. "I believe in Bee. She seems different from the other witches. Not prodding us for payment and insisting she has to leave right away."

I grimaced because those exact thoughts had crossed my mind, and I'd said something to that effect to Leven and Raze last night.

Still, Ash was a star, and already my favorite of the brothers.

"Hold on," Raze said. "Bee," he called out, "you can join us!"

Rocking on my heels, I stopped myself from bolting out of there. Instead, I tucked the pouches of ingredients under an arm and marched into the kitchen with my chin high.

"I...I didn't hear a thing you were talking about."

Four sets of eyes fixed on me. Yeah, I didn't believe me, either. But each of their expressions couldn't be more different, from Talin's wrinkled brow to Ash's soft smile to Leven's stoic mien. Then there was Raze and his devilish grin. Oh, he *so* knew I'd read his message, so I held his gaze and stuck out my tongue.

"Now, I could grill your asses for a week straight before I even make sense of the mess you're all in. But let's be honest, that's none of my business." I set the pouches on the table. "And I doubt you'd want to indulge my curiosity. So I need someone to bring me a handheld mirror. And a bowl with fresh, clean water big enough for the mirror to be dunked into."

Within seconds, three of the men left the room, though two would have been sufficient, and only Talin and myself remained. I collected a small, empty bowl and a knife from the pantry, then returned to the table, positioning myself right next to Talin.

He looked up at me from his seat, one corner of his mouth lifting, as if he weren't sure if he was ready to smile or not. "You going to cut me as payback for last night?"

"Nope. But you'll do it yourself." I set the blade in front of him and poured the powder from the satchel into the bowl. When he didn't pick up the knife, I added, "I need your blood."

"You sure this will work?" The tone beneath his voice carried a desperation I'd picked up on from the others. From Ash when he'd spoken of Talin. My dad had sounded the same when he'd realized that Mom's time had been ending. He'd say all the right things, but his words had been dead, empty, barren things.

I sat next to Talin and placed a hand on his. "I can't guarantee anything. I wish life came with such guarantees. Then I wouldn't have lost my mom. You wouldn't have had to bury your parents and sister, and you wouldn't be facing this fucked-up predicament. But that doesn't mean we need to accept it. We have two days until the full moon, so I'll work day and night to save you."

He smiled, his eyes wrinkling at the corners. "Ash was right. You *are* different from the others, but I'm curious, why are you so generous?"

"Because I hate nasty pieces of work, like Rek. I've known a few in my life and they won't stop until they get what they want!" I hissed, my hands clenching, thinking of the priestess in Terra, even Tristan and his guards, harassing my dad. "And if I can help fight him, I'll do it."

The sorrow in Talin's gaze thickened my throat and screams of frustration at his cousin exploded in my head. Was it too much to ask for Rek to love the princes? Goddamn, they were his family. I'd move the world for my dad.

Talin frowned and rubbed a hand across his brow. For that moment, he looked lost, as if he saw his demise and found it too hard to keep fighting.

"Why haven't you gotten married yet? If that's not too personal a question?" I asked. Maybe he hadn't met the right woman — though to me he seemed like the perfect catch. Not that he'd be interested in me because I was a commoner, carried no royal blood, and I wasn't a shifter. Three things that were probably on his future-wife list. Anyway, that kind of stuff only happened in fairy tales and I was being foolish for indulging in such thoughts.

Seeing the rigid way he sat while staring at me blankly, I regretted my query. "Look, it's—"

"In White Peak, wives gain equality and ownership of half their mate's possessions. Father always told me to not rush into the decision and first make sure my mate's love is genuine and that she isn't marrying me for dominance or wealth. Bear shifters mate for life. There's no such thing as a separation. So I will not jeopardize this realm and those who call the mountains home to Rek or anyone until I find my right mate."

In the little time I'd been with him, he seemed like he'd be a fair and caring ruler. Not like the priestess over in Terra. What would he do with the guards who were harassing Dad and me? Maybe if Talin became king, the solution was for Dad and me to move into White Peak — after making some state-of-the-art bear repellent.

And I remembered Ash explaining how Rek wanted Talin to marry a fourteen-year-old girl. Like that wasn't an obvious power-grabbing decision. I couldn't help but admire Talin for sticking to his principles despite the shitload of trouble they'd landed him in.

He slouched in his seat. "The same night I showed initial symptoms of the illness, all castle staff changed as if they were under a spell. They picked up and left without a word. They returned to their homes and even when we followed them, they insisted they couldn't work for us. No reason, just a feeling they had to follow. It was as if they were mind-controlled. That's why we have no one in the castle. I suspect Rek was responsible. He's trying to force my hand to wed his granddaughter. That was three weeks ago."

So how was I supposed to ever get home if the rebels patrolled the woods to keep anyone from coming in or going out? I'd almost died reaching the castle.

I tried to sift through everything I'd learned, the corruption within the family, the reason the castle lay empty, the atrocity Rek had thrown on the princes for petty revenge and to gain their throne. Fat chance of the cousin retracting his assault. Goddess, someone had to stop him.

Talin offered me a gentle smile, and my heart sunk. His world had shattered and it wasn't just his life at risk, but his brothers'. He had to be gutted. I took a deep breath, reached over, and placed a hand on his, fear looping around in my head. I wanted to bundle him in my arms, take away the agony etched across his furrowed brow.

"Let's fuck up your cousin's curse and send it back to him." Here I'd thought *my* life was complicated. *Holy crap.*

Talin's fingers curled over mine, and his sincerity touched me. No wonder the townsfolk under his jurisdiction feared losing a compassionate leader.

"Do you have a mate?" he asked, the question so random, I tilted my head, facing him.

"Nope," I said, loathing the answer, because who didn't want to find their perfect match? That was all I wrote in my stories, happily ever afters. The longing to find someone to love me hit me in my chest like a spiked mace.

"When you encounter him, make sure he treats you as you deserve." Talin broke our touch and picked up the blade. With a swift motion of the knife, he sliced the fleshy part of his palm, and red droplets rolled down his fingers. He clenched his fist over the bowl. Blood trickled onto the powdered potion.

His words still haunted me. Despite our initial encounter. He couldn't have been more opposite to the monster I'd met upstairs yesterday.

I jumped to my feet and unraveled the tie-cord of my shirt, my pulse fluttering in Talin's presence.

He eyed me, his mouth widening. "Is stripping part of the spell? Because I'm for it."

"It's not what you think." Yet my blood sizzled at his innuendo. But flirting with the up and coming King of White Peak wasn't a smart move. I couldn't take the heartache later. "I don't want to dirty this gorgeous top I borrowed from the wardrobe upstairs."

"The color suits your hair."

I drew the fabric over my head, pulling down on the white undergarment riding up my stomach.

"When my sister, Vivienne, was alive, I promised to keep her safe. As the eldest, it's my responsibility, but I ruined that. So I made myself a promise to put an end to the tension of the four ruling families in White Peak and unite the tribes. Now I'm losing that chance."

Placing my top on a chair, I pressed my fingers into the mixture, mushing it up. "That's enough blood, thanks. And you wrecked nothing. The world is filled with fuckwits who take pleasure in tearing others down. You should see the idiots who live in Terra. I ought to convince Dad to sell our place and move to another realm." Just thinking of Tristan and his idiotic guards had me tensing. Not to mention the guard I'd spotted near the Golden Lock tavern. I prayed he hadn't seen me.

Talin rose from his chair. "Your honesty is refreshing. Most of the time I'm surrounded by those who say anything they think we want to hear. Never the truth."

"Ha, then you should meet my dad. He has an opinion on everything." That was one of the many things I loved about him and I was happy to have inherited it and more.

Raze entered the room carrying a small handheld mirror encircled by a frame of silver. He blocked Leven's and Ash's path as they drew up behind him, each carrying a large, round bucket filled with water.

"Shit, Raze," Leven growled. "Move your ass out of my way."

"Ash, place the mirror into the water," I said. "Then add the black salt. Then take it out in the main hallway. We're doing this there."

I turned to Talin. "I need to paint your face. The enchant-ment will look at your reflection and not recognize the person who's been cursed, and instead return the hex to the one whose blood was used to cast the magic, placing the burden on them." Part of me hesitated in doing this spell because it wasn't white magic, or black. Maybe gray. But with no sacrifice required, I was happy to try it out. Curses weren't easy to break, so sometimes that meant going a bit heavy-handed on the solution.

"I can't tell you how much you're turning me on right now," Raze said. "Not only are you sexy with your little white number, but if you're about to slap Rek with his own spell, fuck yeah." He punched the air. "Let's do this."

I glanced down at my top, not sure what Raze referred to, and noticed my pebbled nipples pressing against the fabric. Okay fine, if it gave them a show to lighten the mood, I could live with it. Though in the back of my mind, I wasn't fully happy with cursing someone, but technically, wasn't I just returning something that belonged to them? And if the prince was in danger of dying, damn right I would help cleanse him.

Scooping the mixture with my fingers, I faced Talin. "Concentrate on me the whole time."

Sharp green eyes met mine, and he gave a slight nod. The stolen moment between us wasn't helping me stay focused. I could picture myself chatting with him for a full day about anything and everything as he made me feel at ease in his company. But they were foolish dreams. After this spell, I'd help him get his life back, and then I would leave. Even if the knot in my stomach tightened at the thought.

I glanced over my shoulders at the others. "Once we start the spell, be ready to jump in if Talin shows any signs of transforming." So many maybes rolled through my head, like the spell backfiring. Did the curse have too strong a hold on Talin for this to work?

CHAPTER 12

*S*tatic buzzed across my skin, and the telltale signs of dark magic licked the length of my spine. I held myself strong, ignoring the shivers, the doubts, the dread coiling in my head. We had to do this now, and that meant showing no fear, controlling my emotions, and working fast without a distraction. When Mom used to practice using her power, she'd become a different person with a blank expression.

I called out, "The negative energy sent to you shall be revoked. Returned to the individual who cast it, threefold." I spoke directly to Talin, who sat in a chair in the middle of the hallway near the staircase. The herb and blood concoction smeared his cheeks and brow, giving him a tribal look. He wasn't shaking or flinching but held a look of determination. His mouth was thin and tight, while a cord of muscle in his neck pulsed. My earlier admiration of Talin just went up a notch as he sat there, brave, ready. No running away or poking fun at magic.

Around us, his brothers fanned out. Far enough away and

positioned carefully to avoid a reflection in the mirror, but close enough should Talin go feral.

Please, Goddess, fill me with your strength. Give me the power to eradicate this spell.

I turned to the bowl of water placed on a chair behind me and lowered my palm over it. At once, a charge skipped across the surface and crackled up my arm, as if a dozen spiders sank their fangs into my flesh at once. I winced but bit down on my lower lip until I tasted the metallic taste of blood.

Show no weakness. No hesitation. My gut clenched.

I collected the consecrated mirror out of the water by the handle. A sharp ache swept up and over my shoulder from the mirror. A dull hum played in my ears like mosquitoes, and I squirmed inside. This wasn't the time for emotions.

Hexes were nasty things that always fought back. So I had to stay strong, and called to my power. It trickled over my skin.

Thrusting the mirror toward Talin, the reflection facing him, I bellowed, "I repel this curse. Return to your owner."

At first, nothing happened. Then a thread of black energy coiled out of the mirror, swinging left and right as a blind worm might do when unsoiled.

I trembled, my breath caught in my chest, and I fought to find my voice. "Re…Retract your curse. You do not belong here. You have the wrong person."

The mirror in my hand trembled, and I tightened my grip. "I revoke you. Return to sender."

Power surged into my palm. At once, golden shards of energy shot out of my hand and engulfed the mirror in a flaming ball.

The object shook harder, pulled in the opposite direction as if someone else held on to the top. I grasped the handle with both hands, keeping it facing Talin. My muscles ached, screaming for release.

Bastard! Curses didn't usually fight this hard, and dread trickled into my mind that I'd made a mistake, that the spell could spin against me, and I'd harm someone. My teeth locked tight. I couldn't stop or reverse time because I didn't know the full extent of the curse. Who'd placed it? What ingredients had they used? Had a sacrifice been made?

I forced everything I had into the mirror. "Curse, be gone!"

On the last word, an explosion of black tentacles burst out of the mirror, throwing me backward. My feet tangled on the steps, and I fell onto my butt, my breath racing. I gripped the mirror tightly, rage boiling deep inside me. "Fucking son of a bitch."

I pushed myself up, noting all the men were on the ground, groaning, except Talin. Right then, invisible hands seized the front of my top and pants and hurled me forward. The screaming came involuntarily as I slammed into Talin, the chair beneath him smashing and both of us crashing to the ground.

My heart raced, and he had me to my feet in moments, his hands over mine to control the freakin' mirror in my grasp.

"I got you." His panicked voice didn't help my own emotions.

"It shouldn't be doing this," I yelled back. Something was wrong, terribly wrong.

More tentacles shot outward, straight for the three brothers, each one colliding into their chests so fast, they slid back down, convulsing. Paintings fell off their hooks. Howls echoed around us.

"No!" I scrambled forward on trembling legs, Talin by my

side. "Goddess. I ask for your divine intervention. Vanquish this curse from this family."

Nothing. Not a single jolt of energy across my skin.

But when a black viper from the mirror curled around and rushed toward me, the tip splitting into a gaping mouth, I screamed.

Talin flew backward from an invisible force.

"Stop! I command you to halt!" I jutted out a hand, driving every inch of strength I possessed toward the oncoming slaughter.

The tentacle smacked into my chest, winding me, pushing me off my feet. And my world blacked so fast, I couldn't even breathe.

* * *

I woke gasping, my hands batting the air, legs kicking.

"Get up, Sugarplum."

Startled, I flipped open my eyes and stared at Leven's face. Dread wrinkled the bridge of his nose, yet my head fogged, and I couldn't formulate a plan. I glanced around the empty hallway. Portraits had fallen off the walls, some cracked, others lying face down. The chandelier swung wildly. Yet the bucket of salt water lay intact on the chair, untouched. Had it been the spell?

A growing pressure to run and never stop until I reached home filled me. The house was quiet, and heaviness hung in the air.

"Where's everyone? Is Talin okay?" A boulder might as well have been sitting on my chest.

Leven took my hand and yanked me upright in a flash. "We need to go."

"Wait, what's going on?" At my feet I found the mirror,

smashed. Yep, the spell had ended, but what had it unleashed?

A roar erupted from somewhere deeper in the house. I shuddered and flinched as I turned around. "Talin's turned?"

Leven snatched my elbow and dragged me upstairs. "Talin transformed first. Then Ash, and just recently, Raze." His accusing voice hurt.

"I didn't curse them." I pulled free and we stood inches apart, halfway up the steps. "Tell me what's going on! Are you going to change too?"

"I don't know. But they're hunting me. And now that you're awake, you'll be on their radar too."

I couldn't swallow, and fear clung to my ribs. "We're being hunted?" Coldness sunk through me. Yet Leven hauled me up the stairs by an arm. I stumbled after him, trying to make sense of what had happened. The spell had backfired, and instead of reverting to the creator of the curse, it had attacked us. Almost as if whomever had placed it had laid a trap for anyone tampering with the hex.

It hadn't even crossed my mind. My stomach ached. How could I not have suspected a trap? Had I just made the nightmare worse? Were we being attacked by the other brothers?

To lay such a complicated curse meant a sacrifice had been made. Why would Rek stoop to murder? And where had he found a death witch?

"Hurry up," Leven whispered.

Another roar rattled through the house from somewhere downstairs.

"Where are we going?" I rushed up more stairs, realizing quickly I'd been here before. Talin's cage was up here.

Once inside the room, Leven opened the door to the prison cell. "Get inside, and I'll lock you in." He shoved me into the cage.

"Wait! What about you?" The world tilted beneath me as everything happened too fast. I had too many questions.

Leven growled and slapped the cage shut behind me. He tossed a set of keys to the ground near my feet. I whirled around, dread constricting my lungs.

He'd fallen to all fours, his body stretching. I cried out, not forming any words, just releasing the desperate fear collecting in my chest.

"Leven?"

Fur spurted down his legs. He belched a screech, painful and earsplitting. It killed me to watch him suffer, to listen to his yowls of pain. I shuddered and hugged myself. His transformation was nothing like the fluid change I'd seen with Raze. This was rough, painful, and disfiguring.

Tears blurred my vision as my heart trembled. No dignity, just fear etched on his warped face as he screamed.

I grabbed the keys and recoiled, my back hitting the cage wall, and my heart pounded in my chest as a half-bear, half-man raised on two feet, turning toward me with a twisted mouth.

His legs might be furry, but his bare chest was wide, with brown hair growing before my eyes, only his arms and eyes remained the same.

Death gleamed in his gaze as he prowled closer. Behind him, three more predators exploded into the room, tearing down the door in the process.

I gasped and recoiled, my hands pressed to my stomach.

Four beasts glared my way, all half-transformed and snarling. They leaped onto the cage, and the terror caught in my lungs streamed out. I screamed as they shook the prison. Clawed hands stretched inside for me from three sides, and Leven was on top. Snarling.

I curled in on myself in the middle against the back where the cell met the wall. Out of reach, but for how long?

With their teeth bared, they roared, slamming themselves into the bars. I couldn't stop trembling, and I hugged my knees, crying. Would the cage hold them back? For how long?

Talin had said the spell drew him back to the castle, keeping them indoors. That meant there was no chance of them leaving my side to hunt down anyone. I swallowed down the burning bile that scorched my throat.

I gnawed on my hangnail, unable to stop rocking back and forth. *What do I do now?*

And how to undo not only a curse, but also the trap? Would there be more surprises waiting for me when I tried again? I felt sick at the thought of trying to fix this, but I had to do something. I couldn't stay locked up without my herbs. It was only a matter of time before they broke this cage and ripped me apart for their meal.

But that meant playing with dark magic. And I refused to kill anyone to retaliate with a spell on Rek. That would make me no better than him. And I didn't want to open up that portal to make a deal with a demon. What if I released them into our world? Because our situation wasn't bad enough. Nope, that wasn't an option now or ever.

Goddess. What I'd give now to be home living my mundane life, dreaming about adventure, but never actually experiencing it. Yep, that's what I needed right now. For nothing to happen.

Maybe what I needed was to exchange spots with the shifters. Place them in this cage, and keep them locked up until I found a solution. But how?

I patted the lump in my pocket, remembering the sleeping potion I'd thought to carry with me.

Scrambling to my feet, I pulled out the small pouch and opened it by tugging on the string.

The bears growled, shaking the cage, and I swore they

would break in at any moment at this rate. I focused on the potion and whispered under my breath, "I send you to sleep. A deep, peaceful slumber."

But the moment I tapped into the energy in my chest, a chill coiled deep inside me, flooding my veins. It catapulted through me, fighting me as a gust of wind might.

I stumbled backward.

No warmth filled me… this wasn't my usual power, yet it was me. And just like that, a fog drowned my thoughts, pulling me in every direction, laughing maniacally in my head.

And the past came flooding forward. The day I'd turned thirteen and I'd had my first female bleed. Darkness had spread through me, unlocking unimaginable power, but it had come at a cost. The urge to kill had owned me. I'd craved it as if I might starve. Mom had found me rushing through the woods with a kitchen knife, ready to slaughter anyone who crossed my path. She'd stopped me with a calming spell, and that was when I'd learned bloodborne witches like me had two halves inside them,. I'd been born under a blood moon, and that meant the darker side was stronger, more powerful. For years, I'd practiced how to keep it hidden, under control, never tempting it out. Until now.

Sweat dripped down my neck as fear overwhelmed every inch of me, and exhaustion had me stumbling.

"This can't be happening." I'd been careful for so long.

A hunger raced through me, warping my insides into barbed knots.

I screamed and fell to my knees. "You will not cross over. I command you to retreat!"

In that moment, Ash and Talin pulled apart two bars, the metal groaning, and already Raze had pushed his head through, his mouth gaping open with a growl, and his hand pawing the air to get to me.

I shivered, and death flashed before my eyes. Something snapped inside me like cracking bones, and a shuddering of energy burst outward from my mouth, covering the room in a black mist.

CHAPTER 13

Adrenaline coursed through me, along with that delicious craving to cover myself in blood. I stretched my back, feeling as if I'd slept for years, and every part of me tingled. For too long, Bee had followed the rules and kept me under tight restraint. Fuck, I'd almost forgotten what I really was—a goddamn witch who took my magic from the real masters of power. This bullshit of working with the goddess left me weak, gutless, and it was an insult. But no problem. I'd make up for lost time. No more sitting on the side bench, watching, and never taking part. This was my turn to shine.

I stood in the cage. Four princes stared my way, dazed and shaking themselves. They were all twisted, part-bear and part-human. Damn, someone had done a number on these poor suckers.

"Hello, boys!"

Leven crouched near me, sniffing the air. When I stretched an arm out to pat him, he snarled and snapped at the air between us. I snatched my hand back.

"That wasn't very nice now, was it?" Power surged in my palms like a charge. An inky black bolt of energy shot out from my hand, striking him in the chest. "Now behave and do as I say."

Leven whined and flinched, crumpling onto his side, trembling, and his body shifted into human form. Now, a naked man lay in front of me.

Hell and spank me twice, I was in a candy store. A whole different kind of enjoyment played in my mind.

But it was curious how he'd switched to his human side when Bee's attempts with her white hocus pocus had failed.

Leven dragged himself to his feet. "Bee! What did you do to me?"

"Darlin', there's no one here by that name. Call me 'Lilita'. So much sexier, don't you think?"

His upper lip peeled upward. "What the fuck?" His hands curled into balls as he surged forward.

"Stop," I bellowed, my arm raised, palm facing him.

And he did, his eyes widening as he remained in his frozen state. "What's going on?"

Damn, his mouth still worked. "You must be hard of hearing, boy. I told you who I am. But I guess our little friend Bee never explained she has two sides to her, like all bloodborne witches. The weak, fluffy light side that she dabbles in, and the tremendously sexy and powerful darker side only I can control. And now it's my turn to come out and enjoy your company."

The other three outside the cage growled.

With a flick of my fingers in their direction, I struck them all at once with shards of energy sparking from my fingers. Tendrils of power punched into their chests, driving them backward. Each gasped for air, hitting the wall, and Talin even roared. Cute. They all transformed back into their human forms.

My knees wobbled beneath me, and I staggered as lethargy weakened me. Okay, it'd been a while and I forgot how quickly I got drained when I used magic. Didn't help that deep in my mind, Bee shrieked for release. Not happening, baby girl.

The princes faced me, three of them still wearing their pants, and I sighed. No problem. We'll change that soon enough.

I stepped out of the cage. "Interesting." I tapped my chin, facing the four men. I wondered if their change was a temporary or permanent thing. *"Okay, a night of debauchery can wait. But first, some ground rules." I counted them on my fingers. "No trying to kill me behind my back. I die and your precious Bee does too. We are two halves of a whole, so no trying to get her back... I'm here to stay. Second, you do everything I say." I laughed. "And lastly, no leaving me for another woman. That would really tear me up, and I don't want to murder any of you. Got it?"*

"Are you fucking insane?" Raze's lips warped, his shoulders stiffening. "I don't give a shit if you're the devil's favorite lap dog, this arrangement will not work. We are the princes of White Peak. Kneel and beg for your life!" he roared.

With a huff, I strode toward him. "Raze. Raze. This is your final warning and only because of Bee. She adores you—well, she has a thing for all of you, and I don't blame her." I stared at the incredible muscular specimens surrounding me. "If only you could be inside here." I tapped the side of my head. "The things she wants you to do to her. That girl puts me to shame. She's hot for all four of you."

Ash pushed forward, as did Talin, and I chuckled. They were predictable and I needed a challenge.

Raze's fist flew toward my face.

I snapped my palm up. "All four, stop." And that earlier exhaustion rolled through me and I stumbled. "Whoa." I remembered their obvious desires and amorous expressions when they'd looked at Bee, but now they just stared at me with disdain.

No one responded. There were only murmurs on their throats, as they were unable to budge from their spots.

"Now that's better than listening to your yabbering. So this is the new plan of action. I'll get changed out of this plain outfit. I mean, we're in a castle and Bee is wearing pants. Wake up to yourself, girl. Anyway"—I turned to the men—"then we're going for a long walk. Been thinking if I can switch off your hex with such

ease, imagine what I could do to Rek and all the other royal families?"

I glanced at the men still standing there. "Oh, right." I waved at them, and the magic flowed down my arm and threaded out to each of them. "Well, come on. Move. We have White Peak to take over."

By the time I reached the bedroom with a closet full of clothes, I made haste to find something more appropriate to wear. I whirled around in a golden gown cinching at the waist, admiring myself in front of a long mirror, my auburn locks spinning with me. My hair kept frizzing, and I patted it down. Bee's hair never did that, the bitch. Long sleeves and a low-cut V-dress showed off my assets. And why the hell not? When you had them, you flaunted them.

I turned to find all the shifters sitting on the four-poster bed glaring my way. They reminded me of a box of candies, each one different but delicious. "Come on. You can't tell me this doesn't turn you on."

They rewarded me with only frowns, and it hurt. I still looked like Bee, so where was their sexual hunger? "Oh, you shifters are party poopers."

"Just because you control our bodies doesn't mean we're on your side," Leven growled.

Strolling forward, I swung my hips on purpose, noticing Ash's gaze dipping to my chest. I lifted my skirt to my knees and crawled up onto his lap, straddling him. "Tell me how beautiful I am."

His lips thinned as he pulled away from me. "You may look like Bee, but you're not her."

"Kiss me," I said. "Maybe we can squeeze in some action before we head off, big boy."

His grimace turned to revulsion. Fine by me. I reached over and yanked him closer by his hair.

Despite the shock in his eyes, I grabbed the sides of his head and kissed him, tasting him. Salty and musky. Yum.

A shock jolted up between us so hard, an invisible hand yanked

me backward and the corners of my vision blackened at once. "No!"
I yelled and the moment I hit the ground, my world disappeared.

* * *

"Bee! Bee!"

Someone shook me, and I flipped open my eyes to four men staring down at me. "Lilita!" I spat out the name I'd avoided saying for years. There was a reason I never thought or spoke her name — to avoid giving her power. Little good that had done.

"Is that you, Bee?" Leven asked.

"Well, duh." Raze nudged closer. "She's no longer controlling our movements. It's our Bee."

I lay there trembling as fear quietly tore through me, starting with my aching stomach, leaving me gasping for air and every inch of me clammy with sweat. "Lilita was here." It wasn't a question. Ice encased me, throttling me at the core, and deep inside I was terrified she'd now own me for eternity. She would allow me to be possessed by demons, ravaging and raping my mind and body. And the longer she shoved me aside, using her magic from the underworld, the easier it would be for her to lock me into a box forever. The less power I had, the harder it would be for me to keep her imprisoned in my mind.

Talin swept me off the ground and set me on the bed. "It'll be okay," he said.

My voice vanished. Nothing would ever be okay again. I recalled what Lilita had said and done as if I watched it on replay in my head. She hadn't come out since I was thirteen, and even then, she'd taken me over, insisting we needed to kill. And now… she had her sights set on White Peak?

The world tilted. Tears fell, and I sobbed into my hands. A rise of sickness hit my throat. I curled in on myself and couldn't stop crying at how horribly I'd failed with breaking the spell. Saving my mom. And now... The darkness in me had been released. And it wasn't finished.

"Bee." Ash called my name again. I didn't want them to see me, not like this. They had every right to hate me for what I was.

"It'll be okay, Sugarplum." Leven pulled the hair off my face, while another prince rubbed my back in gentle circles. The bed shifted as four of them surrounded me. But I didn't deserve their sympathy or their kindness.

"Lilita?" Talin asked. "I think you need to explain what happened." And there it was, the fear and anger I'd expected.

I stayed still a while and wiped my tears as heaviness sat on my mind. She'd been awakened, and now she lingered close, waiting for her chance to emerge again.

When I drew myself to a sitting position, I hugged my knees. Leven drew me into his arms without a slither of hesitation. "You'll be okay," he kept saying, but I wasn't so sure any more.

And the men deserved the truth, to be aware of the danger to which I'd now exposed them. I pulled free from Leven and forced a smile, but it felt empty and fake.

Four sets of eyes trained on me.

"I'm a bloodborne witch." And I explained about my two sides and Lilita. I lowered my gaze to my fingers, lacing them together. With a deep inhale, I told them how I'd kept Lilita at bay for years, the side effects of her using dark magic, and how if I didn't completely imprison her once more, after a few months, my energy would fade, making her stronger, unbalancing the strength in her favor.

I chanced a glance up, but no one was scowling or giving me death glares. Raze touched my shoulder while Leven took my hand in his. Ash leaned closer too, rubbing my knee, and

Talin… he didn't look at me with disgust, but rather an expression I knew too well. Grief and sympathy.

"So how do we help you control her?" he asked with kindness in his voice. I'd never expected them to show such compassion and understanding.

"I don't know." And that was the truth. "I'm guessing your curse had a trap for anyone trying to break it. And it backfired big time, affecting us all differently. It must have tapped into Lilita, since I wasn't a shifter." I could only assume it hadn't affected me as quickly, because of how long Lilita had been locked away.

"I can still feel the forcefulness of the partial shift," Leven said. "As if being ripped in half stays with me. Does this mean I'm now cursed too?"

"I feel the same," Ash said, and Raze nodded.

My breath caught in my throat. "Maybe. It explains why Lilita was released." And dread curled in my chest because I couldn't accept that my attempt to help had retaliated and cursed all four princes — and me.

"We'll find out tonight, so we need to be ready." Talin's voice darkened. "As much as I love you, this curse wasn't something I wanted to share with you all."

"What I want to understand," Leven said, "is why do all of you still have your pants on from the transformation, and I lost mine?"

"Because you got a fat ass," Raze teased. "And when we changed, our pants didn't split."

I couldn't help but laugh, along with everyone else. Considering the shithole we'd just landed in, nothing ought to have made me laugh until my ribs ached.

I guessed misery loved company.

We all fell silent in a solemn state because what were we meant to do next? A suffocating sensation constricted around my chest.

"What do you think happened when she kissed me?" Ash asked, his hand still on my leg, his warmth spreading across my skin. "The spark throwing her off me sent her packing and brought you back."

"Maybe your breath killed her." Raze shoved a fist against Ash's shoulder and chuckled.

Ash glowered and placed a hand over his mouth, smelling his own breath. "Definitely not my breath. It's my enchanting kiss." He waggled his eyebrows.

I loved how even in the face of adversity, they joked around.

"I don't know why she reacted," I said. "Could be that we're under the curse, and her magic is reacting to it? Once two or more spells overlap, anything can happen. If I was home in Terra, I'd go through my magic books for ideas on what herbs could amplify my ability. I might find a way to protect us, keep Lilita at bay, and find something to tackle the hex without the need to spill blood." I didn't plan on giving Lilita any reasons to return. If Mom were still alive, she'd have told me how to keep my dark side at bay. I'd never seen her struggle with hers, so what was I doing wrong?

"I own a few books on plants," Ash offered. "Might even have a couple on magic."

I did a double take at Ash, gasping. "So magic isn't banned in White Peak?"

Ash shook his head. "No, of course not."

Yeah, because only the insane priestess in Terra had implemented that prehistoric rule.

Raze interrupted my thoughts. "What we need is to lock ourselves up. Our only cage is damaged from when we pried it open together, so it needs to be strengthened. That's our first concern."

"I disagree." Talin had a sneer in his voice. "Our priority is ensuring that psycho Lilita doesn't return. She fucking controlled us! Cages are useless if she's free." His hands balled, and I could see him smashing a fist into the wall.

The urge to curl in on myself and hide flooded me. They feared what lay inside me, but then so did I. But if the curse was to blame for bringing her out, then would she reappear once night settled? Just as all four princes would transform into bears?

A boulder might as well be sitting on my chest because I could barely breathe. We were running out of time. In my heart, I wished I could retract ever accepting this assignment. As much as I was starting to really like these princes, I'd caused more trouble than they'd already been in. It would've been better if we'd never met. At that thought, a pain hit my chest, stealing my breath. But I knew the truth of the severity of what had happened. I'd just signed everyone's death warrant, including my own.

"All right, Ash," I said, "where are your books on herbs? Everyone else needs to come up with a new solution to fixing the damaged cage. Unless you have a dungeon under the castle? We can lock you down there if you do. That's all I can think of. Then, we'll work out a plan for your cousin. Our priority is us not tearing each other apart." And keeping Lilita forever at bay.

With the men all staring at me, I forced a smile.

"We got rid of the dungeon," Leven said. "Turned the cells into entertainment rooms with games."

Ash placed his hand into mine, our fingers intertwined. He drew me across the room. "Come with me."

Nausea whirled through my stomach unrestrained. *Goddess, please help me find a solution to save everyone.*

CHAPTER 14

"*I* know you're nothing like Lilita," Ash said, his hand still around mine. That small gesture gave me the strength to keep going, to stop feeling as if I were alone, to believe we'd find a way out of the mess tangled around the five of us.

Tightening my hold, I glanced up at him. "That means a lot. But you're all probably thinking I'm a monster ready to kill you."

"We're scared of more than just Lilita, but I don't see you as a beast." He drew me downstairs and back through the house, past doors I hadn't explored yet. An old kitchen. Dining room. Restroom. All drab, empty of life, and a constant reminder of what was at stake for the princes should they fail to have the hex removed.

And while I easily agreed to helping them because they deserved support, I'd confess that with the time bomb now ticking under my breastbone, I felt like screaming and running back home. But then what? Try to evade the rebels outside and leave the princes in a worse situation than when I'd arrived? But what if being away from them was for the best? There'd be no Lilita to control them, yet with me gone, where would they find another witch? Right, because I'd been such a huge assistance so far.

Hurrying down a long corridor, windows on one side and decorative shields on the other, I stared at the double doors we approached.

"Aren't you scared?" I asked. "Because I am. I feel like a rabbit surrounded by wolves."

"A little." His hand squeezed mine. "After we retrieved my parents and Vivienne's bodies from the bottom of the cliff, I think a part of me died with them that day. Even since, I've realized that if fate's coming for me, who am I to stop it? At least I might see them again."

"That breaks my heart." What would Dad do if I never returned home? Would he spend the rest of his life searching for me in vain? I'd want him to go on with life, enjoy what he had, not waste it on me. Yet I remembered the weeks and months I'd spent hidden in my room after Mom's death, refusing to talk to anyone. Grief still stung like a bitch.

Ash glanced down at me. "I don't know how else to deal with the loss, even after all these years. And when Talin fell sick, the grief rose through me again, shredding me apart." His voice broke, and he looked away.

I hugged him tight, my arms wrapped around his chest. "So that's why you throw yourself into gardening and trying to get the snow roses to grow."

Slowly, he softened against me, his muscles losing their tension, and he embraced me back. I sunk into the warmth of his body, his strength a shield from the world. His touch made my past somewhat bearable, and I prayed he felt the same.

He pulled back, his eyes lightly glistening. "Guess we all have our escapes. Talin dives into community work, getting the royal families to work together and stop fighting. Raze hides behind his heroic deeds and goes out most nights fighting for anyone in trouble. Leven keeps to himself mostly, not talking for a week at a time, but recently he's hinting it might be time for him to find a wife. Expand the family line. Something I've been telling Talin he needs to do, quickly."

I nodded, curious to understand how everyone dealt with grief in their own way. My way was to hide from the world. Dad's had been to throw himself into inventing everything under the sun, and forgetting to eat and sleep. Yet my thoughts revolved around Leven wanting a wife, and a streak of jealousy filled me, which was stupid and childish. I longed to find my own other half one day.

"And what about you? What's your escape?" His hand slid across my cheek, warm and calloused, but protective. His eyes glimmered against the light pouring in through the windows behind him. Ash stood tall over me, and if he'd wanted to, he could have snapped my neck in a flash with those muscles. But he had a soft expression and reminded me of my friend Scarlet. They might be powerful on the inside, but they treated the world with a feather-soft approach.

I responded in a raspy voice. "I spend a lot of time working on controlling my magic, strengthening my ability." *And keeping Lilita from taking over.* Goddess, would I ever be normal and find happiness? "Plus, there's my writing."

His fingers combed through my hair to the back of my head, and something about his closeness had me pressing closer. Anything to stop feeling as if I carried the world on my shoulders. His lips parted, and I stared at their delicious-ness, hidden amidst his short stubble with golden specks.

"It's definitely your erotic stories," he said.

I stiffened at the men's' inability to separate sex from romance. "It's a romance story, not just sex. But maybe you're right. Throwing myself into these stories is something I enjoy and lets me forget my problems."

He laughed, thick and heavy. "And when you do get around to writing about me, I'd be honored." He winked.

"You're funny," I said. "And if we were anywhere else and you weren't a prince, I might even ask you out on a date. There's this great little coffee shop near my place and we can chat about herbs and plants all day long." As soon as the words left my mouth, I froze on the spot, abashed that I would even say that out loud. Being around Ash made me feel normal, as if he were a friend I had a crush on back home and he felt the same, but neither would make a move. I felt so stupid.

He melted me with his grin. "Who said I'd want to talk about vegetation? I'd rather hear more about you. Shall we head inside then?" Ash drew his hand back, but I grabbed for his wrist, keeping him in place. I didn't want to be apart, or alone. For those few moments, I'd felt normal again, amazed I could even smile. His earlier words about my writing being my escape stayed with me. I'd used it to distract myself from the darkness inside me, to pretend I was someone else without such a burden on her shoulders. What I did find was, that each time I wrote just before my magical training, especially the super raunchy scenes, I'd always cast with precision, feeling stronger. I put that down to feeling horny from the scene, which relaxed my muscles, but what if that state of excitement and distraction strengthened my ability to keep my dark side at bay? To control my magic better?

"Hey, you know upstairs when you kissed Lilita," I said, "and then she was thrown off you... What did you feel?"

"Pretty disgusted."

"That's a bit harsh." And now my earlier slip about a date had me blushing like a beetroot.

"Not from you, sweetie, but knowing it was her. A snap of

energy just lanced across my mouth, ripping her off me. Weird, right?"

I nodded, unsure why a kiss would result in such a reaction. "Just toying with an idea. But what if the kiss drove Lilita away? Like an outlet for all the power I carry inside me. And maybe we're somehow connected because of the curse backfiring."

Ash studied me, his gaze falling to my lips, and his closeness seduced me.

"It's a crazy thought." I broke free, but Ash collected me back into his embrace, our bodies pressed together as he leaned down. "But what if our kiss brings back Lilita?" I asked.

"Considering our circumstances, I think we need to try out every possibility. I read somewhere once that true passion coming from the heart could drive darkness away. Maybe your passion is linked to kinky stuff." He smirked, and I fake-slapped his arm, but he caught it and kissed the center of my palm. Every part of me buzzed, and a fiery desire roared awake inside me.

"Can you feel anything now?" he asked.

"Only you tickling me," I teased.

He drew me closer, his face dipping lower, and without pause, his mouth brushed against mine. Soft at first, as if testing my response or what might happen. With no reaction, I wrapped my hands around his neck and lifted myself on tippy-toes. He kissed me — hard and starved. I pressed my tongue to his lips and he parted them, sucking me in, tangling my tongue with his.

I moaned, and he walked me backward until I hit the wall. He gripped my hips and picked me off my feet with such ease that I lost my breath. Pinned between the wall and Ash, I collected my skirt on either side of my thighs and curled my legs around his waist, holding on. Now, we were at the same height. This huge man undid me. Beneath him, fire spread through my body at the intoxication of his desperate and passionate kiss.

When he broke away, we stayed there, our brows touching. Tenderness lay behind his green eyes. "What about now?" His devilish smile was an addiction.

"Well, I may need more of your sugar before I can really tell," I suggested, butterflies swirling inside my stomach. After his kiss, I was lost and needed more. He left me giddy, hyped up on his attention.

"I get that. And just for your information, I'm feeling incredible right now."

I laughed because I couldn't sense that suppressed heaviness from Lilita, either, and I felt normal, as if she was imprisoned back in my mind. Better yet, being intimate with Ash and controlling my dark side at the same time was a win-win.

Ash inhaled my lips and breath, his hands skipping up the sides of my body and across to my ass. Squeezing, kneading. His warmth cocooned me.

"Shall we go check out those books?" He breathed the words into my mouth, and I made a sound that sounded like *yes*, unable to pull myself away.

With my legs still wrapped around him, he opened the door and walked us inside. That old paper smell hit me at once, but my mouth gaped open at the sight, and I wriggled out of Ash's embrace.

"Are you fucking kidding me? This is 'a few' books on plants?"

"I never said all the books were on vegetation. And you may want to close your mouth, as I'm sure there are moths in here."

"Fucking crapping balls." I darted into the enormous circular room and spun on the spot, my skirt twirling around my ankles. Thin vertical windows across the ceiling were tinted a pale pink, giving the five floors of bookshelves a reddish hue. Each was U-shaped; bookshelves covered every inch of the walls and the wooden railings. An elaborate metal staircase sat dead in the center, curling upward and branching out to each of the floors. A few sofas and tables dotted the area, along with enormous vases painted with rose designs tucked into every nook. Rugs with more roses lead to the steps.

Bunching my skirt in my hands, I raced upstairs and swung left on the first floor, staring at books with leather cases in black, brown, and blues. The spines were varied, but with titles like *Encyclopedia of Fauna*, *The Intricacies of Herding Cattle*, and *Lifecycle of Salmon*, I assumed the area must have been categorized by topic. I tingled all over, unable to stop smiling as I ran from one section to another. From the third floor, I leaned over the railing and spotted Ash lounging on a couch, watching me.

"Holy shit! This is incredible."

He pointed to his ear and shook his head.

I rushed past the collections of books on sea vessels, astrology guides, and history texts on Haven to run down the winding stairs to Ash's side. "I could live here. Seriously." I waved my hands toward the room behind me. "I'd sleep on the couch and you could just slide me some food under the door. I'm in heaven." Laughing like a crazy person, I couldn't stop and bounced on my toes. "Where did all these books come from? Back in Terra the local store consists of my friend attending the market and bringing books from other realms. Maybe twenty tops each time. Nothing like this…" I twisted toward the library and my throat tightened. "If Dad saw this place, he might die from excitement. He's an inventor, you know." Mom would always surprise him with new books from different realms. She never told him where she bought them from, but once I caught her selling one of her family rings for two texts for Dad's birthday.

"Books on inventions through history are on level five. Right next to cookbooks. Many of the castle staff used to spend hours in here. It's open to everyone."

I whirled around, at a loss for words for once, and my throat thickened. Back in Terra, the priestess had once held a book burning because not enough people had been working the fields and she'd blamed the texts that people spent hours studying on various topics. But Mom had always made sure I read every night, saying it would broaden my horizons. A tear trickled down my cheek.

Ash stretched out his hand and took mine. He pulled me toward him and I nestled next to him. "Sure hope they're tears of joy." He ran a thumb across my cheek.

"Hell, yeah. But, books remind me of my mom." And the tears flooded once again, gushing out. I didn't mean to cry like a baby, or for my breaths to hiccup. But I missed Mom and I hated the danger I'd put the princes in, how I might never see my dad again — there was all this fear trapped inside me.

I leaned against his chest, loving how warm and strong he felt .

"You're so beautiful and have the biggest heart." He kissed the top of my head.

I lifted my chin to face him, and he wiped away my tears. "Thanks."

"Well, on the bright side," he said, not releasing his hold of me, "I haven't felt any urges to transform, so hopefully that means my brothers are the same."

I stared into his deep eyes, the warmth behind them, the cheeky way the corners of his mouth twitched. "What does it feel like? You know… to change?"

He shrugged. "It always starts in the solar plexus, a sharp

pain as if someone poured acid down my throat. And it spreads through my body lightning fast."

"Ouch. Sounds painful." I pulled back.

"You get used to it." He slid a lock behind my ear, then stood, taking my hand and drawing me to my feet. "Let's get this done then."

What I appreciated about Ash was that I could tell if I kissed him now, we'd end up sprawled over the sofa, humping like rabbits. But he resisted. And don't get me wrong. Hell, who didn't want that with a hunk god? But first, I had to find a way to fix my mistake and save the princes.

If, by some miracle, it went in our favor, I'd gladly be open to more with Ash. I glanced over at him as took me by the hand and led me to a section of the library behind the staircase. He walked with poise and confidence, chest out, chin high. Just as a royal should.

And that image right there deflated me. Kidding myself into believing there was an 'afterward' for us was ludicrous. We were from different worlds, and I was a mere human with no royalty in my blood that I knew of. So I wouldn't be good enough. Not now, not ever.

CHAPTER 15

*W*e had two days to find a cure for the curse. *Please, Goddess, let the earlier transformations be a one-off freak event, and help me keep Lilita suppressed.* Yeah, easy. That was why the book in my hands shook. I sat cross-legged on the library floor with a stack of texts on either side of me. Ones I'd checked and the rest to review for potential spell-breaking herbs.

Ash climbed the stairs, searching for specific publications he swore he'd seen on the topic of magic.

But it was progress. Neither of us had changed yet, and he'd gone out to check on his brothers, who were still functional, normal bear shifters in human form. They'd even fixed the cage upstairs. *Hooray!*

I grabbed a slice of bread with cheese from the plate Ash had brought back for lunch.

I'd spent years keeping Lilita tucked away, meditating and using protection spells. Layer upon layer, over time, those guards had kept her shackled in place. And now I did my best to ignore the tension filing my gut. What would trigger Lilita to return? Was my kiss with Ash really the reason for her leaving? But why and how?

"Bee, I found something," he yelled from somewhere upstairs, the excitement clear in his voice.

Letting out a long breath to ease some of my pent-up tension, I climbed to my feet and brushed the crumbs off my skirt.

A loud thud sounded, and I snapped around to Ash, who'd leaped down and was already rushing toward me, carrying an oversized manual under his arm.

"What is it?" A prickly uneasiness rolled over me. The eeriness ate at my insides like parasites, and when a menacing chuckle ricocheted in my mind, I felt the cold drain from my face. The change was coming.

"Lilita!" I scrambled backward until I hit the shelves. Iciness swept through me so fast my head swam.

Ash dropped the book in his grip to the ground. "Are you all right?"

"Run. Get out of here." I turned away and already my flesh crawled, and my middle constricted. My vision blurred at the edges.

Ash was there, standing over me in an instant. He wrenched me toward him, his mouth on mine.

A blast of terror rocked my body as Lilita pushed through me.

Ash. His mouth. Soft. Warm. Delicious. His fingers dug into my flesh, drawing me closer.

Focus! I yelled to myself. With every inch of strength, I concentrated on our point of contact. His tongue on mine, his heat leaping over, melting the earlier coldness.

The air crackled with energy. But nothing mattered except Ash and me.

He growled, his kiss forceful, and lifted me into his arms.

When we broke apart, I stared into the eyes of the beast. He shimmied as his body readied for its own change.

Torn between my transformation and his, for those few moments, we remained frozen in time. Urgency drummed in my veins, yet I couldn't budge. Wouldn't. Not when his touch eased the piercing ache of someone slicing me from the inside out.

The pain grew, and I cried out as if the air strangled me.

Ash kissed me again, fast and starved.

The agony softened.

Lilita's screams gathered in my head, driving me toward Ash. I fisted his hair, needing more.

"The book," he half-growled, and his body shuddered as he pointed behind to where it lay on the floor. "Curse is connecting us." A roar rolled off his throat, and he lurched backward, releasing me. But I reached out and snatched his wrist. My gaze shifted to the textbook. His words twirled in my brain along with our earlier kiss and how I had no longer sensed Lilita. I didn't understand it, and the growing sludge in my brain slowed my thoughts.

Lilita was here.

I drew on my last inch of strength and dragged Ash closer.

He staggered, but I pressed my lips to his, powerful and desperate. And at that precise contact, a thread of peacefulness trickled through me.

Undecipherable words filled me; Lilita's, no doubt. I ripped open Ash's shirt, craving his touch on me. He walked us to the table and set me on the edge, his hands already pulling at the cords lacing the front of my dress. Our mouths never unlocked, and I adored how his tongue swept into my mouth, how he chewed on my lower lip, how unrelenting his attention became.

He slid the fabric of my dress off my shoulders, and the

cool air raised goosebumps over my skin. We broke away, yet he still held his form as a human. His hands trembled. But within me, Lilita's rage burst forward.

I winced as the pain started once again. "Are we meant to kiss for eternity?"

Ash grimaced, holding his midsection, clearly in pain. "The book said to consummate the connection." Doubling over, he slumped to his knees.

I jumped to his side and pushed myself into his embrace, adoring the way he felt against me, how his hands always held me as if we'd been doing this for months. "Then let's do this." Before he could respond, we merged. His solid muscles were tense against me. Lilita's presence faded once again, and if Ash was right, I'd gladly take one for the team and give myself to him if it meant controlling our dark sides.

He drove the dress down my body, and I stood, climbing out of it, and his breath washed across my stomach. I looked down at myself. Naked. Of course. Lilita didn't believe in wearing undergarments.

But the moment Ash's hands fell to my waist, a fire consumed me.

Ash drew his top up and over his head, then tossed it aside. With his hands on my hips, he guided me to my knees to join him, and his mouth found mine. His skin was an inferno. I straddled his bent leg and drowned under his passion.

In Ash's world, I floated on clouds.

His hands found my breasts and he kneaded them, pinching my nipples. I moaned, desperate for more. If this was him with just a few touches, had I been wearing under-wear, they would have melted off by now.

"You're incredible." His stubble tickled me as he raised a breast to his mouth. He flicked me, and I grasped his shoulders, arching. In slow motion, he nibbled on my skin and made his way over to the next one. His eyes closed, and I rubbed myself against his leg for extra tingling. His hands grabbed my ass, prying the cheeks apart. He dipped lower, his fingers brushing the fire scorching between my legs.

"Oh, yes, Ash. Please, right there."

He lifted himself. I shivered against him.

He fingered me so hard, I swore I'd self-combust. Reaching down between us, I unbuttoned his pants and pushed them down his thighs. I curled my hand over his steel-hard rod, so thick, I could barely get my hand around him. I bent forward to reach his hardness and slid him into my mouth. Hot, musky, and salty.

He rewarded me with two fingers in my pussy, and I embraced the exhilaration that came with him forcing me open, pumping faster. "You're so tight."

Back and forth, I sucked him, and he aroused me in a way I hadn't known was possible. We hadn't even had sex yet.

With that, I lost all manner of control. My body thundered with the sweetest orgasm, my knees buckling underneath me. He pulled out of my mouth, and I screamed, unable to hold on to the building pressure any longer.

Ash's large hands grabbed my ass and forced me to face away from him. My butt perched high, and I shivered with desire.

"Fuck me!" Out of breath, I glanced over my shoulder as he rubbed the tip of his cock with a thumb.

"Let me know if I hurt you, little one."

"You better make it hurt."

He laughed, the sound liberating and so sexy. Goddess, why couldn't I score a boyfriend like Ash to keep forever?

The moment he pushed into me, I arched. Large and strong, he stretched me, and I fisted the edge of the rug beneath me. His grip tightened on my hips and squeezed in deeper.

I writhed, lifting my pelvis for easier access.

And with a slap to my ass with his large palm, he pulled out and thrust back inside. I screamed with desire. Needing. Hunger. Drowning in elation.

Our groans echoed throughout the library. There was no better place to have sex with a delicious hunk than in the most magnificent library I'd ever seen. We fell in rhythm, our bodies coming together, connecting. Sweat dripped down my spine as he rode me, and our scent of sex filled my nostrils.

Sweet mother. My throat dried, and everything about our union felt perfect. My world faded into an oblivion, along with my problems. If this was the euphoria from him taking me, hell, sign me up for a daily serving.

He reached across to my stomach and dipped his hand to my clit, then rubbed my sensitive nub. And as if he'd switched something on inside me, a surge shot through me, convulsing, shaking me as another orgasm owned me.

"That's it. Squeeze me!" Ash released a feral grunt, slamming into me one last time and pulsing with his own satisfaction.

And just as we quieted, a sense of normality flooded me without an indication of Lilita remaining. I turned to Ash, who smirked, breathing hard. No sign of his bear side. He was reaching out for me when a roar bellowed from deeper in the house.

Ash withdrew and leaped to his feet. "My brothers have changed."

And with those simple words, I was hurled back into the arena of madness that had become my life since arriving in White Peak.

CHAPTER 16

*A*sh shoved the couch across the room, the legs scraping on the marble floor. He pushed it tight against the only set of doors leading into the library, locking us inside. All I could do was stand there, hugging myself as another roar burst from somewhere in the castle. The other shifters had turned and probably ran amuck. How long before they tracked us down and made a feast of us? I broke out in a cold sweat.

Despite having just had the most amazing sex in the world, a terror-ridden straitjacket tightened around me. I fumbled with my discarded gown, dragging it over my head and down my body. My hands shook as I tried to tie the laced cord across my bust.

Ash was at my side in seconds, his face pale and eyes enlarged. "We need to move upstairs." He calmly took the cords from me and tied up the front of my dress.

"We should have locked everyone up instead of fooling around." Regret burned a hole through my chest as I chewed my cheek.

"Then what?" Ash met my gaze and climbed into his

pants. "Lilita would have emerged and controlled us, making us do unspeakable things. What happened between us was a miracle." He lifted my knuckles to his mouth to kiss them, then drew me toward the steps. "And not just because you were the sweetest little thing I could ever have, but now we know how to control the transformations."

Of course he had a point, but that didn't ease the trepidation gnawing on my confidence. Hand in hand, we raced upstairs, and my brain yanked me in a dozen different directions as I tried to make sense of what to do next. I needed two seconds of peace to sort through my mind. Instead, I climbed the circular stairs, my thighs aching, and the apex between my legs still wet. Goddess, what I wouldn't have done for a quick toilet break right then. I supposed not having to worry about that only happened in stories, while in reality, things were so much messier.

On the fifth level, I struggled for air, and Ash dragged me into a secret compartment between two bookshelves and bolted us inside the pitch-dark space.

"Where are we?" A funky stink assaulted my senses, and I covered my nose.

Ash shuffled about and pulled open window slats. Brilliant light flooded the small room. There was a double bed on one side and an empty bookshelf on the other, with a narrow passage down the middle leading to the window. Snow cascaded outside, and in the distance an ocean of trees and mountains spread as far as I could see. It was all so gorgeous, and yet we remained trapped amidst its beauty. Before long, the sun would sink below the horizon, bringing with it the cold temperatures.

"This was Vivienne's hideout," Ash said. His voice lowered, and I caught the hitch in his breath. "She used to stay here with her favorite books and read for most of the day about knights saving a heroine from dragons or going on pirate adventures." He laughed, but he sounded almost sorrowful.

"She must have had a wonderful imagination."

"*Wild* would be the better word." He smiled.

"So she loved romances!" I slapped Ash on the hand. "That's what I write."

"Come on. Raze told us what you wrote, and that's full-on erotica." He rolled his eyes.

"Whatever. There's a plot that's more than just falling in love and sex." I plonked down on the bed, which was covered in throw rugs and cushions. The area had been gutted of any personal artifacts — no photos or knickknacks. "What now? We wait to get mauled to death?"

"The library door is locked, as is this one. Our scents are all over the downstairs floor, so if they do break inside, that will distract them long enough so they won't discover us until morning arrives. And we're in a small space, meaning I could take on one at a time if they find us." He winked my way. "Then once I hold them, you do your thing. I don't intend to hurt my brothers."

I pulled my knees up to my chest. "What's my thing? Put a spell on them?"

"Kiss them so they snap out of their transformation."

"Are you crazy? You want me to kiss a bear shifter in kill-mode?" I stared at the door, my hair standing on end. We were easy targets.

He paced to the window, only wearing his pants — I wondered if he was cold since there was no fireplace in this room. I studied the way his muscles shifted beneath his skin, remembering how amazing he'd made me feel. How much I wanted to crawl into his arms and hide from the world.

"What did you read in that book you found before?" I asked to distract my thoughts and ignore the fear weighing on my ribs.

Ash stood there with his hands by his sides, towering over me like a protector. How I'd love to be home, safe and secure. What was Dad doing right now? Hopefully keeping warm and not forgetting to water the garden.

"It was a book about potions, and there was a section that talked about how when some spells affect multiple people, it's because the spell bound them together. Think about it — Lilita's dark magic suppressed the curse temporarily. And you did the same with me, but in your own way."

That made sense, and while I didn't understand the full dynamics of how this worked, what if the solution to break the hex was somewhere inside me? "That explains why the enchantment affects us at the same time. But did you notice that the change came during the day, not at night?" I breathed in the cold air, hugging my knees. "The curse has morphed into something else. The rules have changed." I felt every beat of my heart pounding, drowning the noise in my head.

He nodded. "With us having sex, maybe our energies have merged and are counteracting the curse, so that might be the reason for the changes in the hex and also why we stopped our transformations."

"Probably. I've always had a stronger handle on my magic after I wrote my erotic scenes — and sometimes it would be even easier to control after I'd pleasured myself." I glanced outside and wished I had wings to fly away.

"Oh, really? Please elaborate in precise details," Ash teased, and I loved that he held on to his sense of humor, even in the face of so much danger.

I grabbed a pillow and threw it at him before sitting back down, as there wasn't much space to move about in with Ash standing there. He ducked, and the cushion hit the bookshelf behind him.

"Just so I get this right," he continued. "The release of your sexual pleasure helps you control Lilita too, right?"

"I guess so." I'd only discovered the surge in energy when I'd started writing about a year ago.

Ash was fiddling with the buttons on his pants.

"What are you doing?" I pushed myself against the wall, lifting another pillow and embracing it against my chest, my breath locked in my chest.

He glanced up at me, mischief in his eyes. "Well, if I bring you to orgasm a few more times, you might cleanse the entire house of evil."

I had no words; I wasn't some performing monkey. "Are you shitting me?"

He chuckled and came over, ruffling my hair. "Had you going there."

"Hell, right now I wouldn't be surprised by anything." So much had happened these past few days. My guard and money problems back in Terra were nothing in comparison to what I'd encountered in White Peak.

Ash joined me on the bed, and we sat there, our backs against the wall, our legs touching. In another time and place, this would have been the perfect moment. Yet no matter what we talked about, at the back of my mind, I kept remembering that crazed shifters were out there on the loose.

So our options had come down to one: sit and wait for their transformations to fade.

"I hope your brothers don't run outside and kill innocents."

"Doubt it. Every time Talin got caught outside during a transformation, he bolted back home as if he were possessed. I'm praying they were smart enough to have shut themselves in the cage once they felt the changes coming on." He fell quiet for a while, staring out of the window into the wilderness. "When I changed from the curse, I had this overwhelming urge to remain inside. I can't explain it, but it didn't even cross my mind to go outdoors."

"Might be part of the curse," I suggested, well aware that complicated incantations came with rules and restrictions on the person being hexed. "Maybe Rek didn't want to involve citizens?"

Ash sighed and stared at the barren bookshelf. "I feel terrible that we dragged you into our problems, Bee. Honestly, we believed you'd come in, do a spell, and be done."

"I thought the same. But my dad says things always happen for a reason. And I want to believe good will come out of all of this."

Silence fell between us. With no sounds coming from outside, either, I prayed the brothers were in their cage, not charging toward us. That tightening sensation in my chest never left me.

"Where do you see yourself in ten years? Married with three or four kids?" Ash asked, nudging me to stop me from biting my nails.

"Three or four kids? That's crazy talk. Before I settle down, I plan to visit every realm in Haven. I've seen three so far. Darkwoods, Terra, and now White Peak. I want to try out all the different cuisines, visit Tritonia and ride a pirate ship — but keep clear of the voodoo witches. They're nasty pieces of work. Anyway, I also want to meet a mermaid there for real."

He scoffed. "You know mermaids are myths, right?"

"What?" I twisted in his direction and shook my head. "You need to get out more. My friend Ariella saw them first-hand, and she doesn't lie."

Ash stroked his thick stubble. "Now you've got me curious. And they wear nothing on top?" He smirked.

I nudged him back. "Is that all men dream about? Breasts?"

"Yours are divine. Soft, and they filled my hands perfect-ly." He held his palms out, his fingers twitching as if he were grasping my breasts at this very moment. The corner of his mouth curled upward. I couldn't help but like his compliment. Then again, admittedly I'd never heard a man say he wished I had smaller boobs.

"You're aware of the effect you have on men, right? You're super sexy and confident — or is that an act?"

I suppressed the chuckle pressing against my throat and studied his flirtatious grin. "This is the real me, just trying to survive in a wild world. But in the company of you and your brothers, I feel caught off guard half the time. Can't really explain it. Probably because I'm not sure if I should curtsey or kiss your hands. You don't behave like royals."

Ash looped an arm around my shoulders and tugged me against his side, his skin warm and soft against me. "The four of us agreed to no royal bullshit in our home. We act normal and treat others the same. None of this bending the knee to us crap. No fancy talk."

I leaned into his side. "That's nice."

Neither of us spoke, and I drowned in my own thoughts. Another couple of days and it would be a full moon. The curse would then claim all four princes. A deep ache settled in my chest, and my eyes prickled. I worried for their plight, their futures, their family line.

I hoped the brothers would be back to normal by morning, because then we had to put a plan into action. Yet my thoughts revolved around the strength of the curse and how it had backfired. I wasn't a fool to ignore that death magic was used. But from what I understood, such hexes required the use of a personal object or artifact. Maybe a figurine, or hair clip. The curse's power was kept in that object. Destroy it and it should destroy the hex.

The herb books didn't offer a solution, and maybe the

answer lay in me heading to his cousin's court with the princes and trying to find this object. If I met Rek, I might be able to cast a persuasion spell where he'd have to tell us where the object was. That was, if his cousin didn't kill me first... for being a human. Would he be able to detect that I was a witch?

CHAPTER 17

I woke with a jolt. Orange light from the early morning sun drenched me as I lay on the bed in the tiny room in the library.

Ash was gone.

I scrambled to my feet, my head filled with images of his brothers having taken him. But that made no sense — otherwise, I wouldn't have been sleeping.

A quick glance outside showed no one was down in the front yard of the castle, so I made my way out of the room.

At first, I stood in the doorway, listening. Not a sound.

"Ash?"

No response. I crept toward the railing and looked down into the library, noticing the couch had been moved from the door, which lay open. My stomach hardened. If he'd left the door open, it had to mean we were safe, right? Or had he gone to check on his brothers and one of them had attacked him? One way or another, I had to find out what had happened. I scrambled down the stairs, scanning each floor as I descended. On the bottom floor, I spotted the book Ash had abandoned yesterday and picked it up, curious to read more about the connection he'd mentioned. With it tucked under my arm, I left the library.

It was silent in the rest of the house.

And that left me shaky. If the men were their beastly selves, surely they'd be grunting or roaring. And while part of me screamed to go back and lock myself in the library, I couldn't just sit there forever. Moving deeper into the castle, I passed doors, and with my bladder ready to burst, I checked a few rooms to find smaller bedrooms, a storage closet, and … a toilet. "Thank you, goddess."

By the time I reached the kitchen, the aroma of porridge had found me. And that delicious smell had me smiling, not because my stomach rumbled, but because the boys were back to normal. I rushed inside to find Talin bending over the fire, stirring a wooden spoon in a black pot. On the table were spoons and a stack of empty bowls.

"Morning." He turned my way, and a new scratch lined the side of his face, two more down his neck and vanishing beneath his black shirt.

"What happened?"

"Just a few fights against Leven and Raze, who ganged up on me in the cage last night. We probably shouldn't lock ourselves up together again." He smiled and winced. "But we'll heal."

Would his injuries get infected? Though I was glad they weren't hurt worse, hearing he'd spent his night fighting off the others had me cringing on the inside. "Have you put anything on the scratches?"

"No need." He carried the pot over to the wooden table and started filling the bowls. "Ash told us what happened last night between you two. Fantastic news."

I couldn't help but detect a dull tone under his words. Was he disappointed? I shouldn't have been embarrassed, but my cheeks flushed.

With the huge book still in my hands, I set it on the table. "He told you *everything?*"

Talin took a seat across the table from me and pushed a bowl of porridge my way. "Ash told us that when we change, so do you. Meaning we need to be with each other at all times. This way, one of us can ensure you don't turn." He wiped an injury on his chin, a smudge of blood streaking his jawline.

"Give me two moments; I'll be right back. I've got something for your scratches." I didn't wait for a response and sprinted upstairs to my bedroom to my bag, grabbed my healing paste from my bag and a towel, and dashed back downstairs.

Talin was eating his breakfast, and I sat next to him. "Where are the others?"

"Gone out to collect firewood."

I unrolled the long green leaf I'd used to stash the paste. "Hold still." After wiping the blood from Talin's injury with a towel, I smeared the green goo across his scratches.

He scrunched up his nose. "What is that? It stinks like mushed bugs."

"No insects were harmed in the making of my remedy." I kept my face serious, though the corners of my mouth twitched as I started breaking into a smile. "Just herbs and saliva."

"Gross. Hope it was *your* saliva." He made a face, then stuffed another mouthful of porridge into his mouth.

I laughed. "A witch's saliva has healing properties and helps bind the herbs. Anyway" — I dabbed more of the mixture on the cut down his neck — "last night I had a thought about us heading to your cousin's place." I explained how hexes required an object to store the cursed magic, and if we destroyed that, the curse was gone. "Only one problem. Okay, there are probably lots of problems, but I'm sure they won't appreciate a non-bear shifter waltzing into their home."

"That makes a lot of sense." Talin glanced at me, his thick brows crowning his spectacular green eyes. The faint stubble gracing his jawline coupled with his messy hair — he had this wild look going for him. He was handsome in my books. Nothing ordinary about him in the slightest. I remembered Ash saying Talin needed a wife to claim the throne and become king. I bet he'd have no trouble finding a willing woman, and for the first time, I wished I'd been born a bear shifter. Whomever he married would be damn lucky, and a tingling spark of jealousy wormed its way through my chest.

"I'll declare you my personal medic," he said. "I'll explain I'd fallen ill, but you healed me, and I appointed you as my personal caretaker. And we are simply paying my cousin a visit."

Being a caretaker made sense, yet goosebumps covered my skin at the idea of something going wrong. "I'll prepare a persuasion spell to get your cousin to talk and tell us where he's hidden the curse's focus."

Talin's lips widened, as did his eyes, and hope beamed across his expression. "This might work."

"But you sure they'll be fine with me there?" Wiping my hand clean on the towel, I collected my bowl and spoon and started eating.

"It's not as if we have any other options. We stay close, and the moment I feel the change coming on, well, I would be honored to receive your kiss."

The air grew thick, and I felt tipsy on Talin's presence. I could watch him all day, listen to his raspy words, imagine his arms around me, never letting go. His bright eyes wandered across my face, and I flushed hot from a simple smile.

"Okay. Well, then we go visit your cousin today. But what about the rebels outside?"

Talin's brow furrowed. "The last few times we tried to visit Rek, we snuck out at early dawn, and there weren't many out that time of the day." He combed his fingers through his hair. "So I agree, we leave as soon as possible."

The book on the table stole my attention, and I pulled it closer. Flicking through the pages, it had no spells but was more of a text on what properties different herbs offered. But it was what I'd searched for yesterday.

Talin was on his feet, and a few moment later brought me a cup of tea. Its peppermint infusion calmed me. "Fill up on food. We should leave once the others return."

And just like that, the reality of me meeting another bear family, a royal one that had tried to kill Talin, churned in my gut. What if they attempted to murder him again? And me?

"Before we leave, I'll create a protection spell over both of us. Something to ease the impact of any magical attacks,"

Talin reached over and placed his hand on mine. His skin burned where we touched, and the idea of him so upset bugged the hell out of me. Why had no other family members or friends come to their aid in such a time?

"You've been a goddess-send, and I don't think just saying 'thank you' is enough for placing you in harm's way.

"I promised to help, and that's what I'll do." Lost for words, something inside me shifted toward Talin. How could I live with myself if I ran from here and chose the easy route? Back home, my life would struggle, but it would be no comparison to what these princes would endure.

This simple job had morphed into a storm. Yet the princes had touched me on a level I'd never expected. Leaving wasn't an option, not now that I'd gotten to know them, each of them striving for life after already losing so much.

Besides, how would that impact our connection? Would our distance set off the transformations? And what if I returned home and Lilita took me over? Then what? She'd probably attempt to take over the priestess and get Dad killed.

In truth, I relied on the princes as much as they did me, and in a strange way, I embraced not facing this alone. Having them by my side lifted my confidence to not give up because it was too hard.

Talin smiled, and he pulled me into a strong hug, his sweet musky scent filling my senses. His sudden show of emotion surprised me, but then again the prince had been fighting his own demons. For once, I saw the real man; scared, yet willing to put others first. That I appreciated more than anything.

"We do this together." I pulled back, and we locked gazes for those few moments. I let myself fall deep into his eyes, believing the world could be wonderful for all of us once again.

Anxiety danced down my spine. I had no idea what to expect. Another part of me didn't want to leave the castle, as I'd gotten used to the place.

Talin's words were muffled by the three other shifters entering the kitchen, each one carrying armfuls of logs and chatting.

"Morning, Bee," Leven said as he set the wood on the dwindling pile near the fireplace.

"Hey, Bee. Sleep well?" Raze waggled his eyebrows, smirking, without a hint of jealousy. That earlier heat crawled up my neck. What details exactly had Ash given them? Men loved to talk about sex, but did they indulge in the finer details as well?

Ash slid in beside me and kissed my cheek, his hand on my back. "Hi, beautiful."

Okay, so did this mean we were officially together? Because in all honesty, I was beaming on the inside. Just having him next to me had my insides buzzing.

"You didn't wake me." I sidled up against Ash.

"Couldn't. You were so peaceful. Plus, I had to check on my brothers."

I reached over and patted down a wild strand of hair above his ear. He took my hand and kissed my fingers.

"Goddess, you two," Leven said, rolling his eyes as he grabbed himself a bowl of porridge.

Talin cleared his throat, and we all turned toward him. "Bee and I discussed going to Rek's manor today." Talin went on to detail what I'd told him earlier about the cursed object and how this could solve our problem with the curse.

"I'm coming," Ash piped up, and he smiled my way. "I want to keep you safe," he added.

"Me too," the other two said in unison.

"So how would this work?" Talin asked. "Let's do worst case scenario. We all start transforming. Bee could be with one or two of us, as she needs to control Lilita too, remember. That worries me more than anything."

My mouth dried. Lilita was a huge thorn in our sides, and not something I'd ever imagined in a million years would have added to our dilemma. But Talin had a point. How in the world was I meant to tame four shifters if we all battled inner demons? With Ash, the moment I'd kissed him, the urges had tampered slightly, so would that be enough to help us remain in control? I wasn't sure how I felt about potentially taking turns to sex up each man. Individually and in the right moment, hell yeah. I ought to feel weird with them being brothers, but I didn't. To me, they were individuals and that was how I saw them.

"It's not going to work," I said. "I can't control all of us." Even though I recalled how easily Lilita had zapped all of them at once, and they'd transformed into their human forms. Then again, jolting them with energy was a different set of rules compared to getting hot and heavy with them.

"Then just you and me go with Bee," Raze said, staring at Talin.

"Why you?" Ash asked, his hand tightening around my waist.

Raze flexed his biceps and grinned. "Who's the best fighter among us?"

Leven shook his head and kept eating. "Talin has a point. And it might be good to have Raze go in there, as Rek is terrified of him. But I suggest Ash and I join you for most of the trip. It's a good half day journey by carriage, and we can ensure you face no problems along the way. Then, Ash and I will hang back in the woods in case you need us."

"And if we transform?" Ash asked.

"The curse instinct will have you rushing back home," Talin said. "That's how it was for me each time we tried to approach the court in the past." He stared around the table at us; we were all silent. "So we have an agreement then?"

A shiver curled down my spine as the goddess sent her warning. It seemed everything I did warranted that response from her. But I didn't see another option.

Ash rubbed my lower back, reminding me that I adored how at ease he made me feel.

I sat there, overwhelmed by all the emotions, the plans, and yet so much still depended on chance. "All right. Let's pray we don't shift beforehand and most importantly, that we get in and out of the manor before night falls."

Everything hinged on this working, their kingdom and all our lives. It felt as if we had nooses dangling over our heads.

CHAPTER 18

Four of us sat in the horse-drawn carriage while Raze rode out front, insisting he'd warn us at the first sign of trouble. Talin lounged on the seat across from me. We'd been traveling for most of the morning and my butt was way past going to sleep. I shifted in my cushioned seat.

Ash, Leven, and I sat on one bench, and Talin was across from us. All of us jostled from the bumpy path, and outside, the snow-coated forest glimmered beneath the sun.

"Have I mentioned how stunning you look?" Leven glanced my way, and my cheeks burned.

Who didn't love compliments? Though I suspected it had a lot to do with my dress. I might not have been royal, but even so, I should get away with pretending in the chiffon gown Ash had insisted I wear. It was golden because he'd insisted it brought out my eyes. Anyone who joined royalty had to dress the part, apparently. With my hair pulled off my face by a tiara, my cheeks and lips tainted red with rose powder, I'd never felt more princess-like.

Talin snarled. "Only ten times already."

"Hey, the lady *is* gorgeous. Nothing wrong with telling it like it is. Half the men in Rek's court will attempt to claim her."

I snorted a laugh and froze in horror. Princesses didn't laugh that way. "Yeah, until they realize I'm not a bear shifter." Then they'd probably turn on the princes for breaking some insane rule they followed.

"They won't care," Ash said, cutting me a side look before blowing me a kiss. Heavens, the way he stared at me with his sexy eyes made me forget myself.

I smiled and took his hand in mine, adoring how warm he always felt.

"Well, you three don't look too bad yourselves." Leven and Ash wore several layers of jackets with black pants and woolen tops to block the cold, as they wouldn't be attending court with the rest of us.

Talin and Raze each wore a long cloak with golden trim embroidered around the collar that was split at the middle to reveal black trousers and a doublet. Leven straightened his collar. He'd trimmed his beard, making him look younger. Still cute in my eyes. With his dark hair slicked and pulled off his face, my attention fell to the coat of arms sewn onto his lapel.

Seeing them in their finest made this somehow real, and for once, they felt like princes. I fingered the ruby necklace with a shimmering rose pendant sitting above my cleavage. This pendant alone might have bought a new house and paid off our debts.

"Why is there a red rose on your coat of arms?"

"Dad once told me," Leven began, "that our mother's grandma grafted the first plant with magic."

Ash had told me about their family's rose. But something was missing. And I'd never seen this flower that was on their coat of arms. "How did your great-grandma get the snow rose to begin with?"

"The sorcerer had added her blood to the soil to feed the first snow rose, which is why it can resist the coldest winter nights. While the flower grew on our family's property, everyone in the household would always be blessed with luck, so every generation since continued growing the thorny flower and it was added to our coat of arms."

"So magic you say," I asked.

He nodded. "A rose she'd received from a witch in Tritonia."

"Whoa, back up!" My pulse spiked. "Tritonia? You mean from a voodoo witch? Every tale I've heard from that place involving magic always comes with death." So how would a beautiful rose bring a family luck if it had emerged from darkness?

Talin shrugged. "Even in the darkest of places, there are people who won't blindly follow the majority."

"Maybe you're right." The magic might explain why the roses had died once their parents and sister had passed? They must have been linked to the family lineage... and right then I couldn't ignore the notion that maybe the roses hadn't revived since because they'd known what fate awaited the princes. I shivered, hating that I'd had that thought.

I glanced out the window as a family of deer froze in the distance, staring our way, alert and watchful over their little ones.

Saving the princes pressed on my chest, yet as I sat in the carriage with them, I couldn't deny we'd formed a bond. It felt as if we'd known each other for so long, but now a desperation clung to my ribs, reminding me that I might lose them.

"So how do you think today will go?" I fidgeted with the ribbon tied around my waist, pretending to sit at peace, but my pulse raced. Should I bow or curtsey? Did I wait to be addressed before speaking or never meet the cousin's eyes until called upon? "What do I need to know about being in a court?" Dread clenched my gut.

Leven sat across from me, his legs spread on either side of mine, and he leaned forward. "It's easy." He took my hand in his. "They'll know you're human and won't expect you to know our customs. Be polite, answer when they ask you a question, and stay close to Raze and Talin. They'll keep you safe."

His thumb caressed the back of my hand, pushing away my primal urge to run in the opposite direction.

Talin's gaze fell to his feet. "As soon as this is sorted, I'll put this mess to an end and do what I've been putting off for too long."

"I wish you could convince our priestess in Terra to change. She's maniacal and inflicts punishment without a trial." Like the family who'd been accused of bartering for magic spells with someone from Darkwoods. A week later, the whole family had vanished, and I bet the priestess had played a hand in their banishing.

Leven reclined, my hand falling into my lap. "I doubt she'd listen. Most in power are stubborn as mules."

I burst out laughing. "Shit yeah. I mean…" I straightened my back, lifting my chin and putting on my best serious voice, "why yes, I agree most heartedly, fine gentleman." I supposed I'd better practice to see if I could blend in, no matter what Leven had said. I had a feeling they were biased after everything we'd been through so far. Plus, they weren't like anyone in power I'd met before.

Leven chuckled. "Is that your royal impersonation?"

I slouched. "It sucks, right?"

"I prefer you as you are," Ash said.

"You're such a sweet-talker. All of you are." My voice

caught in my throat, and I admired the way they smiled at me, as if everything in the world was perfect. And part of me wished so desperately that it would turn out that way for all of us. "If I had to choose between the four of you, I'm not sure I ever could pick just one."

"Who said you had to select just one?" Leven shuffled to the edge of his seat, his hands on my knees, and a trickle of warmth raced up my thighs. It suddenly got hot in the carriage.

"What do you mean? Do bear shifters have more than one mate?"

"Doesn't everyone?" Leven asked, his expression deadly serious.

My mouth must have fallen open. "Are you teasing me?" Because I wouldn't have put it past any of the men to make me believe something and then make a joke of it. "Ha, you're so funny, thinking I'm gullible."

"You don't get it, Bee," Ash said, his hand on my lap. "We've met so many people, and you're the first who's genuine. But it's more than that. You're honest, and you're risking your life for us. Who does that for just anyone these days?"

At first, I sat there, swallowed by an inferno. I shouldn't have been attracted to any of the princes, yet I was drawn to each one. But all I was doing was setting myself up to fail. "I have a few friends back home who would do that for me."

Leven patted my leg and sat back. "Hold on to them. If they're anything like you, you're lucky."

Someone tapped the carriage from outside and we came to a halt. I looked outside the window to a forest. "Are we there?"

"This is where Ash and I get off," Leven said.

"Already?" My breaths came in wheezing pants. I wasn't ready to tackle meeting other bear shifters or pretend to be a caretaker. What if I panicked? What if someone detected I did magic?

Leven inclined toward me, his hands on my cheeks, and drew me to him. "I promise to do everything in my power to protect you. Just like my brothers mean the world to me, you have wiggled yourself into my heart." His mouth pressed to mine, and my brain sloshed from his sudden movement, but I held on to his arms, returning the kiss. Soft, passionate, and unyielding.

He stole my breath, and I drew him closer, unable to get close enough. Like with Ash, the unease in my gut unraveled, filling me with warmth and a readiness to take over the world.

Leven pulled back and licked his lips. "I'll see you soon, Bee."

"Be careful." My voice was breathless, yet there was a tightness in my chest at the fact that he was leaving.

He lifted my hand to his mouth. "I'd do anything for you." He hopped out of the carriage.

"Everyone's so sentimental today," Talin said, sitting back, arms folded across his stomach, watching with amusement. Was he jealous or truly put off by how sweet his brothers were to me?

Ash shifted between us and made his way out. He took my hand and kneeled on one leg in front of me. "If anything happens to you, I'll tear the White Peak forest apart to find and make the person who harmed you suffer."

His words had me grinning, and when he kissed me, my body lit on fire. I remembered our time in the library, an experience that would remain with me for eternity. Now, tingles and desire claimed me, and swirls of emotions made me gasp. When he stepped back, I missed him already.

"Won't be long until we see each other again." He left the

carriage and closed the door behind him. I was left with an inferno inside from their kisses.

Each one made me crave them as if we were going on a first date. But these were four brothers. Surely, they didn't want to be with the same girl? Or was Leven kissing me a reassurance to keep his bear side under control? Yes, that had to be the reason. Then why had he stared at me as if he'd been ready to rip off my dress and devour me? And Leven's words about not needing to select just one partner twirled in my head. Except I suspected he'd been teasing me.

I exchanged a glance with Talin who hadn't stopped looking my way with a strange expression I couldn't quite read.

When the carriage took off again, I stared out at Leven and Ash, who were sending us off with smiles. I collapsed back into the seat, Talin moving next to me and wrapping an arm around my shoulders, holding me against his side.

"They truly care for you. We all do."

I chewed on my lower lip, emotions tugging me in a dozen different directions. And letting my emotions about the princes blossom into anything but this simple attraction was insanity. I didn't belong in their world, and I had Dad to look after. My life, my friends. If we survived, they would return to ruling their realm, and Talin would find a bear shifter wife, probably followed by each of the brothers shortly thereafter.

This small stint was a job. And I had to remind myself not to fall head over heels for men who were out of my league. Once I got us untangled from one another, I'd hightail it out of White Peak and never come back. But as I curled in on myself and stared out at the passing landscape, I wasn't sure I was ready to leave them yet — or if I ever would be.

CHAPTER 19

The next time the carriage stopped, we were still in the woods, and my skin prickled. Talin opened the door and climbed out before offering me his hand to help me disembark. In the distance, there was a huge set of oversized iron gates with curls along the top and a stone wall stretching outward. Beyond the entrance lay a winding road leading to a massive manor house.

Raze jumped down from the carriage and stared out in the same direction.

"Why are we stopping?" Talin asked.

"Figured we should brush up on a kiss with Bee just in case the change came. Might help us control ourselves while in the manor," Raze explained. "I already feel the change deep in my chest."

Talin's face paled, and he nodded, balling his fists.

They both exchanged knowing glances, then looked my way. "I can feel it too," I said.

"Okay, I'm first," Raze said and he'd already taken me into his arms. "Where shall we go for some privacy?" He winked.

I laughed, slapping his shoulder. "You're so funny. We're

only kissing. When I was with Ash and we kissed, that drove the dark side away at first, and I'm hoping that will suffice here." *Goddess, please let that work.*

"You sure that's all?" Raze teased. "There are blankets in the carriage to keep you comfortable."

"Raze," Talin growled. "Maybe you ought to get out of the way and let me show you how it's done if you're struggling."

"Ha." Raze stuck his palm out to Talin. "I've got this." He brought me closer, and my hands snapped forward, plastered to this chest.

His breath washed over my face, and my heart raced. Raze had me tripping over myself. He drove me crazy with his flirtatious manner. Tingles swirled in my gut, and when his lips met mine, a snap of energy zipped down my body. His hands pressed into my back, squeezing us together. His mouth devoured mine. Sparks flew through me, and my world faded. I focused on his solid arms folded around me, the electrifying intimacy he made me feel.

My thoughts soared through the heavens, lost beneath Raze's touch, adoring how he sucked on my tongue, how his fingers crawled up my back and cradled my head. My hands stretched up and tangled around his thick neck, and his passion deepened, as did his hands against my ass, forcing me against his hardness. I softened, loving how his body reacted.

His lips glided across my cheek and my ears, nibbling on my neck. "You may have just ruined me for anyone else."

His words had me trembling because no one had ever said anything remotely close to that to me, and I didn't want to move or lose this moment.

When he pulled back, I stumbled, still drifting on a cloud. Bewildered at how sharp my magic felt within me. Raze caught me with an arm.

"I've never felt this clearheaded." He kissed my hand and turned to Talin. "Now try beating that."

His brother rubbed his hands. "Step aside."

I admired how competitive they were, especially when the object of their desire was me. I still struggled with the whole idea of two men kissing me one after the other, but they didn't seem to have an issue with it.

Talin took me behind the carriage and away from Raze. "I believe in giving a lady privacy."

Raze laughed. "Don't take too long."

Talin stepped up behind me, his hands caressing my arms.

I shivered at his softness. "You know, we're just meant to kiss." Trees surrounded us, and I hoped no one hid in the woods, watching us.

He slid my hair back and let his lips fall to my neckline. "If you were anyone else, maybe. But since first meeting you, I haven't been able to get your scent out of my head, and I've been dreaming of tasting you. I can smell your sexual hunger." His hand slid across my chest, dipping down the front of my dress. "Do you want me to stop?"

When I tried to respond, a moan fell free.

He laughed in my ear, and my legs wobbled. "Thought so."

I gulped for air because his forcefulness had me squeezing my thighs together for additional tingles. He had me riled up.

His hand groped my breast, his fingers pinching a nipple so hard, I groaned with pleasure. With his other hand on my jawline, he twisted my head toward him and his mouth clasped mine. That same sizzling power jolted down my body, worming around my core.

"Did you feel that?" he whispered.

"Yes." I reached up and pulled him back down. I wasn't finished yet.

I'd fallen under his spell and enjoyed the rough play. His

dominance had me soaking wet. Our tongues tangled, and I lost myself to Talin.

"You can open your eyes now." His hand released my breast and he turned me by the shoulders to face him. "You're so delicate and gorgeous. I hope to get to taste you for real one day."

I gasped, still catching my breath because if I readied to explode into an orgasm each time the princes kissed me, I didn't think I'd have time for anything else.

"Shall we go?" His fingers intertwined with mine and we strolled to the front of the carriage.

With a hand, he helped me up at the front to sit next to Raze, then he squeezed in beside me.

"Where did all of you learn to kiss?"

Talin smirked and picked up the reins, while Raze placed an arm around my shoulders, holding me close and kissing the side of my head.

None of us exchanged a word as we traveled onward, the road bumpy, and the whole time I concentrated on enveloping us in a white bubble. Fizzing and popping energy crackled across my arms, and I pictured a shield protecting us. I clenched my fists and steadied my energy, keeping us safe. Untouched. Unaffected. *We are safe. We won't change.*

Talin drove the horses through the open gates and down the long cobblestone path, flanked by pines, cloaked in snow.

My nerves stirred as we approached the huge manor house made of red stone. It looked more like an enormous treasure box with dozens of windows and a pointy roof.

One guard stood outside, wearing a long, black coat, hands stiff by his sides. What if he killed me? Was it even legal in their world to bring humans onto royal grounds? But if that were the case, surely the princes wouldn't have brought me here.

Raze climbed down from the carriage and offered me his hand. "My lady."

I half-laughed, half-choked, and whispered, "I don't think I can do this."

"All you need to do is smile and leave the rest with us. Be yourself. Remember, you're Talin's personal caretaker. And I promise, nothing will happen to you." His smile tugged on my heart.

I swallowed past my dried throat. Talin looked my way with a raised brow. So much depended on this, and rather than fall into a puddle of panic, I accepted Raze's hand and stepped down.

A chilly breeze fluttered through my hair, and I joined Raze. We strolled behind Talin, who headed into the house past the solid metal doors.

Gazes followed us, and I glanced over to a guard who sniffed the air, his nose wrinkling my way. Yep. This would be fun. And I couldn't stop shaking, feeling like such a fake. I was terrible at pretending to be someone else. At school, I'd once gotten booed off the stage at eleven years old because I hadn't been able to remember my lines.

Summoning my strength, I lifted my chin and strode into a carpeted room with paintings in golden frames everywhere. In the center of the first room a marble statue of a bear on hind legs towered over us.

Raze nudged me and pointed his chin to the carving, then pointed to himself. He mouthed the words, "I'm bigger than that."

I couldn't help but laugh as we entered a room with velvet-covered seats fanned out in front of a grand fireplace. The fire crackled and spat embers into the metal guard. A carved mantel displayed a scene of bears in battle. Too vicious for my liking. Cream curtains framed the oversized windows. Sunlight pouring in bathed the elaborately carved display cabinets filled with various figurines of bears in various poses. Bronze candelabras stood tall against the walls every few feet, the white candles unlit.

"Welcome. Welcome," came a man's voice from behind us.

We turned in unison.

An older man with graying hair and his middle as round as a barrel rushed toward us. He was buttoning up a black and golden jacket around himself. When he glanced up, I saw he only sported one eye, the other covered by a patch. Healed claw marks, which I assumed were from his initiation as a child, crossed that missing eye.

"Your Majesty, Talin?" His voice rose, and he halted in the doorway, his expression fell, and his mouth hung open. "How are you feeling?" He half-bowed in front of Talin, yet his gaze bounced from Talin to Raze. He approached Talin and embraced him.

"Why would you assume he wasn't well?" Raze asked.

"Rumors had said you were gravely ill."

"And yet as your prince, the Medved house hasn't paid me a visit to confirm firsthand if such rumors were true."

The older man rubbed a hand over his mouth and glanced over his shoulder at the guards in the hallway. He waved a hand at them, and they dispersed. "Prince Talin Ursa, I am but a servant in this house, and despite my protests, we were forbidden to contact you or your brothers."

"We are here now." Talin's voice climbed, his frown deepening. "Where is my cousin Rek?"

"The duke is hunting in the woods. He should return before dusk."

"Dusk?" The word burst from my mouth, and I cringed at once, lowering my gaze. *Stupid*. What was I thinking? Except we couldn't wait until dusk. The transformation would take us before that time.

With a sniff of the air, his gaze swept from Talin to me. "Why have you brought a human into our home?"

"She's with me," Talin said, his voice sharp and authoritative. "My personal caretaker. I have been ill, but not gravely so, as others seem to have insisted."

The old man's laughter left me shifting uncomfortably, his double chins wobbling, but the way his eyes left Talin told me it was all a show. "Please, take a seat. I will arrange for refreshments." He rushed out of the room.

"Who was that man?" I whispered, hating his judging expression. Bear shifters like him probably saw humans as a snack, nothing more.

"Len is one of many advisors to our cousin." Raze took my hand and guided me to a chair, both of us sitting close together, while Talin remained near the snapping fire, staring into the flames. "He used to work with us, but after a falling out with Leven, who caught him stealing from us, he left. But weeks later we discovered he's now working for our cousin."

"Untrustworthy," I said. "You could see it in his eyes and how he could never hold your gaze."

Raze nodded.

Talin faced us. "I was hoping we'd be in and out quick. Maybe we ought to leave before we all change and Lilita makes a show, then massacres everyone in this house."

I wrung my hands in my lap, because staying around could get us all killed. But tomorrow was the full moon and we had to find the object to break the curse. I bounced my knees but Raze placed his hand on them to quiet them.

"And the moment you feel yourself transforming into a half-bear, half-human," — I lowered my voice — "we excuse ourselves damn fast."

Talin raised a brow. "All of us? So we'll sneak into a room for a kiss, then pray that's enough to keep us under control?"

Talin turned away, his posture curving forward as he gripped the grand cherry-wood mantel.

"Do you have any other ideas?" I sure hadn't planned on his cousin being out hunting.

A young girl scurried into the room carrying a silver platter and set it down on the table near Raze and me. A silver teapot, three cups, and a plate filled with sweets. I would never have guessed this was a shifter bear's house. Back in Terra, they were painted as barbaric and vicious. And yet, they had tiny drinking cups decorated with blue florets. I guessed this whole elaborate lifestyle thing was a carryover from when Haven had split into seven realms and the first royals had taken over each town, both kings and queens. Most of those original family lines had passed, but the decorum of royalty still continued.

As the girl left the room, Raze reached for the food. I nudged him and shook my head. "What if they poisoned it?"

His brow furrowed, and he pulled his hand back.

By the time Len returned, Raze was pacing near the window, while Talin hadn't shifted around in front of the fireplace. Me, I remained quiet and chewed on my fingernails, unsure what our next move was, and prayed the duke caught whatever he was hunting and returned home fast.

Len faced me but stood next to Talin. "Your Majesty, you said your human is a caretaker of illness, correct?"

Nothing like being talked about as if I weren't in the room, and despite gritting my teeth, I planted a fake smile on my face as Raze had instructed. *Bring no attention to myself. None.* Not even if I wanted to walk over there and kick him in the shins.

"Yes," Talin responded. "Is there any way you can send someone to notify the duke I am waiting? I have pressing matters I must attend to at home and will not wait much longer."

"Of course." Len bowed, his hands clasped to his belly. "I will arrange that at once." He glanced my way, and my skin crawled. "But may I ask for usage of your human, please?"

"What for?" Raze's voice boomed from behind me, his footsteps closing in. I shifted in my seat, not loving where this was going one bit. My mission was to smile and act polite. Nothing else.

"Your Majesty, we have a slight problem, and your human couldn't have arrived at a more opportune time. Please, my prince. I would never impose, but..." He leaned closer to Talin. "Rek's mistress is in labor and is having complications. His wife refuses to send help, insisting it is up to the gods to decide their fate. Perhaps your caretaker could just inspect the girl and advise our midwife of the issue."

Coldness hit my core, and a protest pressed at the forefront of my mind. "Umm, actually, my specialty is normal illnesses. Coughs. Chest colds. Broken bones. That sort of thing. Not childbirth. I've never—"

Len waved a hand to cut me off. "Nonsense. It all falls under the same medical roof." He turned to Talin. "Please, I ask for your assistance and I'm sure, it will be considered an honorable boon by your cousin. I will advise him of your graciousness in such a situation."

"Talin," I said. "Can I have a quick moment?"

"Excuse me, please." He addressed Len, who bowed and retreated.

"I will return soon. Time is of the essence."

I dragged Talin by the hand to the farthest corner of the room next to a gaudy statue of a man holding three bear cubs, and Raze followed us. "Are you insane?!" I hissed. "I know nothing about childbirth. Zilch. Never seen one. Never want to. And what do I know about bear births? And he said they're having complications!"

Raze rubbed my lower back. "It's straightforward. The woman pushes and the baby comes out."

I slapped his hand away, as it irritated me. Right now, I felt as if I were about to be thrown into quicksand. "Then why don't you go in there? Oh, my goddess." I paced in a small circle. "I can't do this. Last time I saw someone with a broken leg with their bone coming through their skin, I fainted."

Talin grabbed my arms and forced me to face him. "Just breathe. Go in and inspect the situation. Ask the midwife if it's a breech birth. If so, let no one help the mother push the baby out as it could kill them both. But once the legs are out, then they can pull the baby out."

"What? How in the world do you know?"

"Once I got stuck in a house during a snowstorm with a mother and three kids, and the wife was in labor. So guess who delivered the baby, per her instructions?"

"Oh, shit. Why don't you do it then?" I crossed my arms. This was insane and no way in this universe would I be delivering a shifter baby.

Raze's laugh burst out. "Yeah, the prince of White Peak, assisting in the labor of his cousin's mistress. He'd be a joke — plus, he wouldn't be allowed in. Men aren't permitted to attend births."

"That's ridiculous." I dropped my hands and buzzed with the dread biting in my flesh. "I swear, if I ever have a baby, the father will be there the entire time, suffering with me."

Raze smirked. "I can see you demanding that. But I agree with Talin here. It would be considered an insult for us to turn down the plea for help, and it could rouse suspicion if you don't."

"Are you ready?" Len's voice came from over by the doorway.

Talin smiled and gave me a slight nod. He lowered

himself to my level and whispered, "This might help us convince the duke to remove the curse. Please, Bee. Do this for me."

Because my life hadn't become bizarre enough. My legs had hardened to stone, and my breaths grew ragged. I'd rather face a bear shifter in attack mode over helping someone give birth.

"She'll do it." Talin forced me to turn around and nudged me toward Len.

CHAPTER 20

The moment I opened the door to the room, a woman screamed from inside. I froze, but Len nudged me in the back. "Quick now."

"Yes, of course." I stepped inside and found a heavily pregnant woman crouching over a towel, naked and yelling. Sweat coated her body, and her hair was slick with perspiration.

Nope, this was a mistake, but as I reached for the door handle, the midwife was at my side.

"Len said you could assist. Please." She grasped my hand with such desperation, it hurt as she drew me deeper into the room. "Gwenth's been in labor since last night and still the baby hasn't come."

I hugged myself, standing against the side of the bed, unable to stop staring at the poor woman in agonizing pain, unable to think of anything else. My heartbeat banged in my ears. I didn't want to be here or see this.

"What do you suggest?" The midwife was a thin woman, maybe no older than twenty-five, and right then I doubted she was even a real nurse.

"Is this a breech birth?" I blurted.

The girl nodded. "Yes. One of the other midwives snuck in earlier and confirmed it was a breech. Maybe we should get Gwenth to lie on the bed so we can pull the baby out?"

"No!" Thank goddess for Talin's instructions, as I would have probably agreed. "In a breech, I think the butt wants to come out first as the baby is curved the wrong way around in the womb. Then, we can pull him or her out."

The girl nodded, her face stricken white, and we were both thrown in the deep end.

"Let's massage her back, release the pressure." Whenever I had cramps, a hot water bottle also eased the soreness. "And bring lukewarm water so we can warm the towels to assist with the pain."

The girl dashed from the room so fast. Who could blame her? When Gwenth howled with agony, I flinched. Okay, I could do this. It wasn't in my nature to walk away from something hurting.

I approached the mistress and rubbed her shoulder. "Take my hand and let's get you to lean over the bed so you can hold onto the post as you squat." Someone had once told me she'd given birth to all her kids that way, as it was easier.

"Nice to meet you, Gwenth. I'm Bee." I dragged her onto her feet and took her weight against me, her body coated in sweat. We wobbled over to the bed and she leaned over, gripping the post. Her body trembled, and she let out a low shriek, my ears ringing.

"Take deep breaths." I rubbed her lower back, massaging her in slow motion.

When the other girl hurried into the room with a bucket, she set the water down and kicked the door shut.

"All right, soak a towel and then wring it dry. Let's put warmth on her back to assist with the pressure."

Was this even right? What in the world did I know about

childbirth, aside from my rushed lesson from Talin, and what friends had told me back in Terra? Most of the time I'd tuned out because the idea of pushing a watermelon out of my body terrified me.

What felt like a lifetime passed, the walls echoing with screams, when finally the midwife yelled, "I see a bum." She crouched right in front of Gwenth.

I kneeled down and grabbed a clean towel for the baby, hoping this was right. Letting it drop on the floor was wrong... even I knew that much.

"Okay, we'll give you a helping hand." The midwife gently placed her fingers into the crease of the baby's thighs, and the child's legs spontaneously released out from the opening. She gave a light pull. "Keep pushing; the baby seems to be stuck."

Gwenth hissed, her face twisting and turning red.

I wiped her perspiration-soaked hair off her brow. "You can do this. Keep going."

And as if she'd turned on a waterfall, the little thing gushed out, covered in white sticky stuff. I jutted my hands out, catching the bundle with my towel.

Gwenth huffed and cried with excitement.

I gasped, cradling the little angel in my arms, but the midwife was fast to take her from me and wash the white coating off the baby. Climbing to my feet, I took a clean towel to the midwife, who placed a wailing baby in my arms. She returned to cleanse Gwenth as blood and other goo followed the baby. I gagged and turned away, staring at the precious bundle. *Wow.* I couldn't believe I'd helped bring this little girl into the world. A new life, a new start. All lives were precious, and a newfound determination flooded me. We'd come this far, and I would save my princes. After this delivery, their cousin had to be grateful enough to remove the curse.

When I turned, Gwenth was in bed. I approached her and handed her the little baby. "She's adorable," I said.

Tears filled her eyes as she held the munchkin and kissed her head. "I thought today I would die in childbirth and lose her. Thank you."

"I didn't do anything."

"You were there for me, even though you're not from our house. For that, I am grateful beyond words."

The midwife carried the bucket of water and birthing goo out of the room, and I closed the door behind her. My mind spun with how appreciative she was and what an opportune moment this offered me.

"Listen, Gwenth, can I ask you something in private? Woman to woman?"

"Anything." Her baby already suckled at her breast.

"Is there a witch living in this manor?" The time for subtlety was out the window since I doubted I had the time to ask anyone else who exactly did magic.

She stared at me with a piercing expression. "Why would you ask such a question?" Her voice squeaked.

"Please, Gwenth. Someone I know is in grave danger."

She licked her dried lips and looked at the door, then back at me. "This can't be repeated to anyone or I'll lose my baby."

"I would do nothing to bring harm to her or you." I reached over and touched her arm, reassuring her.

"Rek brought a witch into our home a few weeks ago. A voodoo witch from Tritonia. I saw them in the basement. One of the servant girls was down there too." She looked down at her baby, tears cramming her eyes. "If I hadn't been pregnant, I would have left this house that night."

I flinched at the words voodoo witch from Tritonia. "What happened?" I stroked her arm. "Please."

Her breath hitched. "Rek cut his palm and let the witch

drink from his blood. Then the witch gutted the poor servant girl like a pig before bathing in the blood." She trembled, and a tear fell down her cheek. "After that, I left. I couldn't watch anymore."

A chill clasped around my heart, and I loathed Rek. Death magic. "Where is the witch now?"

"Gone. She most likely returned to her vile home."

And just like that, my worries were confirmed. Blood had been spilled, so the curse couldn't be broken by a simple spell.

"Did you see Rek or the witch holding an object in their hand? A charm or jewelry box. Anything out of the usual?"

Gwenth shook her head. "Actually, the witch held something silvery in her fist, but it was too dark for me to see exactly what it was."

Fuck! If we found the item, it would break the curse. We had to convince Rek to hand it over. I cringed at how ridiculously impossible that sounded. But we were so close. And I'd brought all the herbs I could find to create a persuasion spell.

Talin and Raze had to get their cousin alone for me to attempt my spell. We'd show him we'd saved his mistress and baby. Surely, the man carried some empathy.

With my hands washed and wiped clean, I left Gwenth and her newborn in the room with the midwife. Despite my initial shock of aiding Gwenth, part of me wouldn't change the experience, and now I couldn't stop smiling. Something about seeing a new life enter the world, so innocent and vulnerable, reminded me of how precious life was, and why we fought so hard to stay alive. I had to find my princes.

I rushed down a long corridor, my steps lighter than when I'd first arrived at the manor. Shields, painted with coats of arms designs, littered the white walls. I passed one decorated with a rose and crossed swords as I'd seen back in the ballroom in the castle.

Up ahead, a young girl came around the corner. She had dark, raven hair that fell to her hips, and she strolled toward me, her chin high and fingers laced across her middle. She wore a gorgeous off-the-shoulder green gown with a black ribbon on her tiny waist and a matching one curled around her neck. Definitely not a servant, and she had to be thirteen or fourteen years old. A child. And just with that last thought, my mind careened back to Ash's words about Rek's grand-daughter.

"Hello, you are the prince's caretaker, is that right?" The girl stopped two feet in front of me, her face blank as if she'd been taught the fine art of showing no emotions. Unlike me who couldn't hide anything if I my life depended on it.

"Yes, that's me. My name is Bee."

She studied me, and a smile crept across her rose lips. Even though she only reached my shoulders, she held an air of arrogance about her. No doubt she'd been brought up in a well-do-to family. But had she ever had the chance to explore the realm, run around with her friends, play games in the woods, twirl in the rain and get her clothes soaked? I sure hope she hadn't wasted her childhood following rules on becoming the perfect royal without really experiencing life.

"I'm Cleo, and my grandpa promised me to the prince of White Peak." Her mouth widened into a smirk. "You may have heard of me?" Her stare pierced into me, and yet I'd picked up on the trickle of uncertainty in her words.

I couldn't help but pity the poor girl. Had her grandfather not told her Talin refused the offer, or was he planning to offer her to the next prince once Talin died?

"Cleo, it's a pleasure to meet you. I'm new to the realm, so I'm sorry I don't know many people here." I wasn't sure anything I could say would provide her with the ease she craved. "But just between us two, woman to woman," I

167

leaned closer. "I'm a big believer in finding my own future husband, rather than my family dictating. Don't you think?"

Her face twisted in a wry expression as if I'd suddenly grown horns. "It's a privilege for my family to find my suitor. Plus, I would marry the most handsome man in the realm. And I will become his queen." She bounced on her toes, then stopped and straightened her posture.

"Grandpa told me Talin was a gentle prince and would treat me as a lady. He would care for me. Grandpa said me he would never marry me to anyone who would harm me." She glanced over her shoulder and back, lowering her voice. "My father always pushes and hits my mother, but grandpa promised me a different future."

At her words, my response jammed in my mind, and an ache coiled tight in my stomach. Rek might be an evil bastard, but he adored Cleo. Or were his explanations simply a way to placate her so she held no doubts about the arranged marriage?

"Is the prince as kind as my grandpa says he is?" Cleo stared at me with hopeful eyes, and it broke me to see a young child wishing for a kind husband at such a young age. I wanted to embrace her until the thickness in my throat settled, but I couldn't bring myself to shred her heart by telling her the truth. Rek's motivation for the arranged marriage, Talin's insistence he intended to select his bride, or even the sharpness in my chest that reminded me how much I longed for Talin and his brothers.

"He is that and so much more," I said. "But sometimes life doesn't always play out according to our plans. I always believe it's because there's something better waiting for us."

"Cleo," a woman yelled from behind me, and I turned to find a stocky servant in a black dress and white apron, gripping her hips. "Cleo, hurry, I must finish your hair before you meet the prince."

"Got to go." Cleo touched my hand, he warmth traveling through my arm. "Thank you." She smirked and ran down the hallway, her skirt swaying around her legs.

I felt terrible not being upfront with the girl, but who was I to squash her dreams. Besides, that might draw unwanted attention while we remained in the manor and waited for Rek to return.

With a deep inhale, I made my way in the opposite direction. I didn't want to bring Cleo heartache, but Talin was right to turn her down because she was too young to know exactly what she wanted and not allow her grandpa to use as a pawn. I prayed she didn't get married to another man for the sake of politics but rather to someone of her choosing and who loved her.

I hurried back to the main room where I found Talin and Raze.

"How did it go?" Talin asked, getting up from his seat.

"Good, both mother and child are safe. Any news on Rek?"

He shook his head.

"I don't want to alarm you, but…" Raze's gaze was on the window, and his words expelled as a growl.

Panic strangled my lungs, and I felt a sharpening ache settle in my chest, and laughter burst through my skull. *Lilita.*

Desperation swallowed me. I snatched Raze's shirt and hauled him toward me. We clashed, me on tippy toes, his hands on my back, his starved fingers pressing into my flesh. Our mouths met, fast and ferocious. Energy zapped between us, his tongue pushing forward with such ease, and I parted my lips, taking him. Shivers scaled up my spine, a mixture of the goddess's warning and my power holding Lilita back.

"What in the world?" Len's raw voice boomed behind me.

We jerked apart and still my skin sizzled with the need to finish what we'd started, because Lilita lingered in my mind.

Len stood in the doorway, mouth hung open, and his limp arms hanging by his sides, as if the shock had truly left him immobile. "Raze, you've brought your whore to my home?"

A growl rolled through Raze's chest, but that was the least of my problems, because a prince was gone. "Where's Talin?" I darted into the hallway with the giant bear statue. The front door remained closed.

"Is she even a caretaker for Talin, or are you taking privileges?" Len continued.

My stomach ached. What if Talin had turned, and we'd lost him? Regret chewed me because I should have taken him too, but I'd gone for Raze, as he'd shown symptoms first, and my head had spun.

A faint menacing chuckle echoed in my head, and the earlier dread fisted my lungs.

"Where did Talin go?" Raze's voice climbed.

Len huffed. "You boys need a lesson in etiquette and manners. No bringing whores to a royal family home, no—"

"Enough," I bellowed, and Len shuddered to a halt. When he faced me, his glare sucked the confidence out of me as if he'd willed my heart to stop beating.

"How dare you address me—?"

"Talin's in danger. Where did he go?" I moved to Len's side and grabbed his arm. "Did you see him? Quick!"

Raze had already thundered out of the manor and vanished outside.

"And this is why the princes are not suited to rule White Peak." Len pulled out of my grasp, his nose wrinkled, as if I were mud on his shoes. "They need to step aside. They're impulsive and rash, and they have no respect."

I faced the shifter. "From what I've seen, if following the rules means leaving a poor mistress at the mercy of childbirth and angering a wife, then you don't know what being a true leader means." Not to mention sacrificing servants to gain power.

Rage pushed against me, throttling me at the core, and my mind kept swaying between the present and falling into a pit of darkness. I whirled toward the door to head after Raze when Len seized my hand, his fat fingers constricting the blood from flowing down my arm.

"Go back to your human world. White Peak is too much for grubby girls." His voice was brutal and angry. "There's only one use for someone like you." He licked his lips, and I gagged.

"Ew!" Coldness flooded me, and my rational thinking vanished. I yanked free from his grip.

Bee. Lilita's thin voice echoed in the recesses of my mind like rusty hinges creaking.

My mind swayed in so many directions, and with no sign of Raze or Talin, would she explode out of me like a hurricane and destroy the manor with everyone in it?

"What is wrong with you?" Len asked, his eyebrow pinching together. "Why are you shaking that way? You better not have brought any human diseases into our home."

I was desperate: maybe kissing Len would do the trick? Too many reasons for why that would be a bad idea flooded me, but I didn't listen, and I lunged at him, my hands gripping his shoulders. Despite my stomach turning over, I kissed him, hard, holding myself against him. Not a single spark.

His hands shoved into my chest, throwing me backward, and I stumbled a few feet, wiping my mouth of his disgusting taste.

"Whore!"

I gasped but pushed the angry words to the back of my

mind. He wouldn't understand, so I bent over, pretending to scratch my leg. Instead, I retrieved the pouch of herbs with my persuasion spell from my boot. "You are what's wrong with the world," I said, noting a few servants peering at us from farther down the corridor. When they saw me looking, their eyes widened, and they ran away.

They must have seen me as a mad woman, but I didn't care. Not when I had to find my princes, and the thorny pain indicating Lilita's presence crawled through my chest.

She pressed on the forefront of my mind, chuckling.

"What's in your hand?" Len's smug expression fell when I poured a few herbs into my palm. It should wear off in a few days. "You shall never speak ill of anyone again. Never mouth a word about me, and every word you voice will be a compliment."

He grimaced. With his fat fingers flying toward my face, I blew the contents toward him.

"Speak no evil and forget me."

He stumbled backward, coughing as if something had caught in his throat. "W-Witch!"

His eyes rolled backward, and his body trembled. For good measure, I kicked him in the balls for calling me 'grubby.'

Len sunk to his knees, then slumped to his side like a sack of potatoes, groaning in pain. "A f-f-f…antastic k…ick."

"Where did Talin go?" I demanded.

"Ou…O…" Shaking, he pointed to the front door before curling in on himself, crying.

I turned on my heels, smirked, and ran outside, having wasted enough time.

The guard turned my way, his glares promising me torture. "Len is dying. Something happened to him," I lied. "Please help him — now!"

Without so much as a question, his darted inside.

The sun hovered over the horizon, painting the skies in bloody streaks, as trees beyond the manor gates shook violently in the winds. There was no sign of Talin or Raze.

A blade might as well have pierced my heart.

CHAPTER 21

*L*ilita's voice fluttered through my skull, her laughter shredding my grasp on reality as my vision blurred in and out. I clasped my head with both hands, trying to steady the spinning. Dread punched me in the gut, emptying my lungs. I gasped for each breath as if it were my last.

Focus. Raze's kiss, his touch. Electric warmth. I have control. I repeated the chant, picturing myself surrounded by white light, its energy passing through me, cleansing me.

When a roar exploded from the woods in the distance to my left, I sprinted faster. With a quick look over my shoulder, I didn't see any guards following. My spell would have confused Len, and he wouldn't remember me, so that bought us time. But not much.

Terror raged within me, Lilita lingering closer in my mind. My kiss with Raze hadn't been enough. Attempting to do the same with Len had failed, but I'd tried out of sheer desperation. The curse connected the princes and me. But it was more than that, I felt it in my bones. They'd shown me their caring natures and returned my desires for them threefold. I craved them every moment of the day. And I wasn't saying it was right to feel that way about all four men, but I could barely hold on to my sanity, let alone sort through my emotions.

We should have left the manor the moment we'd found out the duke was hunting and no way should I have taken my eyes off Talin and Raze. I'd hate myself for eternity if they died. I kept picturing them stuck mid-transformation, bolting home toward the castle, exactly as Talin had said he'd done on their previous attempts to visit his cousin.

Then I'd be stuck in White Peak woods, and Lilita would make a meal of me — and probably kill everyone in her path. My knees wobbled beneath me. I'd rather die first.

Once I passed through the gates, I veered left towards where the roar had come from, trampling snow-coated shrubs and foliage. The constant heaviness of my thoughts lingered.

Raze, where are you? I rubbed the cold out of my arms, thankful my dress had layers of fabric.

As I jumped over a dead log, a snap of energy shook me at the core.

Bee. Lilita repeated my name over and over.

"Shut up!" I pushed onward, hitting my palm against my temple. "You're not coming out." I staggered through the woods and ducked under low-hanging branches. "Raze," I yelled. "Talin?" *Please let that be one of them growling.*

My vision toggled between blurring and sharpening.

Another roar from my left, and the promise of finding the princes propelled me forward. I wove through the trees, the chill in the air freezing me.

Night crawled across the heavens. But that didn't matter if I didn't track down my bear shifters.

When the land sloped downhill, I lost my footing. Snatching the air, I caught a branch, righting myself. My stomach swirled with bile. Falling down a gorge and killing myself would be a painful way to go. But at least Lilita would no longer have been a problem.

When a grunt came from behind me, I scrambled upright, the tree to my back, and found Talin, disfigured and snarling in his half-bear, half-human form.

He sneered, the corded muscles in his neck tense and ready to snap. His eyes narrowed, and his long, furry ears twitched as if he heard sounds I didn't.

I froze, unable to find my words. Kissing him seemed an impossibility in his state.

His lips peeled back over sharpened fangs.

Trembling, I recoiled away with the tree at my back, well aware of what an attack posture looked like. He charged. My foot slipped out from under me.

Arms flayed outward, I hit the ground and slid down the snow, the momentum dragging me fast, foliage and shrubs tearing my dress and hair, stabbing and ripping at my flesh. I screamed, the world tumbling around me.

Darkness snapped across my vision, and all sounds faded, replaced with the repetitive thud of my heart, the constricting sensation of being strangled.

And in my head, Lilita shoved me aside like a rag doll and charged forward.

I cracked my neck and pulled myself up. I stood at the bottom of a hill — on a damn iced-over river. "Well, one could go worse ways. About time that whiny Bee got out of the way." Enough of this being nice bullshit, and who the hell delivers a stranger's baby? Seriously. *Now, if there had been an option to use the bundle for a spell, then there would have been a purpose. Though, that was still a possibility once I got the manor.*

The baby would help me open the doorway to the underworld. I'd build myself a small army made up of a few thousand demonic spirits. Then the rest of the pieces would fall into place. Take over all of Haven, destroy anyone who stood in my way, and rule this world how the ancients had intended. With war and bloodshed.

Shaking snow out of my hair, I huffed and stomped up the slope. I jutted my hand outward, drawing on the energy Bee had ignored for so long. A spark of black threads snapped out from the tips of my fingers, hitting the forest floor. "Winds, lift me. Carry me to the duke's manor."

The ground trembled beneath me, as if it had thundered. Wind battered into me. I smirked, slightly turned on by my power.

Someone tackled me from the side, and I yelled from sheer surprise, falling over.

Raze grasped my wrists, pinning me down.

"Oh, boy. Didn't know you had it in you. You so want some Lilita candy, don't you?"

He lay on top of me, his body transforming, bones cracking, fur bursting across his flesh, his clothes ripping.

Ah, how delicious they sounded.

Bee's shrieks galloped across my thoughts.

No way in the seven kingdoms of hell would she reach him. I flicked my fingers toward Raze, my floundering power zapping him. He flinched off me in a flash, groaning, and rolled across the ground several feet away.

"Son of a demon's ass." I climbed up, rage boiling through my veins.

Raze lay there in his human form, spent, naked, and vulnerable, with his clothes pooled around him in shreds.

Bee loitered in my ear, and a sense of warming passion swept through me for this bear shifter. "Disgusting." I turned away and hiked up the hill. Girl, you need to get your priorities straight. What do you think he'll do to you when he turns? You're lucky I was here to save us.

And who walked these days, anyway?

Energy snaked down my arm, and I unleashed the power. "Winds. Take me into your arms."

A gale curled around me, causing my gown to flutter around my legs, my hair to blow across my face, and a tiara to fall off my head. I stepped on it, crushing the piece. In that moment, the gale lifted me off my feet as if it were an invisible hand.

Raze smacked into me from behind, knocking the wind out of me, and I lurched forward. His arms and legs latched around my body midair, him on top of me. We were still floating and the current whistled in my ears, tearing at me. I bucked against him and elbowed him in the gut.

That arousal owned me again. Damn, I might actually fall for Raze if he kept teasing me like this.

He fisted my hair and twisted my chin to face him. His lips clasped mine, and in that precise moment, a sharp jolt shuddered through me. I screamed into his mouth, and panic sliced through me.

We fell with a thud, and my vision darkened. The earlier pulse across my skin dampened. And Bee was right there, yelling in my skull to fuck off.

* * *

"RAZE!" I gasped as I found myself tangled in his arms, my head pounding, my whole body drenched in sweat despite the cold.

"Bee? Is that you?" He stared at me for an instant and raised himself to kiss me. I grabbed hold of his face and met his lips. I lay in the snow, drowning in his arousal, ecstatic we'd shoved the bitch back into her place. Because taking over White Peak hadn't been enough, now she threatened to open a portal and dominate all of Haven? What next? Declare herself a goddess? Yep, nothing like having a deranged psycho living inside me.

Our bodies bonded, burned up, fit perfectly as one.

"I thought I lost you," I managed.

"Me too." His voice grew raspy and dark, as if he still fought the change. Our foreheads touched, and I kissed his chilled lips once more. I let out a whimper as he rolled me on top of him and kissed me down my neck. His hands groped my ass. The fiery desire ignited between my legs, but this was the wrong time and place.

I pulled away, battling to fill my lungs despite the arousal pulling me to Raze. "We can't do this here," I breathed.

The corners of Raze's eyes wrinkled and with a low grunt in his throat, he got up and yanked me to my feet. His hand looped around my back in a hug. He trembled against me, naked.

I pulled off my cloak and offered it to him.

He accepted the clothing with no hesitation and threw it over his shoulders, drawing the ribbon at his neck. "How long will the effect last?" he asked, his teeth chattering.

"No idea. But we must find Talin before he hurts someone or himself."

"He's in the forest with us, attacking anything that moves. He hasn't bolted home like before. Could it be because we're within the range of the magic object in the duke's house?"

"Maybe." I swallowed the boulder in my throat, unable to calm my breathing or the terror leaching to my lungs. The constant shivers were racing up and down my spine with the goddess's warnings. What a nightmare we'd landed in.

"We have a day to get Talin under control and wait for Rek to return before the full moon tomorrow night." Without waiting, Raze took my hand and hauled me up the steep slope with such strength and mobility — his agility impressed me.

I gulped for air. "I found out what Rek did to create the curse. He paid a voodoo witch, and they killed a young servant girl. But—"

"Who told you this?" His voice crackled.

179

"His mistress. She saw it firsthand." We reached the crest of the hill in no time. Only a slither of sunlight remained, and shadows filled the woods.

Raze stiffened and sniffed the air. He pushed me behind him. "Talin's here."

I shuddered, so exhausted from running for my life, from someone trying to eat me. If I survived, I swore I was taking a trip to the sea with Ariella and sunbathing for a week straight. No drama. No fighting. No being terrified out of my mind.

Raze darted to my right so fast, I stumbled into a tree. *Fuck, fuck!* I reached into my boot, retrieved my pouch of persuasion herbs, and poured some into my hand.

Snow crunched behind me, and I snapped around to find Talin. His shoulders hunched forward, his face twisted into a wild beast's.

Coldness sank through me, and terror froze me on the spot. "Talin, it's me." I couldn't catch my breath.

"Don't move," Raze said from somewhere in the woods.

Facing my death in Talin's gaze terrified me because this wasn't the person I'd craved, who loved his brothers, who'd nearly brought me to orgasm from a kiss. Patches of fur covered his torso and arms, one leg resembled a bear's, the other a human, giving him a slant as he stood. But his face and eyes were his, and my heart broke to see him this way. I recalled his agony at losing his heritage and having no control over himself. He hated what the duke had done to him.

Talin charged.

I flinched backward just as another blur whizzed through my peripheral vision. Raze, in human form, collided into Talin's side, bringing them both down. Not wasting time, I rushed after them and blew the herbs into Talin's face as he snarled from underneath his brother's weight.

"Stop fighting."

Talin thrashed, his teeth biting the air between him. No change.

Raze held down his clawed paws, his strength impressive.

"It's not working," he hissed. "Kiss him — now!"

My heart slammed into my ribcage. "Are you crazy?"

Talin snarled, his fangs practically exploding out of his maw.

"I can't hold him much longer. Do it!"

Every inch of me ached, and I couldn't get myself to move closer. Because when they read out my obituary, they'd say, "Bee died by having her face chewed off by a bear shifter."

CHAPTER 22

"*T*alin." I collapsed to my knees on the forest floor next to the prince pinned to the ground by his brother, Raze.

He trashed and snarled, his body convulsing.

"Hurry," Raze growled.

I stretched out a shaky hand. With my palm over Talin's brow, I pressed his head to keep him from biting me.

Raze shuddered from the strain of his brother's attempts to get free. He straddled his brother's waist, keeping his arms locked under his knees. He clasped his shoulders down. Talin snapped his teeth, unable to reach Raze's arms.

Talin floundered and twisted, but when his eyes met mine, he eased, his expression softening.

"I don't want to hurt you," I pleaded, hating to see him this way. But it was for his own safety.

"Do it now," Raze demanded.

My breath hitched, but I kept Talin's gaze, his attention. With my other hand pressed to his chin, I lowered myself. "Listen to me, Talin," I continued. "Remember our earlier kiss, how you had me burning up, how I haven't been able to stop thinking about you since."

A faint whimper rolled from his throat, and my gut clenched at hearing the agony, knowing he suffered and struggled to escape his imprisonment.

I inched lower.

Foliage crunched from up ahead, and someone gasped.

Before I could react, Talin roared in my face and kicked into a raving animal, exploding with energy. He bucked Raze off and shoved me aside with a hand, catching me in the face. Blood smeared my mouth from my split lip.

Fear collected in my chest as I dragged myself backward on my butt in the snow, expecting him to pounce.

But he lunged toward an enormous man with golden locks who was standing between two trees, carrying a dead boar over his shoulder.

"Rek," Raze yelled. "Run!"

Fuck! That was his cousin! Everything happened too fast, and I staggered to my feet. "Talin, no!" I chased after them, terror bleeding into my veins. Talin would butcher the one person who knew where the cursed object was so we could break the spell.

Raze darted ahead of me.

"Don't let him kill Rek," I wailed.

He vanished into the darkness of the forest. I raced after them and jumped over the dropped boar.

Sweat drenched my skin as my pulse vibrated in my ears. Snow swallowed my boots, making my gait slow and clumsy. I dodged trees, ignoring the branches snagging my clothes and hair. I pumped my arms.

A roar from my right, and I veered in that direction. Up ahead, dark shapes bounced about. A newfound energy exploded within me and I raced toward them. My feet kept slipping outward, but nothing would stop me.

Fail and we all paid the price.

I cried on the inside, begging Talin to stop. Where the fuck had Rek come from, anyway? Why had he crossed our path? But he knew where the cursed object was, so maybe I could convince him to tell us where he'd hidden the item. We'd break the hex tonight! Then we'd return to the castle, laugh at the close call, and breathe normally for a change.

"Raze, hold Talin back!" I yelled.

The shadows dissolved into the night, and I emerged on the scene, my pulse hammering into my breastbone.

Raze lugged Talin away by an arm with his cloak fluttering behind him, as if the wind aided him.

Rek was in bear form, dragging himself in the opposite direction. His legs lay limp, and wounds riddled his brown coat.

Talin growled, blood dripping from his lips.

My feet were glued to the ground and terror shacked me. Tingles filled my muscles with the urgency to run and help Raze.

"Bee," Raze growled, "I can't hold on." His body shimmied with the telltale sign of the change coming.

Ice daggers pierced my chest as the darkness slinked through me as well.

"Hold him!" I couldn't stop shaking. This was my nightmare, facing off with bear shifters, but the alternative was unleashing my evil side if this didn't work.

Raze's arms trembled, but he snarled and hauled his brother farther backward.

I scrambled after them.

Talin turned and catapulted himself at Raze, bellowing, and Raze's face paled, his eyes widening with horror.

The pair crashed into a tree with Talin's mouth latched on to Raze's shoulder.

I screamed.

Raze growled, his face distorted with torture, his menacing eyes blazing with rage.

Instinct took over, and I swiped a branch off the ground, then closed the distance between us. I brought the weapon down across Talin's head. The sudden release of pressure made the stick crack in half.

I shuddered, my gaze swinging left and right as I searched for something to defend myself with. My mind drowned in the horrible death coming my way and a strangled cry rolled from my throat.

Talin flinched, staggering on all fours at first, shaking his head. His brother grimaced and pushed himself to his knees, yet he swayed on the spot.

"Raze, get up," I bellowed and bent over, patting for my pouch in my boots. Nothing there. Shit! I must have dropped the herbs.

Talin's jerky movements had me retreating, but he pivoted toward Rek and charged with a mighty growl.

At first, I hesitated, torn between being scared out of my head and confronting a savage Talin. I burst after him. "Talin! Please, don't do this."

The moment he crashed against Rek, his claws tore at his cousin's throat, so fast and deep, and red splattered the snow and trees.

I halted, a hollowness swallowing me whole. Our efforts were lost. Wasted.

Rek slumped in the snow as his body shook, and he changed form back into a human.

The world tilted beneath me from our poisonous predicament. I yelled from pure frustration, the hopelessness, the rage burning me up from the inside out. I stood unmoving. My life had become one twisted pile of knots.

Lilita was in my head, howling with laughter.

Talin, still in his half-bear form, snapped in my direction, his mouth gaping open, blood staining his teeth and chin. No humanity was left in his cold, wild eyes.

Shivers climbed my spine.

Talin had killed his cousin.

Did that mean all-out warfare? Worse yet, I had no way of finding out what object he'd used for the curse. And to top things off, the slicing ache of Lilita shoving herself forward pierced through me.

In a flash, Raze darted up behind Talin and whacked him in the head with a huge rock. Talin's eyes rolled upward as he fell to his knees, then face-planted into the snow. Raze tossed the stone aside and pushed his brother onto his back.

"Shit! Is he going to be okay?" My words shook, and grief tore me apart. Rek was dead, and so was our chance to find out from him the location of the cursed object that could break the spell. Anguish surged forward, and tears flooded my cheeks.

Raze joined me, and his skin twitched as his eyes glazed over. Blood tainted the corner of his mouth. Before I could say a word, he had me in his arms, our mouths plastered together. And goddess forgive me, but even surrounded by death and chaos, falling beneath Raze's passion undid me.

He clenched my hair in his fists, tilting my chin up as he drove me up against a tree. His hardness pressed into my lower abdomen, grinding against my stomach, and I mewled. A growl thundered in his chest.

His tongue surged into my mouth, and I tasted something coppery, metallic. Blood. His along with mine.

In that same moment, a spark of energy rattled me at the core, and threads of energy zipped down my flesh like hundreds of blades cutting into me. Raze flinched against me.

A calmness flooded me. Lilita disappeared in an instant, along with her echoing screams.

Raze broke free, gasping. "Did you feel that?"

I gulped for air. "There's magic in the air, and it's affecting all of us."

"It's eradicated every urge from my bear. Your earlier kisses pushed him aside, but not like this."

So maybe I'd been wrong, and the connection wasn't sexual but linked to our blood? I struggled to understand how this worked. What could I do to save the princes? It felt as if the answer stared me right in the face, but I was blind to it.

Raze kissed my nose. "If we ever get out of this, I promise you I will never leave you. I want you like no other, and it's not just the lure of the curse, but to do something other than running for our lives. To show you how beautiful White Peak is, and that it's not all danger and gloom. To take you around the realm. To make love to you at every exquisite place we find."

"How can you say that, Raze?" I cried. My emotions turned ragged and my insides constricted. "You're a prince. I'm a nobody who only brought death to your doors!"

His brows pinched together. "Do you care for me? Do you want a future together?"

I nodded, my throat thickening, and all I craved was to crawl into his embrace, or any of the princes', and forget myself. But when I looked over at Talin, my heart broke. Like the other brothers, he'd touched me, showing me that beneath the insanity of their predicament, he was a shifter who wanted peace for his people. And I couldn't deny my attraction to each brother equally, yet for such different reasons.

"Each one of you means the world to me." I hiccupped on my breath. "But this isn't the place to talk about emotions."

I pulled free from Raze's hold and moved to Talin's side. "What are we going to do about Rek? And we need to get

Talin warm before he freezes to death." But before Raze responded, I wiped the blood from Talin's lips with a thumb, assuming it was from Rek.

I recalled the way the coppery tang on Raze's tongue had shoved Lilita into her place. And that got me curious. The curse had bound us, connected us, so what if... I touched the open wound on Talin's collarbone and red dripped down my hand. I sucked on my finger and a metallic and salty taste coated my mouth.

Without waiting, I bent over on my knees and kissed Talin. Immediately, the energy crackled across my skin, leaving me shaking as if lightning had struck me.

Talin's body morphed into his human form, his shirt shredded, and only the collar barely hung on him.

"How did you do that?" Raze lifted his brother into his arms.

"I think we're all connected through blood. And it keeps our dark sides away." Just as our intimacy did, but I also suspected my blood was needed for the exchange.

"Fuck. That's great, right? How can we use it against the curse?"

My voice faltered, and I ached all over from exhaustion. "I don't know yet."

"Well, let's leave before anyone finds Rek dead. We'll say he attacked Talin first, but we have more pressing problems."

Raze walked away from Rek without looking back.

Drawing on my last bit of strength, I reminded myself that tomorrow was the full moon. We'd lost the chance to save ourselves, but I'd discovered new things, like how tasting our blood pushed aside our curse. Now to determine how I could use that to help us survive the full moon tomorrow night, when the curse would kill the princes.

"Quick," Raze said, speed-walking, his brother slumped in his arms.

I dredged onward in the snow, trying to rack my brain for a blood spell. I blinked hard as dizziness flooded me and I fell. Back on my feet, I pressed on, my breathing labored as fatigue pulled at my every step.

Despite the ugliness of what Rek had done to the princes, part of me hated that we'd left him there without a burial or at least bringing him to his family — we'd left his mistress's newborn child without a father. Albeit, he was a father who scarified people, so perhaps it was for the best.

The night carried a heavy coldness. At the edge of the woods, I stared at the manor's front gates in the distance, hidden by shadows. Being so close to the place left me itching to run in the opposite direction. No guard manned the front door. Were they in the forest searching for us?

I scanned the surrounding yard, the building, the woods.

"Where's our carriage?" I asked.

Raze set down the unconscious Talin, propping him up against a tree. "Stay with him. I'll collect it."

"You have a massive bite mark on your neck. And blood everywhere on your body. How will you explain that?"

He checked his injury, as if just noticing his wounds. He pulled off the cloak he miraculously still wore, folded it long-wise, and flung it over the bite mark on his shoulder and under his arm like a bandage. The rest of him was completely naked.

"Better?" Nerves danced beneath his voice.

"Sure. If you're going for the sexy injured look." I cleaned the splashes of blood across his cheek and chin with my hand. "Please be quick and careful."

With a smile and a quick kiss that heated me, he darted toward the house.

I kneeled in the snow next to Talin, who breathed heavily and remained out of it. I rubbed his arms to keep the circulation going. "We'll find a solution. No real idea how." Staring into the forest from the direction we'd come, I sent my prayers to Rek's family. To his mistress, Gwenth, and their newborn child, who hopefully wouldn't be tossed out of the manor. *Goddess, please send them protection.*

And I hoped Ash and Leven were okay back in the woods. They would have transformed by now for sure, so were they headed back to the castle?

I waited for what seemed like an eternity, shivering not just from the cold, but from the idea that anyone who found Rek would raise the alarm. Would they blame the princes? Though, as Raze said, how could they prove who'd killed him?

As heartless as it sounded, my worries revolved around the dangers we all still faced as the full moon approached.

When the familiar clip-clop rhythm of hoofs hitting the ground reached my ears, I jerked to my feet, finding the black carriage passing the gates and leaving behind the manor.

"Oh, *damn*." My nerves twitched. He'd done it.

By the time Raze reached us, his face was blanked. "We have to leave now. They're sending out a search party for Rek."

I trembled and rushed to open the door. Raze carried Talin inside and set him down on a seat.

"Get in," Raze insisted as he jumped out. "I'll be out front to steer the horses out of here and fast." And just like that, my pulse jackhammered once again. I climbed inside the carriage. As soon as Raze shut the door behind us, we lurched forward, the rapid movement throwing me flat against my seat.

CHAPTER 23

Talin slept inside the carriage, unconscious, and in his human form. We'd covered him with two blankets for warmth. In the opposite seat, I curled up, my head in Raze's lap as he stroked my hair. Once we left behind the duchy once ruled by the duke, Raze joined Talin and I, insisting the horses knew the rest of the way home. Now, his soft touch calmed me.

"Who would look after that manor now, with Rek dead?" I asked out of curiosity.

"He has two sons who could step into the role, but under normal circumstances, I might spend time with them first and teach them how we want our lands ruled."

"Do you think Ash and Leven are all right?" I wasn't ready to face more terrible possibilities. Sleep tugged on my mind, and even the smallest thing seemed difficult.

"They're resilient, and I pray they are safe. When we changed, they would have transformed as well, and the curse would have driven them to bolt back to the castle." His tone darkened.

"I hope you're right." I swallowed past my dry throat. "We

lost the chance to break the curse." Anguish burrowed through me. "Rek would have stashed the cursed object in a private location. And with him now dead, I doubt we'd have the chance to scour the manor for secret compartments."

Talin still hadn't snapped out of his state or stirred. How hard had Raze hit him across the head? *Goddess, please aid his fast recovery,* and I pictured an invisible white bubble around him, sending him healing energies.

"It never occurred to me that Rek would bring a voodoo witch from Tritonia. I assumed someone local practiced dark magic."

"Rek was a fuckwit and let jealousy drive him to madness. He used to joke that if Talin didn't find a wife soon, he might challenge us for the throne. His father had always loathed our parents. He loved our mother and could never forgive losing her to our father." Raze sighed. "Dad would tell us that a kingdom will fall if all families are not in unison."

"There's always a relative who stirs problems, causes heartache for others." With only Dad and me left, I was lucky not to have that problem. But most of my friends had troublemakers in their families.

"True, but I think what my father had in mind was that despite squabbles, the king would bring all the other three dukes under the same direction. To provide a better life for all bear shifters in White Peak. Not that we'd squabble amongst ourselves for higher-ranked positions."

"Your father and I would have gotten along well."

Silence fell over us. We jolted about with every pothole we crossed over. Raze raked his fingers through my hair. Heaviness tugged on my eyelids.

I bathed in their company. Raze's caring nature showed, and Talin wasn't trying to eat someone.

* * *

THE WORLD SOFTENED BENEATH ME, and I startled awake. I opened my eyes and stared into Raze's smiling face. Behind him lay the fishnet material covering the four-poster bed I'd slept in the first night I'd arrived at the castle.

"How did I get here? Where's Talin? What about Ash and Leven?" Night still cloaked the sky outside, and I must have been in a deep sleep to not feel Raze carrying me indoors.

"It's all fine. Talin is in the cage with Ash and Leven in case he transforms again. I found the other two had crashed from exhaustion in the library. Ash loves that room, even when he's under a curse, it seems. So I carried them both and locked them in the cage. I worry they'll fight, but it's not as if I had any other option." Raze chuckled, his eyes creasing at the edges, and his fingers stroked my cheek. "It's late. Tomorrow will be long. Good night."

He pulled away, but I leaned the side of my face against his hand, kissing his palm. "Don't leave, please." After the insane day we'd had, I yearned to be held and forget how close we'd been to breaking the curse. I cringed because it felt as if we were starting from the beginning again.

Raze nodded without a hint of hesitation. "Move over." He kicked off his boots and took off his shirt.

An orange glow from the fireplace lit up his layers of muscles, which had me chewing on my lower lip. I unbuttoned my coat and shuffled my arms out of it. My dress had dried, even if was torn at the hem, but I didn't care when Raze got into bed alongside me. The mattress indented under him, and I rolled toward him.

I shifted to face away from him, and he pressed up against my back, spooning me. My head cradled on his bicep, and his hand slid around me, his musky scent comforting me. Raze seemed to calm my nerves with a single touch. Here, we could pretend we weren't facing the end of the world tomorrow night, but instead that I'd simply found the most amazing shifter, and he was into me too. All four of them affected me in the best possible ways, and it stole my breath each time I thought about losing them.

I wasn't sure I'd recover from such a loss, and that terrified me more than anything.

"You okay?" Raze asked, his sweet lips on my neck. "You're shaking."

I nodded, unable to find my words when it felt as if I was suffocating in my mind.

His arms coiled around me tighter, and he kissed the skin between my neck and shoulder. "I'll always protect you, Bee."

My next breath hiccupped, and the words poured out. "But what if—?"

"No. Don't think like that. I believe in you, in our future, in everything my parents built."

Swallowing past the boulder in my throat seemed an impossibility. "I want that too, but I'm scared."

His breath washed across my jawline. "Even if I only had an hour left in this world, I wouldn't want to spend it fretting."

Shuffling about on the bed, I turned to face him. "How do you push everything aside? My brain feels as if it might explode from the panic gripping me."

He placed a peck on my nose. "What's the use of worrying about something now if you can't do anything about it? Our problems aren't going anywhere, but don't carry the burden with you."

I chewed on the inside of my cheek. "Easier said than done, but I understand what you mean."

With his hand gliding up my arm, his other hand brushed across the top of my dress, and I gasped. "Sometimes," he teased, "a distraction might help with the stress." He offered me a devilish grin.

The moment his mouth brushed across mine, my world

faded. His attention eased away the knotted tension in my muscles. It shoved Lilita back into place quicker than any hour-long meditations could.

I slid a hand over his stubble, through his shoulder-length hair, and then drew him closer, deepening our kiss.

His fingers dug into my arm with urgency. "I've craved no one this much." He plucked at the drawstring across my bust, and I tingled all over.

"Take me," I purred. "Ever since I first met you, I fantasized about having you."

"Oh, I know." He winked, loosening my dress and sliding the fabric down a shoulder. "Remember, I read your story."

"Hey, that—"

He placed two fingers over my mouth. "Hush. Let me show you how that scene should have played out."

The smile splitting my lips sent a tingle to the pits of my libido, caressing me in all the right ways.

Raze's kisses swept over my chin and down my neck, leaving behind a trail of euphoria. He dragged the gown down my arm and chest, revealing a bare breast. He cupped my boobs.

"So sexy." He squeezed it lightly and licked my pebbled nipple.

I quivered beneath him.

When his lips clasped around my breast, his ravenous tongue flicked until I moaned. Fire scorched between my thighs and Goddess, I desired Raze like flowers depended on the sun. Under him, nothing could touch me, and before arriving at the castle, no other man had ever affected me the way these princes had.

Yanking the fabric farther down my body, he moved onto the next breast, paying it equal admiration. The whole time, his hands worked to undress me completely.

He broke free and lifted himself up and out of the bed,

shoving aside the fishnet fabric around us. "I love how you fill my hands, how your pink nipples tighten from my kiss. Now I want to see the rest of you."

I lay there, staring up at a god and the boner nestled against his pants, so I reached over and stroked him through his pants, then flicked open a button.

"No. No." He nudged my hand away. "We're doing this my way. Lift that sweet butt of yours." He grabbed hold of dress sitting at my hips along with my underwear and yanked them off me with such speed, I jolted and gasped from the force.

He tossed the gown over the bed, his roaming gaze never leaving me. With him standing at the edge of the bed, he collected me up to a sitting position by an elbow and kissed me with the passion of a starved bear. He leaned over me, strong and powerful, his heat burning me. Starting with my collarbone, he licked me in long strokes.

I trembled as he left a trail between the valley of my breasts, then back around each one, tugging on my nipples gently enough to have me squirming for something harder, quicker.

"You're driving me wild." I fisted his hair, moaning.

He laughed, the sound almost evil, but so sexy. "Patience." He continued zigzagging over my stomach, reaching farther below.

"I love that your auburn hair graces your sexy pussy." He pushed back up to stand and collected my ankles in each hand, hauling me across the bed until my butt perched on the edge. My chest tingled to high hell as he knelt in front of me. His hands slipped to my knees and widened them.

Excitement owned me as he studied me with smiling eyes. "Fucking gorgeous." He kissed the inside of my thigh and took tiny nips of flesh as he lowered himself deeper toward the apex between my legs.

"Gods, I'm ready to explode from your scent alone." With his hot breath over my sex, I collapsed onto my back, staring at the ceiling, my body thrumming.

When he ran a thumb down my silkiness, I arched, powerless to hold back much longer.

"So wet." He pried open my inner lips. "Remember that note I left you?"

I cranked my head up, loving the sight of Raze between my legs, his expression elated. "*Yeah.*" I breathed the word.

"Spread yourself wider for me. I have it bad for eating pussy and I can't get enough."

And before I could even react, his mouth latched around my sex, sucking and licking. I groaned, my pelvis grinding against him, begging for more.

His hands gripped my waist, and his slurping sounds drove me to an insatiable desire the likes of which I'd never known existed. Working his tongue over my clit, I writhed, unable to believe a hunk like Raze was going down on me.

The pressure on my libido tightened. But the moment he fingered me, I trembled with such ferocity, I couldn't think straight.

"Yes, please yes." I slid my hands to my breasts, plucking at my nipples, needing the release.

Raze's hand brushed them away, breaking his connection. "No, you're all mine."

My breaths heaved. "Raze. Fuck me."

His laughter rushed over me. "Scream my name as you cum." He bent down, driving my legs wider, and pierced me with his tongue, wriggling inside me.

My arousal balanced on a knife's edge, my hips grinding back and forth. His thumb rubbed my clit in circles. And right then, an orgasm detonated through me. I convulsed, screaming, clenching the bedsheets. "Raze! Oh my goddess. *Raze!*"

His face remained buried in my sex, and I clenched my thighs against his head as the pulsing sensation claimed me. With my throat raw and my pussy soaked, I lay there, spent.

My sexy beast of a shifter climbed to his feet, his chin and nose glistening. "Fuck, Bee. I have no plans of ever leaving your side, in this lifetime or the next. I am at your command." He gave me a slight bow of his head.

I laughed and snatched a pillow before tossing it at him. "You're crazy."

The pillow rebounded off his chest and he lifted his gaze, the most devilish grin widening his lips. He popped open the buttons on his pants, dropped them, and kicked the garment aside in record time.

But what stood in front of me had my jaw dropping open. "Oh, my." He was equivalent to Ash, but longer, and I shivered in anticipation.

"Approve?"

"Fuck yeah." I pushed myself up, reaching out to grab his hardened steel, an inferno to the touch. The flesh was silky and his tip wet with pre-cum. Lowering myself, I slid him into my mouth, tasting his saltiness, loving how he filled me.

"No, I'm too close. I need to be inside you." His hands on my shoulders drew me back, and I released him. Glancing up, his eyes glazed over with the look of euphoria.

"Well, then, you better come on down here." I curled a finger for him to join me.

He shook his head and offered me his outstretched hand. Without a word, I accepted, and we climbed off the bed, and he drew me against him, his hardness against my stomach.

His hands were on my waist, and he lifted me up with ease. "Hold on to me."

I gripped his shoulders and my legs wrapped around his hips. He cupped my ass, guiding me over his erection.

"Raze, I adore everything about you."

His kiss reached me, and I tasted myself on him. When his hardness pushed into me, I gasped for air. I wriggled to give him full access and he drove my hips farther down over him. I couldn't stop groaning as this shifter made love to me.

"Bee," he groaned. "I'm not letting you go, now or ever. You're mine." He thrust deep into me, and I lost myself.

I held on to his arms, and he pounded into me. I rode up and down on his cock. Excitement tore through me from his stare and the smell of our sex.

"Raze!" Already another second orgasm drove through me, and I trembled. There wasn't anywhere else in the world I'd rather be.

I drowned in his world, believing for those exhilarating moments I could have a future with the shifters. That somehow Raze would take me as his, just as the other princes would. And for the night, I let myself fall, knowing, in the end, that I would eventually hit the bottom and never recover.

CHAPTER 24

The morning sun beamed across Raze's face, the perfect curve of his stubbled jawline, the dip of his throat, and his delicious muscles. He lay naked, the blanket covering him to his waist. The fabric stuck up like a tent over his rock-hard member... and damn, what a divine muscle. After three orgasms last night, I'd fallen asleep in Raze's arms, spent and satisfied. But it was more than that. The way he'd taken his time to pleasure me, to kiss my neck until I giggled, and his possessive words had won me over. But what did they mean? Was it a promise all bear shifters made to swoon a female? I was fooling myself if I thought I could have a life here... with them. No, this was a fantasy and, as soon as the curse was broken, I'd go back to my life and they... theirs. A shooting pain hit my chest and I winced. Surely they'd get over me in a few weeks, but my heart would never truly recover from them.

With Talin stepping into the position of king, did that allow Raze the liberties of choosing a girl from a non-royal background? I adored Raze and his passion for anything he did. I kept thinking about him heading into the woods at night to help anyone in need. That was why he'd looked all hooded and brooding back in the tavern. It must be a normal escapade for him to be out and about, getting into brawls. And I'd be lucky to have any of the princes as mine. Ash with his sexiness that drove me insane, his caring nature, and his passion for learning — we could converse about herbs for weeks straight. Leven might have been cocky when I'd first him — though, admittedly, that roguish charm had swept me off my feet — but I'd seen the real man since, the man behind the bravado who wanted to settle down and have a family. Who loved hard and didn't hold back. And Talin, with his protective nature, caring for everyone, trying to pull the family together. Plus, he had that darker, dominant side to him that I couldn't get enough of.

How could anyone choose between the four princes? I'd take all of them if it were that easy.

My pulsed raced. They were out of my league. Scarlet had fallen for three wolf shifters, and I still recalled how adoringly they looked at her, as if they'd jump into the pits of the underworld to save her if needed. Which reminded me, if I got out of this in one piece, I intended to grill Scarlet on her experience in the Den realm as inspiration for a future story.

But I didn't want to engage in such thoughts. Not when it was a full moon tonight, and I stood to lose everything. So if I was delusional in letting myself believe they craved me for more than a night or two, then fuck it, I embraced them wanting me.

With pressure on my bladder, I inched out of bed in slow motion to avoid waking Raze. Each part of my body hurt from yesterday's battle, but the ache between my legs came from Raze's incredible attentiveness with his cock. Then again, Ash's had also been big and delicious. And I adored the way he'd made love to me.

After a quick bathroom stop, my mouth grew parched

and I eyed the cup of tea Raze had made me last night on the table near the couch. I drank it, even if it was cold. I dressed, figuring I'd check on the other men and make everyone breakfast. Considering the crap lying ahead of us, I wasn't ready to let dread creep into my chest. At least not until I had a full stomach. Then, I'd speed-read every book in the library if I had to until I worked out how to break the curse.

From the wardrobe, I selected a simple blue dress that reached my ankles and had long sleeves, cinched at the waist with a black belt. It reminded me of a few of my outfits at home, and it looked stunning even without layers underneath. I stepped into my boots and headed into the hallway.

Without another thought, I climbed to the third floor, hearing voices.

Inside, three men sat in the cage, nude and chatting.

Ash was the first to twist around to see me and he smiled.

"Finally," Talin said, and they all got to their feet, waiting to be released.

"How are you all feeling?" I crossed the room, noticing the new bruises, cuts, and bite marks on Talin's body. My heart bled at the memories of last night, how he'd hunted us and fought his cousin. Killed him. When he met my gaze, something shifted behind his eyes, an unspoken connection. Was he thinking about yesterday too? Had he told his brothers what had happened?

"Where's the key to the cage?" I asked.

Ash scratched his hair, making it stick upward. "On the back of the door. Hurry, because I need to pee like no man's business."

I retrieved the key and glanced at three sets of eyes. "Are you all okay, transformation-wise? No one has the urge to go furry or hunt?"

When no one said a word and they simply glared my way, I rushed to unlock them. "Sorry, just had to check."

"Everything hurts, even my toes," Talin said as he marched out, "and I've turned purple from my bruises. But I'm not sensing any other urges."

"Speak for yourself," Leven teased.

I caught his smirk and laughed.

Ash left the cage next, his hair ruffled.

"Morning, big boy." I winked.

There were no words needed because he navigated an arm around my waist and forced me against him, his lips on mine. He kissed me so deeply and passionately that I trembled beneath him. "I missed you," he whispered, and a flinch of guilt filled me from sleeping with his brother. What if they weren't okay with sharing?

Releasing me, he hurried out of the room behind Talin, and as Leven approached me, his expression fell serious. "Are you okay after yesterday? Talin told us everything."

I nodded. "It was insane, and so much happened."

Leven hooked an arm around my neck, smirking, and the sensation sent jolts of desire up my body. I reached for him, kissing him. His breath sped and his arms folded around me tightly and securely. I loved his tenderness. The way his tongue licked my lips, how he massaged my back, his fingers crawling down and over my ass. I craved each one of them. Leven's mouth glided to my ear, and he sucked on the fleshy earlobe.

"Your kiss helps control my transformation, but I'm thinking we need some alone time to be sure." He gripped his arms and wore his smug expression, then kissed me hard. My legs shook beneath me.

"I don't know if it's the effect of the curse bonding us, but I've been thinking about jumping your bones." I giggled and rolled my eyes at how sweet and innocent my voice sounded. Hell, the truth was the complete opposite, considering I'd flirted with and kissed four shifters... and had sex already with two. From the moments I'd first met each one, I'd wanted to be with them all.

He smirked. "I'm yours anytime."

"But you know it's not just lust — otherwise, I wouldn't adore the way you care for your brothers, how you put family first. Those are qualities of someone with love in their heart. And it drives me wild how you've recently been thinking about finding a wife to settle down with."

His brow arched, and he sighed. "Let me guess… Ash told you that?"

"Was he wrong?" I held Leven close, curious if he was the marrying kind.

"No. I've spent too long keeping to myself, unsure what my next move was. And I always came back to the happiness I missed… the same my parents used to have, because they supported each other no matter what. I want that too."

"Hell, yes! Don't we all dream of having someone special to share our lives with? I sure do."

His whisper of a smile had me snuggling up against him, even if his hardness pressed against me. I'd been getting used to their nakedness and not complaining one bit.

With another kiss, he took my hand and led me out of the room. "Let's get food first. I'm starving — and if I don't feed the beast, I might have to start on you first." He lifted my elbow to his mouth, and he nibbled on it.

I burst out laughing and batted him away. "That's for later."

"I'll see you in a moment." He vanished down a hallway and into a bedroom.

In the kitchen, Talin wore only pants and was beating a huge bowl of eggs.

Ash, also dressed, tossed logs onto the dwindling fire. Leven soon joined us and marched into the pantry room. He reemerged with half a loaf of bread and a tub, the edges lined with cheesecloth. With the cold, it wasn't as if they had problems with foods spoiling too quickly.

The atmosphere remained calm, as if it were any other day. No one brought up the dreaded topic of tonight when the curse would claim their lives. My knees bounced under the table, not wanting to think about it, either.

"Have you kissed Bee this morning?" Leven nudged Talin in the arm as he passed and made his way to the walk-in pantry. "To keep the curse in check, and because she tastes delicious." His laughter faded as he vanished into the room stacked with preserves and foods.

Heat climbed my cheeks. I didn't need them ordering Talin to make a move. If he wanted to, he'd do it when he was ready. Sure, back in the woods, I'd almost exploded with an orgasm brought to life by his passion, but there was this uncertainty between us, as if he were holding back. As the rightful king to the throne, he would have reservations, and I fully expected him to see me as a solution to his problem — no emotions involved.

Ash glanced my way and winked, his smirk reassuring, seemingly uncaring that Talin approached me.

"Is that okay?" he asked, offering me his hand.

"Yeah." My voice wavered, and I cleared my throat. "I don't need you all turning into uncontrollable beasts and hunting me down. Plus, it helps me manage Lilita." I laughed, feeling as if maybe I'd misinterpreted their affection as a need to control themselves. But then why did Leven share his emotions, or Ash, or Raze?

I accepted Talin's hand, which was soft in mine. He guided me out of the kitchen just as Raze waltzed in, his smile beaming. My heart palpitated at the way he stared at me with grinning eyes, and his gaze fell to our fingers intertwined. I froze at first, but I shouldn't have. Would he think I jumped from one man to the next without a care? A blaze climbed up my neck.

"Where are you two off too?" he asked and then leaned over, placing a peck on my nose as he groped my butt.

"Talin's getting his morning kiss," Ash said, breaking the white cheese into bite-size chunks. "But he's too shy to do it in front of us."

Raze roared with laughter, his eyes watering with amusement. "Come on. None of us have issues with sharing. Stop acting weird."

I did a double take in Raze's direction. They had no problems with them all sharing me, or was he referring to whole taming-the-curse thing?

Talin huffed and stuck out his chest. "Do you think I want to show you all my moves?" He whisked me outside into the hallway before shutting the kitchen door.

"I'm starved," Raze said from inside, but Talin drew me deeper into the corridor.

"Why are you so shy?" I asked. "I would never have guessed a future king would be that way. Especially with the way your brothers are."

"You mistake respect for shyness. I love my brothers. I won't get into a deep passionate kiss with a girl I admire in front of them. Not my style."

So he admired me, and here I thought he saw me as a means to an end. Though that hadn't stopped me from fantasizing about him too. Butterflies swarmed in my gut as if I were going on a first date. I followed him into a room with a chestnut table running down the middle and six chairs. Nothing else, not even a chandelier and candles. Sunlight poured in from the uncovered window, and beyond that lay a snowy landscape with pine and mountains in the distance. "Wow. That's beautiful."

Talin stood behind me, pushing his chest against my back,

and I inhaled his musky scent. His arms hooked around me. "Everything about the castle reminds me of my childhood. The festivals my parents would hold, the laughter booming throughout the halls. I'd hide in a different room when bedtime came to avoid going to sleep. My dad always found me and carried me to bed on his shoulders. That's the type of future I dream of for my family."

I leaned into his arms, loathing that Rek had dragged Talin into this mess. "I promise to do everything to make it a reality."

His kiss on my neck incited tingles that ran through my chest. "I wouldn't want anyone else helping us."

"But I made things worse, and couldn't stop you before you killed Rek. We could have forced him to tell us where the magical object from the curse was so we could break the hex."

"Sweetie, don't blame yourself." His fingers skimmed the fabric off my shoulder, his mouth finding the soft flesh, and I melted against him. "This whole situation is fucked. And I refuse to look at the past. We'll get through this. If us kissing and getting personal keeps the curse at bay, then the answer may lay there."

I nodded, unsure how to respond. But he was right. The solution lay in my magic drawing us together. Why else would tasting each other's blood have snapped Raze and me back to normal in the woods?

And while the easier solution might have been for Talin to taste my blood on my lips, I enjoyed this side of him better — sexy and unafraid to speak his mind.

He clasped my breasts, and my libido sparked. As if I hadn't had enough last night, a warm trickle of my desire coated my sex. Nope, this was definitely the best solution. And I wasn't complaining one damn bit.

The moan on my throat propelled Talin to spin me

around and face him. His mouth fell to mine, fast and desperate. Arousal shuddered through me, and I pawed at his bare chest. The overwhelming longing to have Talin take me clawed at my insides, rousing the inferno calming me.

"Talin," I cried.

His hands skipped to my hips, and he yanked my skirt up, bunching it around my hips, the coldness of the room a reprieve on my bare ass because I hadn't got dressed properly for the day yet. But the moment his fingers caressed my pussy, I moaned.

"One touch and I'm intoxicated." His chest expanded. He lifted me to sit on the table's edge. "If I'd known you weren't wearing any underwear, I would have ravaged you the instant I got out of the cage."

I fell back and arched in anticipation as he spread me. Before I replied, he crouched and took my sex into his mouth, devouring me, licking every inch. His tongue was silk, and my toes curled. Raw intensity rolled through me — breathing faster, pulse speeding.

My head rocked from side to side, a mewl escaping my lips.

He pushed two digits into me, pumping so fast, I raised my pelvis, meeting each thrust.

"I'm going to explode."

And with that, Talin pulled out, and I groaned. "What are you doing?"

He grinned, his handsome face taking on a different look from the usual solemn expression he'd worn for days. "I could stare at your pussy for eternity, the delicious folds and how they glisten."

Out of instinct, my knees come together, but he shook his head. "Keep them open. Show me all of your assets." He pushed them wider and stood back, staring. "Touch yourself for me."

I swallowed past the fire climbing me, but an inferno blazed through me. My palm traced down my chest, over my stomach, and grazed the curls between my thighs.

Talin dropped his pants and stepped out of them.

I couldn't stop admiring his thickness. Not only were these princes the most handsome men I'd ever met, but they packed a punch in their trousers. Equally.

"Don't stop," he demanded. "Open yourself."

As I lay on the table, I rubbed a finger down the middle of my slit, trembling from the sensitivity, and how much I craved to have Talin pound me. I pried open my inner lips. Just having a hunk like Talin watch my pussy while I stroked myself, turned me on beyond measure. I shook, and my gut clenched.

"Please, Talin." How quick had he brought me to arousal?

Without a word, he edged his tip into me, while his hands collected my legs and placed them against his chest and over his shoulder.

When he plunged into me, I exploded with a scream. The forcefulness coupled with his size left me convulsing with excitement. He hammered fast and deep, grasping my waist.

Barely able to keep up with my racing heart, I gasped for air, drowning beneath his attention. Needing more, I moaned louder. And Talin didn't back down or stop.

Something inside me gripped my libido. And in an instant, my orgasm unleashed. My skin tingled in a frenzy.

I screamed with the most satisfying euphoria rattling through me, my inner walls squeezing Talin as he slammed into me once more before grunting, pulsing. His eyes were on me, with a new look of admiration, as if he saw me for the first time.

After a long pause of us gasping for air, he said, "Is it wrong of me to dream of keeping you forever?"

I gasped for air, convinced he was high on sex. "You don't know what you're saying."

"Maybe not, but right now, I could marry you."

And with those few words, he'd undone me. Not only had he said what I'd desired to hear, but a sharpness pierced my heart. Every moment I spent with the princes carried me closer to them. Made me crave them and fantasize for a future that might never exist.

CHAPTER 25

*B*y the time Talin and I returned to the kitchen, everyone had vacated the room. Scrambled eggs on bread remained on a plate, and Talin had already helped himself, and I joined him.

"Where are they?" Had they transformed? There wasn't any roaring from deeper in the house and they would have busted in on us in the other room if they'd turned. Part of me worried that they'd listened in on Talin and me doing more than just kissing… Were they pissed, or jealous? I struggled to keep my emotions in check or understand what the men thought about our relationships. Not that I'd call it that, yet the idea of losing them left me hollow, which was stupid. Yet in their company, they made me happier than I'd been in the longest time. They calmed me, had me laughing, aroused me to no end, and I adored our conversations. But none of that would matter if I didn't find a solution. The full moon arrived tonight, and a shiver gripped me.

Talin smacked his lips with food and was at my side, embracing me. "You look pale."

I nodded but said, "I'm fine; just need to eat." Trepidation

211

wormed through me, and I ate my meal, staring at the herb book still there from yesterday.

Talin's strong hand rubbed my back, and he pulled up next to me and dragged my chair with me in it closer to him. "We're all scared of tonight. But we've got each other."

"What if we fail?" My throat tightened, and panic clawed up my spine. I fumbled with the cord on my dress. "You all die and I turn into Lilita forever, killing everyone in my path." Hiccupping, I blinked fast to keep the tears at bay. This wasn't the time to break down or lose myself to what-ifs. Yeah, my logical brain made easy sense of the obvious, yet my heart bled, and I gasped for air to fill my strangled lungs.

"Take slow breaths. You're not alone. The four of us adore you so much, Bee. More than you could imagine, and in the past few days, you've touched each of us in different ways. I can't speak for the others, but I'm falling for you." His voice deepened and took on a serious tone.

I lifted my chin, his face blurring behind tears. "Goddess. Why would you say that when I'm already struggling with losing you?" Whatever happens, I wasn't an idiot to think the princes of White Peak would take a mere human as their partner and share me. I almost laughed out loud at how ridiculous it sounded. I'd be the luckiest woman in the world if I had one of these men in my life, yet I cried for all four.

Talin wrapped me in a warm embrace of his chest and arms. "You've got the biggest heart of anyone I've ever met. That's one reason I'm drawn to you."

I softened against his hard muscles, adoring his way he ran his hand over my head.

He was right... time wasn't on our side, and as much I wanted to hide and pretend we weren't up against the odds, I had to pull myself together. With a deep breath, I looked up at Talin. He studied me with a smile that reached his eyes.

"Remember," he said, "No matter what happens, you've

already won over our hearts. There's nothing you can do that will disappoint us."

I nodded and wiped my eyes. "Thank you." Dozens of ideas fluttered across my mind, but they blended into a fog. This wasn't an ordinary transformation. The hex came with an expiration date — they were all going to die when the full moon reached its highest point in the night sky unless I stopped it. Would my efforts be enough?

Talin kissed my wet cheeks and climbed to his feet, taking my hand in his. He consoled me, yet he was about to lose everything, his family line wiped out, and his brothers gone.

The time for feeling sorry for myself ended now. "I'm going herb hunting in the greenhouse. Hoping to find sage and rue." I hugged him. "Thank you."

"I'll find the others and we'll meet you in the library. We have books on every topic in the world. There has to be an answer we haven't thought of yet."

I trekked outdoors and entered the glass house, and the snowy iciness on my skin melted. Vegetables, fruit trees, ripe vines, and other greenery surrounded me, some covered by a white cloth to help the plants avoid frostbite.

Once I reached the two bronze benches where I'd first met Ash, I searched the rows of plants around me, surprised by the lack of herbs. I eyed the wooden stem of the roses Ash had planted in a dozen pots. They huddled close near the glass wall. His belief was that one day they'd grow again — it was a way for him to connect with his lost family members on an emotional level, I assumed. And I understood, as I still kept Mom's button collection, for no reason other than she collected them and every time I stuck my hands in the jar, I'd hear her in my ear telling me not to drop them.

I crouched down next to a stem and prodded the soil. Dark and moist. Looked healthy. The outer layer of the stem remained green, as if it were fresh. If Ash was right, and these were ten years old, then there had to be magic still in the flowers from when they'd first been created.

The stem was bumpy under my touch.

"A complete waste of time," Ash grumbled from behind me.

I flinched, and my finger pricked a thorn. "Ouch." With my cut finger in my mouth, I tasted the coppery flavor and lifted myself to face Ash.

"You okay?" he asked.

"Damn thing stabbed me." I showed him my injury and it must have been deep, as a fresh droplet rolled down my skin. Ash was there, and he kissed the tip of my cut and licked it clean.

He brushed past me and crouched near the flower. "Got to be careful. Some still have thorns."

I joined him, gawking at my blood snaking down the stem in slow motion. The soil hungrily absorbed it.

Ash nodded, inspecting his plant with such dedication. He loved those roses, and his passion made me adore him even more.

When he looked my way, I stole a kiss. "You're so cute," I said. "But your glasshouse is missing something."

"And what's that?" He tilted his head to the side, studying my lips. Was he considering kissing me?

"You have no herbs in your garden."

He tapped his nose. "You're looking in the wrong place. They're all the way at the back on the shelves, after the berry bushes."

"Of course they are." At the rear, I found an array of herbs from hyssop to myrtle to thyme.

"I'll leave you here," Ash said, hugging me from behind and kissing my head. Then, he vanished, and I turned to the herbs, figuring I'd make as many spells as I could remember, taking into account everything I'd learned. We were dealing with a bitch of a curse crafted with death magic. Nothing like tackling the impossible.

* * *

THREE POTENTIAL CONCOCTIONS done and yet bile bubbled in my gut, and with each passing moment I spent in the greenhouse trying to create a solution, my chest constricted. I'd never read about such a complicated enchantment involving various individuals. Add to that mix, my magic *and* Lilita's. As much as it terrified me, my thoughts kept pointing in one direction. Could tapping into Lilita's dark powers offer a possibility of counteracting the curse? Except I had zero idea how to do that without releasing her. And she would not save the men, only herself. Then she'd go on a rampage.

I stared down at my palms, wishing I'd learned to better manipulate magic, not only to control what lay inside me. Most spells I worked came from books, and they usually worked amazingly. But Mom used to put things together from thought alone, while I memorized them to look like I knew what I was doing. Half the time, I was terrified of trying something different in case I opened the portal to my darkness. Sticking to safe spells had kept everyone around me protected.

Mom would say my fear blocked me from spreading my wings. Maybe she was right, but for too long I'd lived with dread, and now I didn't know how to free myself.

I collected the small bowls of paste I'd created and crossed the greenhouse when something red caught my attention, and I turned my head.

My sights landed on a tiny red rose, blossoming on a new branch where the stem had jabbed me.

I stood frozen, trying to make sense of what I was looking at. That wasn't there before.

Ash had said his ancestor had used blood and enchantment to create these snow roses, and how everything he'd tried to regrow them had failed. But did they normally grow this fast?

In the herb book, there was a section on the power of rose petals. A shudder rocked me. These flowers had the most positive vibration of any living thing. And, coupled with these specific ones being borne through magic... What else did it say about them?

Hope burst across my chest. I dumped the bowls in my hands on the ground, grabbed the smaller pot with the flower, and sprinted back into the house.

I took a detour to the kitchen, snatched the book I'd left there, and made a dash toward the library. Juggling the plant and the book, I shoved open the door with a shoulder.

Ash and Talin were upstairs, while Leven sat a table, his nose in a book. There was no sign of Raze.

"I found something," I yelled, plonking the stuff in front of Leven. "This might help us." My voice squeaked, and I bounced on my toes, the earlier dread dissected by the joy.

"What is it?" Ash and Talin said in unison, huffing as they rushed closer.

Raze appeared from behind the stairs, but Ash had already gasped and pointed to the plant. "Fuck! It grew a flower."

"Yes," I said. "But remember how I cut my finger on a thorn?"

"Your blood awakened the plant?" Raze blurted out. "How does that help us?"

I pulled up a chair and flipped through the fat book until I landed on the page about roses. "Here, it says to use crushed petals to reverse a spell." I glanced across at the men, who clearly weren't believers, judging by their arched brows and pinched lips. "I saw this before, but thought nothing of it since we had no roses and half the stuff in here talks about curing an ailment. But now we have a plant we know grows with magic and reacted to my blood, like Raze did in the woods. What if this helps? It could purify us of the curse and energize me to control Lilita."

Leven's brow creased. "It says that in there?" He leaned over my shoulder.

"It doesn't talk about an enchanted rose," I said. "But combined with my ability, this spell might work. Mom often grew normal roses around the house, insisting they kept the property purified and clear of evil."

"We all need to take baths with the rose petals," Leven explained.

"Together or each of us with Bee?" Raze asked, smirking.

I pulled the book back and read the passage about the cure needing petals from twelve red roses.

"Sounds easy enough," Talin said.

I swallowed the boulder in my throat and stared at the men. My knees bounced under the table.

They all nodded without a word exchanged. Getting my hopes too high was out of the question, but this was the closest thing to a potential cure I'd found.

"Okay, so I guess I need to now donate blood. Who's coming with me to the greenhouse?"

CHAPTER 26

*L*even gasped and nudged me in the arm as another rose blossomed before our eyes. Red petals unraveled outward, springing from the bud's green casing and spreading its wings.

"I could never tire of watching them grow. Beautiful. I remember Dad used to spend hours in the greenhouse pruning the roses," Leven said.

The candles on shelves around the greenhouse threw shadows about while outside night had settled over the landscape. Strangely, the rest of the day had flown past without a single incident of me or the princes transforming. I'd researched the books for backup spells with no luck. It almost felt as if the universe had given us our last day of reprieve before snuffing away our lives. Still, my pulse was a raging bull.

Last I saw, the other men were moving a huge porcelain tub from inside the house to the backyard, as we had to be outside for moon magic. It was a bath that could easily fit all five us, and if I had known such a large tub existed, I would have taken a dip on my first night at the castle.

Leven's fingers intertwined with mine, his thumb caressing the back of my hand. "So what now?" Despite his stature and half-smile, I heard the quiver beneath his words. No one had spoken about their fear, but it lingered at the forefront of my mind. I could tell because of how everyone stared off into the distance now and then while they ran around to keep busy. What was lacking were the jokes and laughter.

"We make a paste out of half the roses. The rest we need to leave whole," I explained.

Without a word, Leven started dividing the pots at our feet between us. I crouched and gently pulled the delicate red petals free, placing them in my bowl. By the time we'd finished, I'd crushed mine into paste. Leven and I grabbed everything, and we traipsed outside.

A dusting of snowflakes fell from the heavens, and the cold closed in around me. I trembled. Overhead, a heavily pregnant moon scaled the sky, glorious and with a silvery tinge.

A light tingle wriggled down my arms, and on cue, the goddess's warning shivered down my spine. *I'm well aware of the danger headed my way, Goddess. If there was ever a time for your intervention, it's now. And if you do, I promise to never pester you again with inconsequential things like finding the right date for the town ball or helping Dad sell an invention.*

I hiccupped my next breath. *I'm not ready to die, or be replaced by Lilita.*

By the time we reached the rear of the castle, we stood on an open balcony, staring out over a snow-covered maze made of oversize hedges. I'd always dreamed of entering one of these — and there were so many other things I wanted to experience in life. Travel the world. Earn enough money to let Dad focus on his inventions in peace. Find a man or four who loved me for who I was. *And, Goddess, as I face my mortality, I've come to the realization that I do want children, to grow old, and enjoy life. To stop hiding behind fear. So, just saying... any help would be appreciated.*

Leven and I took our time going down the steps to avoid slipping on the slick surface and set our bowls next to the huge porcelain tub. This was more of a pool than a bath. Wooden steps rested against one side offered an easy way to get into the water. A fire burned on either side of the tub and warmed up the bath. Steam curled upward from the glimmering surface, and the snow falling inside melted in an instant.

Leven cuddled up against my back, his arms wrapped around my stomach. I leaned against him, and my words fell out, as if I had no control of them. "I'm scared of losing all of you, of never seeing my dad again, of unleashing Lilita onto the world."

His cheek grazed the side of mine, our breaths floating in front of us. "Don't think like that. We will succeed. Grab hold of that and let your ability shine." That time, his voice strengthened, and it filled me with power.

I turned toward him, desperate to accept his words, to empty my mind of worries. "You're right." Mom hadn't raised me to fall apart. She'd told me to face the world without hesitation, do anything I wanted. I had to believe in myself and harness my confidence.

Lifting my chin, I met Leven's mouth. Our lips pressed together, bonding, reminding me how much all four princes had affected me since first arriving in White Peak.

"Hey, what about me?" Raze teased. When I twisted my head left, he rushed closer with arms open and hugged Leven and me. "We've got this. Nothing will get in our way."

The crunch of snow came from my right. Ash smirked and strolled over, then joined our huddle. The men's warmth flooded me. "This isn't the end," Leven added.

"Talin," Ash howled. "Get over here. Group hug."

Before I could turn, Talin stood behind me, his body glued to mine. They crowded around me, showering me in their heat, their scents, their love.

"Bee, you burst into our lives like a storm," Talin began. "But now I can't imagine not having you by our sides. If my brothers and I don't make it out of this, I've prepared and signed a decree that makes you the sole owner of our castle and all belongings. You won't have any authority to rule over White Peak, but I am giving you everything we own, so you and your father will never endure hardship again."

His words weren't sinking in at first and they twirled through my head. "What are you talking about?" I turned to face him amid the closed in walls of four bear shifters. "I will *not* let any of you die."

Talin kissed my mouth, soft and endearing, his hand against my cheek, shaking. "It's a precaution, sweetie. There are no guarantees in life, but if anyone has a stronger chance of surviving tonight, it's you. And I want to leave you something to remember us by."

Rage pumped through my veins, loathing his words, because with them came defeat. And if I lost all four princes, how I could ever walk the halls of the castle without remembering our adventures, or enjoy a meal in the kitchen without recalling their laughter and jokes?

"No." I pushed my way out of the group, and tears pricked the corners of my eyes. "Don't you get it? If I lose any of you, and by some miracle I survive, part of me will die tonight. I'd never be able to step foot in the castle again."

Talin stretched an arm out in my direction. "We just want to rest easy knowing… Knowing you'll be okay."

"We want to provide for you," Raze added.

Leven pushed his hair off his face, and I adored the way

his eyes melted when he looked at me. "Sugarplum, don't you understand? We've all fallen so hard for you."

My heart shattered into pieces. They were offering me security in case they lost their fight, and they were smiling, while inside I was falling apart. Tears drenched my cheeks. I wanted to scream, run — anything to stop what might come our way, but I knew it was fruitless. I clenched my hands so hard, my nails dug into my palms.

"I've given you my heart," Ash said, placing a palm on his chest.

The ragged beating of my pulse rattled me. My heart iced over, feeling as chilled as an iceberg. They had no right to say those things, not now, not when anything could happen. I'd prefer to think they showed me the affection to keep their beasts at bay, nothing else. That I could live with… but having all four of them stare at me with admiration, and admitting their emotions were deeper and waiting for me respond… It was too much.

My throat thickened, unable to take enough air into my lungs. *Goddess, help me!* Agony squeezed my stomach with invisible claws. I needed to say something, give my farewells should shit fly sideways.

A chorus of shouting carried on the wind from the front of the castle.

I shuddered, my thoughts flying to Rek's family sending an army after us. Had they found the body and were coming for revenge? I had no idea who'd shouted. We were already in danger from the curse, let alone someone else coming for us.

"What the fuck was that?" Raze didn't wait for a response and vanished around the side of the castle. Leven took the other side, along with Talin.

Ash grabbed my arm, his fast breath screaming dread, and he dragged me toward the stairs, leading us through the rear doors.

But a surge of power sizzled through me as if someone had punched me. I gasped and folded over, my knees buckling, my arm falling loose from Ash's grip.

Pain seared through me and burned down to my hands, as if I'd thrust them into a fire. I screamed as the agony increased in waves.

Energy crackled across my fingers like barbed wire whipping my hands.

My heart clanged against my breastbone, and fear engulfed me, knocking all thoughts aside.

Bee! Lilita's voice reverberated in my skull over and over, in a maddening chant. My nightmare had just awakened.

CHAPTER 27

*H*olding my middle, I pushed past the darkness spreading through me. I scrambled across the snowy lawn behind the castle, my eyes focused on the bowls with rose petals. The moon sat right above us, and I had expected a buildup, a warning, but the curse had hit like a storm. Ready to smite us.

"Ash!" I cried out. "It's happening now."

His footfalls grew heavy and sluggish behind me, his breaths wheezing. I fumbled with the rose petals in a bowl and pressed it into his hand.

"Put them into the water." My words raced.

His eyes glazed over, and his body shimmered with the telltale signs of the onset of his change.

I clenched his coat in my fists and dragged him closer, kissing him, hoping to buy us a few moments so I could gather the rest of the princes. Our lips merged, soft against me, starved… but nothing. Not a spark. I found emptiness.

We broke apart and panic crawled across his gaze. "It's not working."

Coldness tightened my throat. My thoughts flew to the

woods when I'd kissed Raze with blood in his mouth, how quick we'd healed. I pulled the knife from my belt and without a single thread of hesitation, I slashed the meaty part of my palm, the blade biting into flesh. I gritted my teeth through the sting and stuck on the wound. The distinct coppery taste inundated my senses.

"Try again," I yelled.

Ash gripped my shoulders and our lips locked. He took my tongue into his mouth, devouring me, and I trembled from his assertiveness.

But there was still nothing, and I pulled away, my stomach churning. "Goddess!" Tears stabbed my eyes.

"Why isn't it working?" He grabbed the knife out of my grasp and cut his hand. He pulled me to him once again, but even before we kissed, a sickening sensation flooded me as Lilita grew stronger in my head.

"Fuck!" Ash broke away, growling and swaying on his feet.

"Get in the water. Add the petals," I hissed, but my knees buckled out from under me. My head sang with Lilita's humming.

Ash, still holding on to the bowl of rose petals, grabbed my arm and hauled me up the steps toward the bath.

In that moment, the three princes careened out from the edge of the castle. They ran along the stone veranda and down the steps.

They were shouting something, their bodies flinching and convulsing. Each step had them stumbling. A paralyzing fear owned me as my mind emptied on what to do next. The corners of my eyes blurred, and at once, an invisible force ripped me backward and away from Ash.

I tumbled to the ground.

Ash tethered sideways and tripped into the water. The bowl in his arm tossed upward. Red petals flew everywhere. Half of them landed into the bath, the rest on the snow.

Fear shook me, but I couldn't lose everything. Not after Mom. Scrambling to my feet, I collected as many petals as I could find, then threw them into the water. Ash, still shaking, stumbled up and over the edge, falling onto his side and groaning. He got to his hands and knees and reached for the rest of the petals.

I wobbled on my feet, my head spinning.

Mom had always controlled her emotions during a spell, insisting they interfered with the enchantment's intention. But I couldn't stop the terror leaching to my insides. Nearby lay the bowl of crushed-up roses. I ran my fingers through the cold sludge and smeared the mixture over my palms.

Lilita drummed in my skull, but I sank back on my heels and called forward my own powers. "Goddess, I call upon your guidance. Your strength."

In the face of no reaction, I raised my voice and summoned the force lying deep in my chest, the pure white light that always engulfed me kept me safe and fueled my ability.

A faint trickle washed over my fingertips, but it sizzled with black lines that bounced over my fingers.

Terror rattled me at the core.

Lilita rammed forward.

But so much hung in the balance. Dad's face floated in my thoughts, followed by the princes'. I bit down on my lip until I tasted blood. "With the purity of the snow rose, I cleanse you, Lilita," I repeated the words.

A violent shiver tangled through me, shaking me.

Lilita remained in my ear, shrieking, and I could have sworn she stood right next to me. But I never stopped chanting.

Movement caught my eye and I saw the princes contorting, their bodies stretching, bones cracking, skin splitting. Ash was by their side, hauling Leven toward the water. But his legs buckled under him, and he growled into the night.

There was movement near the house. I glanced at the top of the steps and spotted a group of ten men, their shadows stretching out behind them. Who were they? My insides constricted. We didn't need additional complications.

Without a pause in my chant, I watched Ash get to his feet and shove his brothers, one at time, toward the tub.

"Bee! There she is! Save her." The voice rang in my ears... so familiar.

Leven exploded into a roar, then two others followed. Ash collapsed, his body stretching, elongating. His cries tore me apart.

My palms burned, and I stared down at the black threads twisting tight around my fingers except, where I'd cut myself earlier, the wound had healed and the lightest trickle of white sparked.

"Bee!" The voice came again, but Lilita thrashed inside me as if I had swallowed a serpent that now battled for escape.

"I call upon the goddess of light. Cleanse me. Purify me."

The newcomers ran down the stairs. The glow from their flaming torches illuminated them. They wore the gray Terra guard uniforms.

Then their faces came into focus. The dicks who'd bullied Dad and... his face. The cropped hair. Tristan!

I shouldn't have cared, but his presence left me twitching. No one knew I did magic, and here I was with glowing hands as if I'd been hit by lightning. But that wasn't the problem at all. It was that I had my princes to save, and no time to deal with an over-domineering ex.

"Bee," Tristan yelled. "I've come to save you. I've thought hard about us, and I will change for you. Marry me."

Stunned at first, I couldn't believe he'd think that after

coming to my rescue, I'd fall over myself to accept his proposal. Never happening, even if he was the last man alive.

"Go back home," I cried out. Idiot would get himself killed.

The princes' growls quaked through the air. Even in their warped half-bear forms, they shuddered. The end was near.

The curse would kill them.

"Beasts!" Tristan bellowed, taking a knife from his belt as she scanned the ground where my four princes writhed, deformed and fighting the curse. "Kill all the beasts."

Dread locked my gut, and my world faded in and out.

Darkness pressed in on me, stealing my vision. I kicked and punched, needing to escape Lilita's hold. I slid back to reality, then back into the pits of the underworld in my mind. I caught flashes of the guards attacking the bears.

I screamed, my chest burning with anger, ready to explode. "Stop! Tristan, no!"

Bee! Lilita sang in my ears.

I threw myself on hands and knees, remembering that Ash had dropped the knife. I patted the snowy ground as my vision seesawed back and forth. I found the rose mixture and scooped some into my mouth. The bitter taste was slippery and gross, but for those few moments, Lilita flinched to the recesses of my mind.

Something silver glinted up ahead, and I scrambled for the weapon. I snatched the knife and slashed the blade across my forearm. Swallowing past the sharp pain, I coated blood onto my hand still caked with the rose paste.

"Cleanse me!" I cried out. "Eradicate Lilita. Purify the princes."

To my left, a guard hovered over a fallen Leven, gripping a knife. Coldness rocked me, then fire surged and gushed from my palm. The energy jutted outward, white and black sparks intertwined. They struck the guard in the chest, throwing him off-balance. He landed with a thud, convulsing.

The last tendrils of power drained and fizzled. Exhaustion had me teetering on the spot. I was running out of time.

I staggered up, and a darkness swept through me once again like a tsunami, swallowing my thoughts, my emotions.

Talin lunged and chomped on a guard's arm. The man howled. But Tristan was coming up behind the prince. He leaped up and drove a punch at his back.

Talin wailed and collapsed.

My heart throbbed with dread, and I cried out, "Tristan, please stop!"

The others battled with savagery; teeth, fur, and blood. Chaos.

Fear buried me, and I pushed up. My body spiraled with overtiredness. One leg in front of the other, I approached the fight and raised my arms. "Goddess, fill me with your ability."

Nothing came out. No pop or flicker.

Lilita hummed in my ears once more, unrelenting.

A sense of hopelessness enveloped me, my muscles aching at my inability to keep Lilita back. Yet I didn't stop trying, and I staggered toward the guards, needing to protect my princes.

Tears drenched my cheeks as a guard drove his boot into Raze's gut. His chest heaved with each breath. Talin wobbled on his feet, and five guards circled him.

Overhead, the moon shone like a beacon, but it wasn't a salvation, only death.

Lilita crowded my mind, shrieking, deafening me. In my haste, I tripped over my own legs and fell into the snow. But I hurried back up, rushing toward the men who'd captured my heart.

Maybe it wasn't too late if I could get them into the water

and try the reversal spell. "Goddess, please, I beg for your help."

Tristan slammed into Talin, and my prince grunted, folding over.

Rage owned me, and a sudden explosion of pain seared down my arms. I unleashed it from my palms, striking all the guards. They all fell over at once, including Tristan.

An invisible wall of fatigue smacked into me. I wavered as my vision danced.

I gulped for air and found Talin staggering back up, half-bear, bloody, and bruised. The wind pulled at his hair, one sleeve still hanging on an arm but the rest of him was naked.

"Talin," I called out.

He turned in slow motion, his mouth agape, and my gaze fell to the blade stuck in his gut. Talin's eyes rolled back, and he collapsed.

I screamed, my throat raw. "No!" Terror tore my heart to pieces, and tears gathered in my eyes. The other bear shifters weren't moving, either. Talin lay on the ground, still.

Each breath rattled my lungs, but I hurried to Talin. They had to survive. Skidding next to him, I cupped his face, warm to the touch. He gasped for air, gurgling. Blood trickled out from the side of his mouth.

A jolt of desperation took me. I tapped into my reserves, remembering who I was. A bloodborne. The curse was moon-related, straddled between light and dark. Magic coursed through my veins.

I controlled my destiny. I had the ability to do anything. *Don't fight who you are*, Mom would tell me.

Yet I'd never understood what she'd meant, terrified of working with the darkness and Lilita taking over.

Her magic was stronger. She'd snapped the princes out of their transformation states with a single zap from her enchantment.

My princes were dying.

Despite the terror chewing on me, I raised my hands and pinpricks fluttered down my flesh. I imagined myself pulling back the shackles I'd worn for years to keep Lilita controlled, tearing back the layers, and stood there vulnerable.

I opened myself to the darkness.

Lilita shuddered through me, gushing out like a starved wolf. I flinched but instead of crumbling, I inhaled the darkness. Mom's words swamped my head about accepting who I was. Tears rolled down my cheeks. Numbness owned me, and my heart battled between fighting and staying open to Lilita's magic.

I concentrated, grinding my teeth, curling my fists. Earlier, our threads of energy, light and dark, had woven together.

That was the answer: working as one, not divided. Without Lilita taking over.

Summoning every ounce of strength forward, I felt the tendrils creeping along the surface of my skin. "No division. One person. One magic. One heart."

Lilita's scream boomed and talons clawed at the inside of my skull.

"Goddess of the moon, I draw upon your help. Unify me. Empower me." Adrenaline awakened in my body as every inch of me cracked with sharpness. Golden light struck down from the heavens, rotating around my arms, sliding down my body. A scream of pain pierced through me. My head yelled to run, but I'd done that my entire life.

The light burned, and I wailed.

The ground shook and black serpents slithered upward, curling up my legs and hips.

No more fear. I was finishing this now.

"Unify me. Empower me." I chanted over and over, biting past the sensation of drowning.

I shook, unable to feel where I started and ended. Half of me scorched with fire; the other froze with ice.

"Unify me. Empower me," I sobbed.

The two opposing energies collided above my heart and shattered outward into a brilliant light, blinding me, cutting through me. I screamed from the sharpness spearing into me, as if someone were dissecting me into thousands of pieces.

Gasping for a sliver of air, I hit the ground. My ears rang with each heartbeat. Thumping. Pounding.

Stars twinkled in the tapestry overhead and the moon hung low, almost glowing. Each breath I took rasped in my lungs.

Within me, an inferno blazed. But it felt different from before, less smooth and warming. Now it came with thorns. And not a single sensation of Lilita stirred. Had the goddess driven her away or had I merged our magic?

Rolling onto my side, I stared at Talin, his eyes wide open, not breathing.

I scrambled to his side. Butchered bodies riddled the land, including Tristan. Their chests rose and fell with each breath... thank the goddess he was still alive. I recalled how rudely I'd spoken to him, then stolen his horse. Those memories would have stayed with me forever if I'd killed him. He was controlling, manipulative, and made a terrible boyfriend, but he didn't deserve to die.

My gaze shifted to the fallen princes, who lay motionless, and a strangled cry pressed against my throat. A shear nothingness took hold of me as I stared at my four shifters, and I choked on my tears. My reversal spell had cursed Talin's brothers. Now I'd delivered them to their deaths. I sank to my knees next to Talin.

"Please, come back." I shook his shoulders. My chest constricted and crushed my ribs. I remembered the way he would stare at me with desire in his eyes. I locked that away for eternity.

Tears flooded my cheeks. I shouldn't have survived without them. Not like this, never like this.

I reached a shaky hand for Talin's chest. Fire singed my insides, but I refused to believe that this was the end. A crack of energy pinched my skin, and I forced my magic down my arm. It danced across my fingers, the tethers twisting together. At once, it speared into his chest, and I jolted from the impact.

He didn't respond, and I broke out into a desperate cry. I couldn't be too late.

Popping sparks of dark and white flames encased my hands. I lifted myself and raised my arms. "Lift my princes. Ash, Talin, Leven, and Raze."

Power pebbled through me, and each of their bodies elevated. *Focus.* I lifted my arms and guided the men toward the tub. Two at a time, I placed them inside, in a sitting position. "Stay upright."

And they did as I commanded, the water lapping at their necks, without an herb in sight, just as Lilita had done. Darkness spread within my chest, swirling together with the light, as if together they balanced one another to perfect harmony. Had I been wrong to believe I only needed one side?

Had I fought against Lilita because the unknown had scared me when the whole time she'd just been a part of me...?

Hell. She *was* me! My power divided.

I shoved that aside and ran to my princes, tears dripping down my cheeks. But I couldn't fall apart yet. I collected the bowl with what remained of the rose paste, then climbed into the cool water.

My hands shook as I reached Talin and yanked out the blade sticking out of his stomach. Blood gushed forth, pouring from his body like a dam had burst, tainting the water. Had I been too late to save them?

Not thinking, just focusing as Mom used to, I sliced my wrist and dropped the knife. I blinked to clear my dancing vision, and emptiness swirled through me. Blood trickled into the water, spreading outward, and I collected blood into the bowl I still held. I mixed it with the rose contents. Dizziness swirled through my brain.

No time. I approached each prince and smeared the paste onto their cheeks and lips, pushing some into their mouths. A swirl of red trailed me, and the world tilted.

I clasped my earlier cut on my arm to my lips, tasting myself, swallowing the blood.

I cried out, "Heal my princes. Take my blood and bestow it upon them. Give them life."

A new force prickled across my skin, different, yet similar, as if it had always been there within my reach.

"Princes." My voice shook. "Return to me."

I lowered my palms into the water and a golden charge sparked. At once, the jagged lines of magic shot outward, grasping the shifters in its hold, and the bright light streamed out of the bath, racing across the yard in every direction, as far as I could see, at lightning speed.

A violent current pulsed through me, and I convulsed, my nerves shuddering. My vision darkened. For once, it wasn't fear that embraced me. That was a most welcome change.

* * *

COLD WATER LAPPED AGAINST ME, and someone was shaking my shoulder.

"Is she awake?"

The world revolved as memories slammed through me. I snapped open my eyes.

Four princes looked down at me, each with dread in their gazes. Behind them the sun shone, giving them a halo glow… had we all died and now awoke in the afterlife?

The lump in my throat swelled at seeing the men who filled me with life. The earlier darkness had vanished and now a flicker of hope swept through my mind. I hadn't lost my shifters.

Leven collected me into his arms out of the freezing water. "You're alive, sugarplum."

I rubbed my eyes and scanned the castle grounds. The Terra guards who'd attacked the castle last night were groaning and pulling themselves up, as if they hadn't been injured or beaten.

"No one's dead!" I stated. Had the energy that had shot out from me healed them completely, just as it had my princes?

Confusion knotted through me, and I stared over at Talin's stomach. "Your stabbing injury. It's healed!"

He ran a hand across his skin where he'd been stabbed. "I've never felt stronger." His widening lips beamed. "This is incredible. Bee, you saved us."

Talin reached over and guided hair off my face, his warm touch reminding me that the world swarmed with possibilities. And I had a full life ahead of me.

"The spell worked on everyone? Including the guards?" I was convinced any moment now Lilita would pop up and scream, *fooled you*. But I remembered merging with her, binding our magic. And now I was whole, as if all these years, I'd been living as half a person.

"Sure hope so," Raze said. "Otherwise, we've all become the undead." He chuckled, and I adored that sound more than anything.

My gaze settled on my princes, and I couldn't resist

smiling and falling into a happiness that I hadn't felt since I'd lost Mom.

Raze nudged Ash, and they laughed. The heaviness from my shoulders had vanished.

Once we were out of the tub, Leven lowered me to my feet and all four men towered over me, alive, healthy, and sexy as ever.

"I don't know how you did it," Ash said. "But I feel strong enough to lift the entire castle."

Talin slid his hand into mine. "We owe you our lives. Anything you want is yours."

I grinned and stared from one shifter to the other. "I know exactly what I desire." Chewing on my cheek, I lifted my chin and said, "All of you."

Raze leaned closer and pushed aside a strand of my hair caught in my eyelashes. "That was already a given. Right?"

"Yep, that was my understanding," Ash added.

Leven slouched, his hands gripping his hips. "You would have major problems trying to leave us behind."

Talin kissed my brow. "You belong to us and we are yours. We almost died, and I won't waste another moment waiting to take what's mine."

All the princes nodded.

Hope beaded within me, and a radiating sensation soothed me from head to toe. Lightness burst through my heart. Maybe it was the excitement over the fact that I hadn't lost my future, and had gained more than I'd ever thought I deserved. I smiled so hard, it hurt my cheeks.

"You don't know how much I've waited to hear you say those words." They meant the world, and finally I'd get to live a life without always worrying about unleashing my darkness.

"Let's get you warmed up inside." Leven took my other hand.

Talin released his hold and regarded the guards staring our way. "The rest of us will get rid of the attackers from last night."

With a quick glance over my shoulder at Tristan, I pitied him. He'd only known one way to face what he didn't understand. Attack it. In a way I appreciated him coming to rescue me, but now he had to comprehend that I'd moved on. He had no control over me. There was nothing left for us. So I raised Leven's hand to my mouth and kissed it. He hugged me, and I leaned against him.

Tristan lowered his head and looked away. But I still worried how they'd treat Dad now that they'd seen me do magic. So, I lifted my hand and with a flick of my finger and a wave of newfound fire rushing down my arm, I shot out a golden surge of power that struck all the humans in the chests. "As soon as you all leave here, you won't remember a thing from White Peak. Oh, and Tristan, you give up on Bee." They shuddered, and within moments, they stumbled around like lost sheep.

"Damn, girl," Leven whispered. "That was impressive."

I turned to Talin. "Don't hurt them; they're just dumb guards from Terra. They need to go home."

Raze snorted. "What do you take us for? Beasts?"

y stomach tossed like a stormy gale. I glanced around, terrified that a guard might patrol the Terra woods near my house. I mean, the four hunky princes at my side stood out like sore thumbs in their blue pants, golden tunics, and cloaks. Everyone in Terra knew everyone, but I wanted no more trouble for my family. Not after the crap Tristan and his goon buddies had pulled by turning up at the castle and then trying to kill the bear shifters. They must have tracked me from the Golden Lock to rescue me or some bullshit. But they'd been lucky to survive. Raze and Ash had escorted Tristan and the guards to the Golden Lock tavern and left them there, disorientated and confused. With my spell, they wouldn't remember me using magic, the bear shifters, or anything else from White Peak.

That idea still hadn't settled in my mind. The whole event still tortured me, as everything had happened too fast. But I'd saved my princes - and everyone else. My shifters had declared their love for me, and I hadn't felt a sign of Lilita.

I hadn't expected to actually succeed in folding my energies back together. To think, as a child, the terror of working with dark magic had affected me so much that I'd manifested Lilita in my head. She represented everything I dreaded, and that explained why my abilities weren't strong enough. The half of me that I feared had controlled me all along. And the scary part was, when she'd spoken, it had been me, taking on her persona, but I hadn't realized it because I'd divided myself.

Yep, some fucked-up shit there. But I planned to work through that with my four amazing new men. If anyone understood me, it was them.

A few days ago, I'd joined them on a visit back to their cousin's manor to check up on them. Rek's wife had discovered from his mistress that he'd worked with death voodoo magic and sacrificed a young girl. They admitted he'd gone too far. No one spoke of who had killed him, but I suspected they knew it was either Talin or Raze. Maybe they didn't have proof, or worried about Talin's reaction, but they agreed to put the past behind them and work together. For the interim, Leven, as the second eldest brother, had taken over Rek's territory and realm, and his first priority was determining if either of Rek's sons were right for the position of Duke. I told Leven I'd join him on a few occasions as I wanted to spend more time with Cleo, Rek's granddaughter. I intended to show her how amazing she could be and do more with her life than wait for marriage.

The wind brushed past me, rustling the leaves in the woods, and I couldn't stop perspiring.

"Perhaps going home isn't the best idea," I told my men. A knot formed in my stomach at the thought. "Maybe we should ease Dad into the idea. This is a bit sudden."

"Don't back down now, sugarplum," Leven said. "Talin needs a queen."

Goddess! Did he have to remind me? Was I even queen

239

material? What if I could never meet the expectations, or the other bear shifters never accepted me? But the princes insisted they would, as it wasn't unusual for shifters to mate with different races.

"Keep your voice down," I said, glancing around again. I didn't need a guard overhearing us and realizing I'd illegally brought four bear shifters into Terra.

Talin took my hand, kissed it and warmed it between his palms. "We're asking your father for your hand today. No more waiting. Officially, you will wed all of us."

My knees went weak from his touch. *Damn him!* He could say anything, and I'd be his. All of theirs. But how would Dad react?

The uneasiness tumbling inside me flared. My dad would freak when he opened the door and found me escorted by these four. Then I'd probably give him a heart attack when I told him I was marrying not one, but four princes, and I would become the queen of White Peak.

We stopped near my house, and my heart drummed; it felt like a lifetime since I'd left home.

"A deal's a deal," Ash chimed in, stroking the roses planted out front along the path to my home. "I owe you a magnificent garden to complement these gorgeous roses."

True. I was excited. But how was that going to work if I married the shifters and moved into the castle?

"Maybe you could have these in your bouquet?" Ash suggested.

What a perfect idea. My dad would be touched. I imagined my mother smiling down on me. Tears pricked the corners of my eyes.

But first things first. Tackle one thing at a time, Dad being top of the list. The boulder in my stomach hardened just thinking about facing him.

"Okay." I took a deep breath, stretching out my shaking

arm to the latch, but the door was locked. Reaching up, I tapped the top ledge of the doorframe for the spare key when the door flung open.

Father stood there, his expression flickering from a joyous smile to tight lips. He seemed ready to shake me for being gone so long.

"Bee, thank the goddess you're back. I was so worried." He enveloped me in a warm embrace.

Dad warily eyed all the princes with suspicion. "*Are* you in trouble?"

My throat clogged up with nerves. I couldn't get a word out. What was with me? I could stand up to a guard no problem when he bothered my dad, but admitting wanting to marry four princes had me all bothered.

"Is she ever," joked Raze, and my dad's eyes widened.

My stomach churned, making me want to vomit.

"No trouble, sir," Ash assured my father, elbowing his brother. "We're ensuring your daughter's safe passage home."

Dad's eyes widened, and his shoulders stiffened. "Thank you for returning my daughter." He wrapped an arm around my waist and bundled me inside the home.

I didn't blame him for wanting to get me inside and away from the strangers. Having the princes on his doorstep could amount to no end of trouble for us if guards spotted them. But Talin shot a foot out into the doorway before Dad could close the door behind us.

"I'm Talin, prince of White Peak," my hunky bear said, extending a hand in greeting. "These are my younger brothers, Raze, Leven, and Ash. Pleasure to make your acquaintance, sir."

For a few awkward moments, my father stared at Talin's hand before accepting it and shaking it. "Prince?" His gaze drilled into me for an explanation.

Goddess. This was not getting off to a good start. I'd imagined the scenario in my head a thousand times, but never like this, always with Dad smiling and excited to meet the princes. Damn reality. No. Damn me and my writer's brain dreaming the best outcome.

The nerves wedged in my throat refused to budge, even though Talin gently nudged me to say something.

"Lovely to meet you, Talon, Graze, Lever, and Rash," my father said, and I cringed that he'd gotten their names all wrong. "You must be tired from such a long journey. I will allow you to continue on your way to the tavern." He tried to close the door behind us, but Talin pressed a hand to the door.

"May we come inside, sir?" Talin asked.

My father turned to me. "What's going on, Bee?"

I coughed and cleared my throat. "Everything's fine, Dad." My voice was strung taut like a bowstring. "More than fine. Umm, so listen..."

"Perhaps we should have tea," Ash said.

Tea. Brilliant. I was so glad he was holding me together. "Don't be rude, Dad. Let them in." My feet carried me to the kitchen, and I began to prepare the brew.

Dad followed closely behind me.

The footsteps of the men echoed as they entered.

"Bee, why are there princes in our house?"

I pulled cups from the shelves, and my hands shook so hard, I accidentally dropped one on the floor and it smashed.

Get a hold of yourself, Bee. I bent down to pick up the mess, but my dad pushed me away. "I'll clean this up. You get the tea on."

I filled the teapot with water and set it on the hearth to boil.

As I pulled out a jar full of tea leaves, I pondered the best words to answer my father's earlier question, but ended up using the ones I'd rehearsed.

"I met the princes on my travels, Dad." Although I tried using my calm and steady voice, it came out more like a strangled cat. I didn't have the heart to tell him the truth about my magic. The less he knew, the better, especially if the guards came sniffing around again. But here came the bombshell.

"And I fell in love."

My dad's face softened. "Oh. With one of these fine princes?" He gave me another hug. "Which one's the lucky fellow?"

"Er, all of them."

My dad froze at first, his grasp shaking, and panic gripped me. "Are you okay?" I asked.

He shook his head, then kissed the top of mine. "You always had a good sense of humor," he said with a chuckle.

"No." I grabbed his hands. "I'm serious."

Father eased away and retrieved half a loaf of bread along with some cheese from a cupboard. "Bee, this isn't one of your romance stories you always write."

I glanced out into the living room, where the princes sat on the couch, whispering words I couldn't decipher.

The tea leaf container hit the bench but didn't smash. *Shit.* He knew about that? Heat scorched my entire body. *Goddess strike me down with lightning right now!*

"They're good," he said, slicing the bread. "Especially the mermaid one. Stayed up all night to read that one."

This was not a conversation I wanted to be having with my father. Him reading the sex scenes I'd written made me want to run away and never come back. That'd teach me for hiding them under my bed and not locking them up.

"Thanks," I said, tapping my fingers on the bench, praying for the brew to hurry and boil.

Luckily, my dad took the plate of bread and cheese to my princes just then.

I wiped sweat from my forehead, then got busy spooning the tea leaves into the strainer.

A few moments later, I carried the cups on a tray into the sitting room.

My men were munching on the nibbles and smiling. Well, Raze winked at me as I poured the tea, and I was overcome with the urge to sit on his lap. Instead, I shoved a cup into his hands.

Talin grabbed my hand once I was finished serving and drew me onto the sofa beside him.

"I was admiring the lovely roses out front," said Ash. "Do you garden too?"

Small talk. Perfect. Complimenting your future father-in-law's garden and raising topics of mutual interest was a good start… I supposed. Oh, how would I know? I'd never done this before and didn't plan on doing it again. The first time was stressful enough.

The princes engaged in conversation with my father until the tea and snacks had vanished.

Talin set his cup down, and I could tell by the intensity in his face he was going in for the kill. "You must be dying to know the reason for our visit."

"Oh, well… yes," replied my father. "It's not every day four princes turn up at my door. Or that my daughter says she's in love with one of them."

The princes all glanced my way.

"Out with it," Dad said. "Which one of you lucky fellows has stolen my daughter's heart?"

They all stood, then got down on one knee.

"Well, you see, sir," said Talin, "we all came to ask for your daughter's hand in marriage."

My father stiffened, put his shaking cup down, and pressed a hand to his chest. "Don't joke about that with an old man. You'll give me a heart attack."

His gaze drifted between the princes and me.

"We kid you not, sir," Leven said.

Talin nodded. "I need a queen. And I choose your daughter."

"We all do," Leven added.

My father's brows bunched up, and he scratched his head. "I'm not sure about this. You're from White Peak, so you're bear shifters. And I don't want my only daughter surrounded by danger her entire life."

Raze cleared his throat. "Sir, we have nothing but respect and love for Bee. With the four of us, no one would ever dare harm her."

"I don't understand how that would even work," Dad said.

"It is very common in our land for a female to take several males," Ash responded, holding his head high, proud.

Heck, I had no idea either how it would all work, but I didn't care. "Dad, all I want is to be with these four men who have my heart. I love each one equally. This is what I want."

He sighed. "Will there be four weddings?" Dad rubbed his chin. "Goddess. What will our family friends say about this? Will she live in White Peak? May I come visit her?"

The questions just kept coming. My shifters didn't have a chance to answer.

"Who will have the honor of the wedding bed on the night of the ceremony?"

Goddess. Fire claimed my cheeks. Why was he asking that?

"When will I get grandchildren? Will they be princesses and princes too?"

Raze and Leven exchanged a smile. I was glad someone was having fun because I was praying for the torture to end, for my dad to say *yes*, and the opportunity to hide forever in shame.

"Sir," interrupted Talin, "The most important question we

need answered this day is, may we have your daughter's hand?"

I wanted to kiss him for silencing my father. Not just a quick peck either. A long one. But I'd save that for tonight.

"Well..." said my father, as if he really didn't approve. Then he smiled and added, "How can I say *no* to four princes?"

What? Had I heard him correctly? I almost fell off my chair. All this time I'd thought for sure he would say no.

* * *

MONTHS LATER

Bells rung overhead, signaling it was time. The sun beat down on the castle in White Peak, birds flew overhead, and others chirped in the distance. The perfect day.

My stomach bounced with both trepidation and anticipation. By tonight I was going to be a married woman.

"Are you ready?" Scarlet asked and smiled wildly. Her long hair had been curled and bounced over her shoulders from the breeze.

She wore a greenish-blue glittery gown, long and loose, suiting her slim figure. Who else would I ask to be my bridesmaid but my best friend?

"I'm ready, but my stomach is doing somersaults."

She gave me a hug. "It's nerves, but once you're in there, you will be floating on clouds."

Just having Scarlet here made me feel less of a stranger and more as if I belonged.

"You look beautiful," she said and pulled back, her lips pinched to one side. "I noticed you had to outdo me by getting yourself four men, hey?" She arched a brow then chuckled.

I smirked. "I love having four of them to adore me, and in the bedroom…"

Scarlet placed a hand to my mouth. "Not here. Tell me later." She giggled as Dad emerged from the doors and hurried toward us, waving for Scarlet to enter the room.

Scarlet embraced me once more. "Go in there and kill it, Your Majesty." She smirked, straightened her dress, and headed to the door, waiting for our cue.

Dad kissed me on the forehead, pulled my veil down, and linked arms with me. "You look beautiful, Bee. I'm so proud of you. Snagging four princes. Just like in your stories."

He still hadn't stopped talking about that. For the last month while I'd prepared for the wedding, he'd gone on and on about it, bragging to anyone in White Peak who would listen that I was marrying four rich princes. But I hadn't had the heart to tell him to stop embarrassing me. Not when he was so proud, and his face lit up at just the mention of my wedding.

I squeezed the bouquet of my mother's roses, laced with white baby's breath flowers. When my father had presented me with it, we'd both shed a tear in remembrance of my mother. I wished she was with us today.

"Don't cry again. You'll ruin your makeup," Dad said.

I inhaled a deep breath, preparing myself before I commenced my journey down the aisle.

Dad smiled at me and, with my arm curled around his, he guided me up through the open doors leading into the back of the castle.

Scarlet headed inside ahead of us, leading the way, also holding onto a bouquet of roses.

I buzzed on the inside, my throat tightening, but I promised myself not to cry as excitement bubbled in my chest. We entered the ballroom, my princess white gown billowing around my legs, sparkling with every move. Silky fabric covered the bodice, pebbled in diamonds.

There were people everywhere, close to three hundred, and I'd finally got the chance to meet the castle staff who treated the princes like family... and who embraced me without hesitation. The princes had told me that after the ceremony more shifters would attend the reception, which was set up in the yard. But that didn't matter to me as much as the four men awaiting me at the end of my walk.

Every eye followed me, and their smiles beamed. My breath raced. Lanterns and ribbons decorated the walls, creating a magical glow. We stood at one end of the long aisle, visitors sitting on chairs in rows on either side.

I caught sight of Cleo, Rek's granddaughter, sitting next to a young couple who I assumed were her parents. She waved my way, and I smiled back, glad she attended the wedding and wasn't upset when I'd told her I was marrying Talin.

Farther along the aisle, Santos and Ariella, grinned my way. Ariella wore a beautiful floral hat to cover her fae ears. Next to them were Scarlet's three wolf shifters, each with a baby on their laps, and I almost melted at the sight. It took every strength to not run over there and hug the family. Maybe one day that would be my princes with our babies. Nero winked at me, and I grinned. Who would have thought both Scarlet and I would have each gained our very own harem?

I turned my attention to the long path ahead of me, and my gaze fell on my four princes. They were dressed in elaborate cloaks with golden trims, their heads raised high, their faces exploding with joy.

I bounced on the inside, convinced I'd burst out crying any moment to have my wildest dreams come true. I had the men of my dreams, I'd become a princess, and Dad had moved in with us in the castle. When a soft harp ballad played, Dad walked us forward.

It was time. Time to take the first step into my new life.

* * *

LATER THAT NIGHT

"Okay. Ash, Talin, and Raze. Leave. This is my time with Bee." Leven waved his arms toward his brothers who weren't budging.

I stood in the middle of Leven's bedroom with all my princes surrounding me, and if there was ever a perfect moment, this was it. Five of us bound, ready to tackle anything. Despite the whirlwind of my life, the craziness we had all endured, I'd ended up with four of the most incredible husbands in the world. They are all mine. I pinched myself because the whole wedding day had felt surreal as if maybe I imagined everything.

"Why exactly do you get Bee first," Ash asked, his brow wrinkled.

I reached over and touched his arm, and his features softened as he offered me the sweetest smile.

"Because you were all too slow, and I claimed her first." Leven laughed, and damn he was a flirt.

"The way I see it," I interrupted the staring match. "It's all our wedding night, and I intend to spend time with each of you because I love you all."

Ash raised my hand to his lips and kissed me.

"My vote is we stay and watch," Raze demanded with the devilish voice he used when he teased me.

"Not happening," Leven said.

"Yeah, agree with Leven." Talin was at my back and lowered his mouth to my neck. "I'll be seeing you soon, sweetie."

Ash placed kisses up my arm, while Raze approached and kissed me on the lips, his tongue licking me. God, to have the men against me left me dizzy with arousal, and I couldn't wait to have them claim me all night long.

Talin pulled back as did Ash and Raze, and already I missed their company.

By the time, the three princes walked out of the room, Leven was fast to shut the door behind them. He spun toward me, wiggling his eyebrows. "Finally, it's just us two." He strolled over and tickled my sides.

I burst out laughing as his hands swept to my back and unraveled the ribbon keeping my wedding dress bodice in place.

When his mouth grazed mine, all worries faded, and I let myself drown beneath my husband. I loved that word so much. I might have had four husbands, but that made me four times as lucky.

With the bodice loosening around my chest, Leven's deft fingers unwrapped me and tugged the dress up and over my head, leaving me in my underwear. Layers of white chiffon fabric covered his face as he carried the gown and set it on a table.

His bedroom was twice the size of the guest one I'd slept in, and we'd all agreed that I got to select my own room, but most nights I'd take turns snuggling up with a different prince. Best arrangement ever.

"Now, where were we?" Leven dusted his hands and unbuttoned his shirt. He took off his top, and I reached over and caressed the muscles. The fire of his skin felt like an inferno. He removed his pants, and I'd never get enough of staring at his hardness… Huge as I remembered.

He kneeled in front of me. With his hands curled over the band of my panties, he slid them down my legs.

I shivered as his fingers caressed the silkiness of my sex,

his breath a feather gliding along my stomach. The fire behind me warmed me, and outside the night sparkled with stars and a silvery moon peeked out from behind clouds. I never would have thought my life would have turned out so incredible. Perfect. Insatiable. And with four shifters at my side, I was ready to follow my passion, travel the realms with my men, and write my stories for everyone to devour. Oh, and do royal, queen, and political things, which I still needed to learn about.

Leven's mouth pressed to my sex, his tongue long as it swept my length. I melted away like an iceberg in summer. His mouth latched around my bud, sucking me, pulling at my inner folds. Two fingers pushed inside me. I cried out with pleasure and writhed as an inferno claimed me.

When he pulled out, I moaned my protest.

"Sugarplum, I love you. And I plan to fuck you in every position imaginable." His eyes, all seductive and free, brimmed with desire.

Before I could find my words, he swooped me up and off my feet and laid me on his bed, prying open my legs. He lowered himself over me, covering me with his naked body, and parted my mouth with his tongue. The kiss was warm and soft.

He took my hand and placed it above my head, then the second one, and pinned my wrists down. He pressed his cock into my entrance.

"I want to control you," he said. "Is that okay?"

"Leven. Yes. I want you so bad, I'm melting into a puddle." The delight pushing through me heightened, and I rode the wave of pleasure.

I shifted my hips, ready to accept him, my muscles taut. And the groan in his throat was the sexiest sound I'd ever heard.

Once again, his mouth caught mine and sucked on my

tongue as his long cock glided forward, stretching me. I quivered as the sex-god claimed me. He plunged faster, hard, each slap driving me closer to an explosive orgasm. I groaned for more. And he took me so forcefully, the air in my lungs expelled.

This was me falling deeper in love, and I wanted to scream about it to the world.

My moans escalated, and utter bliss crashed through me like waves.

I screamed my pleasure, and Leven hammered into me. I lost myself, drowning in elation. If this was just a hint of what was coming my way from my four princes, I was indeed living a fairy tale.

ABOUT MILA YOUNG

Bestselling author, Mila Young tackles everything with the zeal and bravado of the fairytale heroes she grew up reading about. She slays monsters, real and imaginary, like there's no tomorrow. By day she rocks a keyboard as a marketing extraordinaire. At night she battles with her might pen-sword, creating fairytale retellings, and sexy ever after tales. In her spare time, she loves pretending she's a mighty warrior, walks on the beach with her dogs, cuddling up with her cats, and devouring every fantasy tale she can get her pinkies on.

Ready for the next story from Mila Young? Subscribe today: www.subscribepage.com/milayoung

Mila Young loves to connect with readers.

For more information...
milayoungauthor@gmail.com
www.facebook.com/milayoungauthor
twitter.com/MilaYoungAuthor

12271645R00166

Made in the USA
San Bernardino, CA
09 December 2018